I0762127

IT PAYS TO BE AFRAID OF THE DARK

REVIVE

KIRSTY BRIGHT

REVIVE
The Titanium Trilogy: Book 2
By Kirsty Bright

ISBN: 978-1-7399978-3-0
Published through Untuned Publishings LTD

First Edition: December 2022

Book and Cover design by Untuned Publishings LTD

For information contact:
kirstybrightauthor@gmail.com
Or visit
www.kirstybrightauthor.wixsite.com/welcome

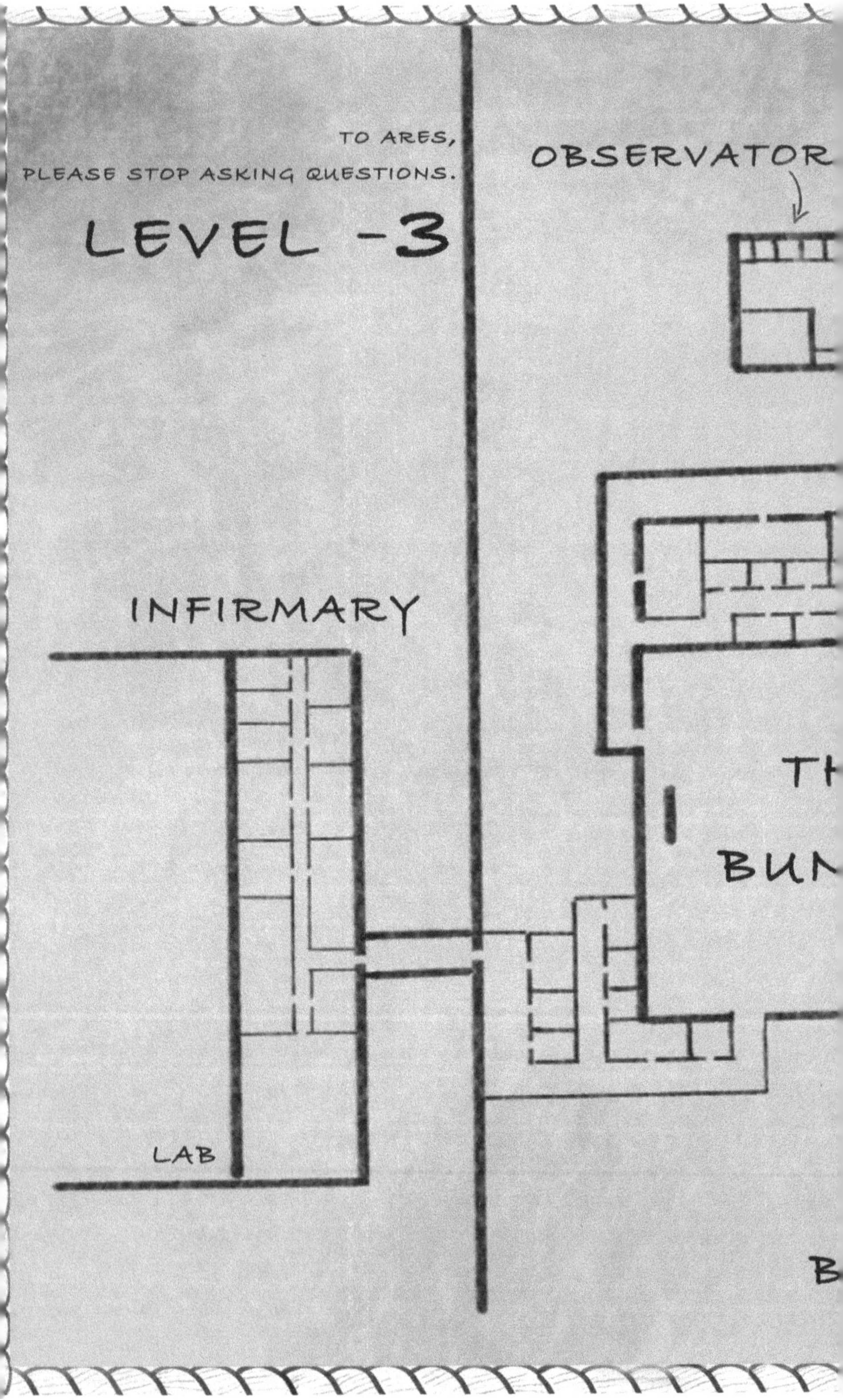

TO ARES,
PLEASE STOP ASKING QUESTIONS.

LEVEL -3

OBSERVATOR

INFIRMARY

TH

BUN

LAB

B

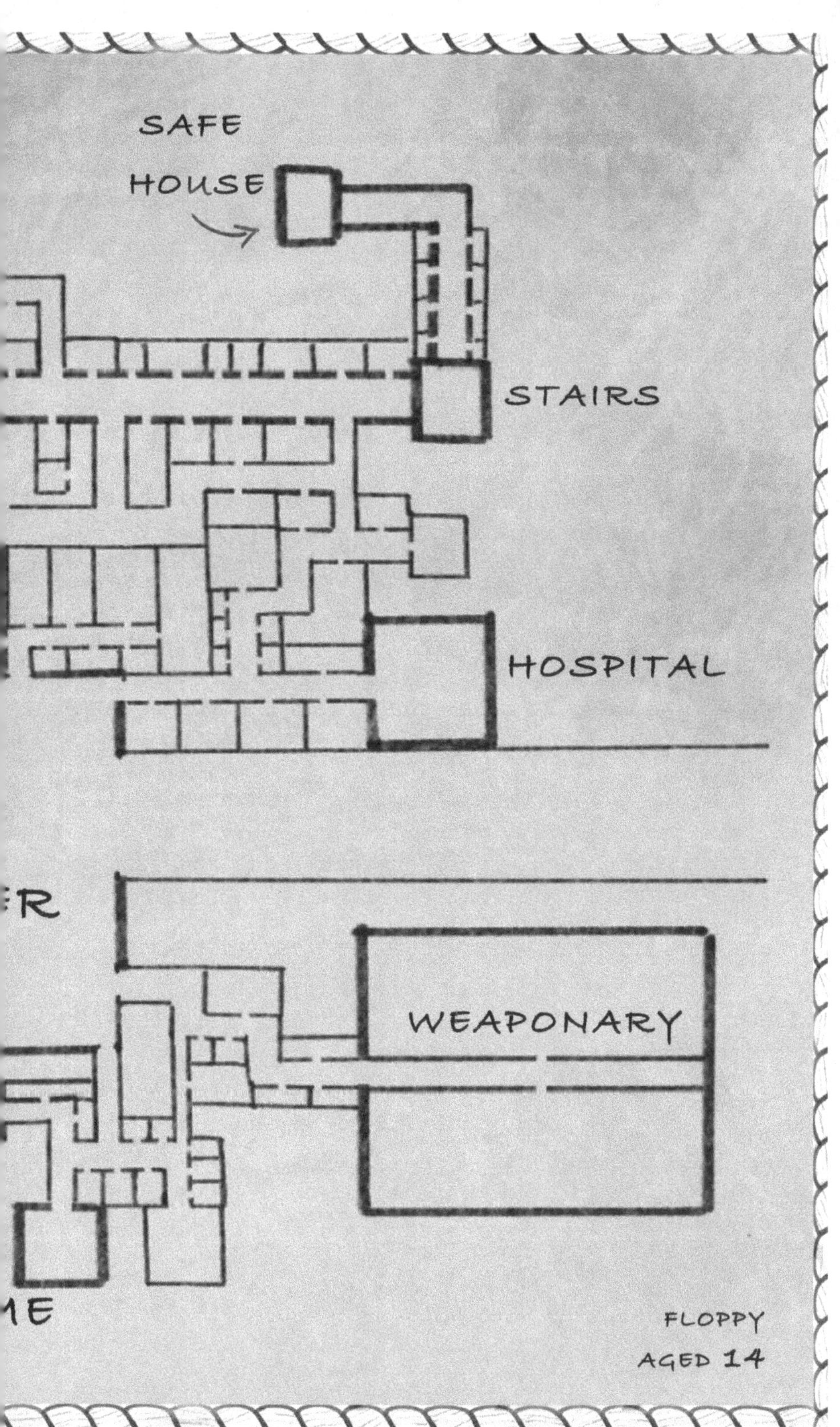
SAFE
HOUSE
STAIRS
HOSPITAL
ER
WEAPONARY
ME
FLOPPY
AGED 14

For those who smile through hard times.

PROLOGUE

HER

I welcomed the darkness like a vein of warm, pulsating blood. My mouth watered, teeth tingling at the thought.

This shadow had been home to me once per week for the past eight months. The cameras didn't cover this tree; it was a blind spot, a fault in the system. Intel informed us that there were four blind spots along The Farm's parameters, and so long as we stayed hidden, we'd be safe to watch and listen. Wait for the go-ahead.

I remained deadly still.

Then the silence revealed something I'd not experienced in eight months. Legs were moving through the grass—a vehicle following close behind.

Yes.

I turned back and waited for the signal. Far in the distance, a light flashed twice. We'd been hacking The Farm's cameras for years, and tonight they revealed that it was safe enough for me to approach the fence.

Two blinks of light. Two beings inside of the fence.

I pulled up my hood to keep my face hidden from the cameras, which would now see me as I stripped away the shadows, and I glided through the moonlight, red cape carried by the wind. Pausing meters away from the intricate panelling of the fence, I waited.

The hybrid came into sight, and I could smell the blood of another on his clothes and skin, mixing with his own. His eyes appeared bruised yet lit in glorious energy which shone like a thousand stars. To drink his blood would be to taste the night sky.

"Hail," I called out to him.

It would never get old, watching confusion turn to horror on the face of my prey. In his evolved state, my call could not compel the hybrid, but that was not the purpose of my mission tonight. I merely toyed with the boy. A smile crossed my face.

Hail backed away slowly, unsure of what exactly I was. I waved as he turned to leave.

My business was not with him but with the farmer who was sure to follow. The vehicle drew nearer.

And then it appeared over the hill, and I focused on the human inside. "Marshall," I whispered, knowing I could easily capture his mind. The truck slowed as he heard my voice, bringing it to a halt beside the fence. "Marshall," I said, his eyes locked on mine this time. That was how the compulsion worked best, as the humans were yet to discover.

"Evacuate the truck," I ordered. Marshall complied. His pupils dilated as he stared at me. He was just a shell for now. "You will return to The Observatorium and ask to rewatch the night's events. You will see this moment captured on camera and not remember a single moment. You will panic." I cast my spell while forcing myself to keep my eyes steady on his, not the veins of his neck. "You will know that we're coming for you, that this is the beginning of the end, Marshall, and you will join us soon enough."

CHAPTER ONE

ARES

My fists drummed against the door. "We need to get out of here!" I yelled to Marshall and tried the handle for the thirtieth time, and as expected, it didn't budge. We were locked in.

"You'd much rather be in here than out there with them, trust me," Marshall mumbled through his grogginess. He was still drifting in and out of consciousness, the drugs in his system yet to wear off.

It had been ten minutes since I'd forced Marshall into telling me about the Night Walkers, and then he was back to sleep, leaving me with no further information other than the fact that they had breached The Farm's parameters.

Night Walkers.

I recognised their name like an itch I couldn't quite scratch. I feared them. And I feared for my friends who were still in the barn, an easy target; sitting ducks.

I needed to get out. They needed my help.

Marshall grumbled as I tried the door once more. It was cold, metal, and sturdy. This room was the safest space on The Farm and, therefore, even the safest place on Earth. I couldn't open it without mutating. Once locked, this door would need unimaginable strength to break through.

The alarm still blared.

The panic still pumped through my veins.

If I busted out, it would leave my long-lost brother even more vulnerable than he already was.

I'd just discovered my family, and although I still didn't like Marshall nor agree with his actions over my time on The Farm, I couldn't leave him defenceless.

I hit my head against the door with force, hoping it would give me an answer to my problems and not just a large purple bruise.

"He shut us in here to save us," I muttered as I sank down the wall.

"A bit late to play the hero, don't you think?" Marshall replied. He wasn't referring to me but to our uncle, Dr. White. He had known of my history since I woke from hibernation and decided to keep it from me, claiming it was what my mother wanted.

They had planned to keep my identity a secret long before my parents died, sacrificing themselves to save The Farm.

Much like Dr. White was doing now.

Once again, my uncle had been hiding things.

He had rushed off during our conversation earlier, claiming that he was needed in the Observatorium now that Marshall was too drugged to run The Farm, and we weren't sure how much trouble my brother's side effects would cause.

Next thing I knew, I'd been escorted from the hospital room and led to the Safe House with sirens wailing and lights flashing.

Dr. White was still out there, trying to organise the farmers and keep the invasion under control. "It's never too late to play the hero, Marshall," I said.

Maybe Dr. White thought I was still too weak to help. It had only been a couple of hours since Marshall had carved a new breathing hole into my neck. Thankfully, my hybrid abilities healed the incision before it became too much of a problem, but I hadn't yet fully recovered. Running my hand over the plaster, the wound underneath felt fresh and tender, likely to reopen if I applied too much pressure.

"I think that you owe me an apology." I faced Marshall. My skin crawled at the sight of him. He'd killed so many hybrids. It would take time to accept that we were of the same blood, and

I was unsure if I'd ever forgive him for his actions. It didn't matter that he was mentally unstable from the unprescribed drugs he'd been taking. He'd taken lives. He had unnecessarily spilt blood and appeared to enjoy it.

His cold brown eyes landed on me, and for a moment, I wondered if mine had been the same colour before the metamorphosis had turned them gray: the symbolic colour of the Titanium hybrid.

"I could say the same." He pointed to the hand-shaped bruise I'd left on his neck after my animal alter ego tried to kill him.

I didn't encourage violence—most of the time, I would run from it—but being a hybrid wasn't simple. Once the anger released mutant hormones into my bloodstream, it became almost impossible not to mutate, making it challenging to think clearly.

But balancing the anger-induced hormones with love-induced hormones didn't allow me to evolve into my ultimate state like the other hybrids, and it returned me to my human state instead. It must have had something to do with the fact that I was the only Gen. 3 hybrid ever to exist, thanks to my scientist mother, who apparently didn't want me to fit in with the other Titanium hybrids.

That was something I still needed to figure out.

But first, I had to decide whether to break out of the Safe House and leave Marshall or stay with him and pray that my fellow hybrids found a way to fight back against the Night Walker invasion.

Part of me wanted the enemy to find Marshall.

"You deserved what I did to you after everything you've put us through," I defended my earlier actions as I pointed to his neck. "You killed my friends."

"I only did what was necessary for the sake of The Farm and the war," Marshall slurred.

"No. What's necessary is giving everybody a fighting chance. You broke your rules and then blamed me for the disruption."

"What the fuck do you know about the rules? Don't you dare…" His eyes rolled slightly, and he returned his head to the pillow.

"I know what Dr. White has told me. You're supposed to help the hybrids, but instead, you've forced us to fight against our own kind. You made Hail kill Beckle, and I could have killed the Veno Alpha last night."

"The Venos aren't supposed to survive anyways. Who gives a shit if you kill one? I don't."

"You are a monster." I felt my nostrils flare as my anger built.

"If you truly believe that, then you're blind, Ares. The real monsters are above us right now."

The anger subsided a little as I tried to picture what the pack was going through. I sighed against the wall, trying not to let the frustration consume me. I needed a distraction.

"Tell me about the Night Walkers. If we're going to be stuck in here until..." I didn't know how to finish the sentence. *Until what? The Night Walkers kill everybody? Until my friends defeat the creatures that roam the night?* Who knew what would happen from here on out. "You may as well make yourself useful and tell me what I need to know."

Marshall scoffed. "I don't owe you anything. You're still one of them, an animal, and you still have to follow the rules."

"To hell with the rules, Marshall!" He flinched back as my anger spiked. "The Night Walkers are up there. The Farm isn't yours to control anymore. You're out of your mind! For all we know, the human race may have just lost the war."

He let out a sigh in what almost sounded like relief. "Then maybe that's how it's supposed to be, and we were just prolonging the inevitable."

My blood boiled; I felt it simmering underneath my skin, thick and struggling to keep up with my rising heart rate.

Marshall was giving up. After all this time and all those lives lost, for what?

Why was I trying to keep him alive if he was happy to roll over so quickly? Brother or not, I couldn't save somebody who didn't want to live.

I made my decision and let the panic and anger set in. My body exploded with a feral feeling, becoming familiar, although I still struggled to cooperate with my animal alter ego. I focused on the door to reduce the risk of turning on Marshall again and yanked at the handle, and it popped open with the creak of bending metal.

"What are you doing? You can't leave me here! Don't you dare walk away from me!"

I focused on the fuzziness in my mind and tuned Marshall out, knowing that if I paid him any slither of attention, my mutant would attack. I couldn't risk it.

If he were to die, it'd be at the hand of a Night Walker, not my own.

I leapt through the door without a second thought.

And then I was retracing my steps down the corridor with the windows and onto the stairwell, which would take me to the surface several hundred feet above.

The mutant lurched from the railings, swinging from side to side as my body climbed. Mutating was like taking the backseat within my own body. I couldn't feel a thing, and my sight vignetted in red. I could influence the animal alter ego and give direction, but the decisions were not entirely my own. Apparently, the more a hybrid mutated, the more influence they could have over their mutant state, but I'd not allowed myself to find out, too scared I'd hurt those I care about in the process.

My body swung up the handrails, floor by floor. In less than a minute, I reached the door which led to the outside world, opening it into a room I didn't recognise. The animal didn't care for it, only for my plan to reach the barn. I smashed through a window within the guesthouse and ran towards the wooden building I had come to consider home.

But the barn sat empty.

The doors hung open, and not a farmer was in sight.

I ran into the barn to find the stalls unoccupied. It was eerily silent beside the wailing of the siren. I had expected gunfire, screaming, proof that the war had crossed onto The Farm's land. But instead, I was met by a deserted shell of my home.

Where was everyone?

I'm too late. I've left it too long.

The anger erupted from me as a harsh scream into the night.

And that's when I heard her voice.

It cut through the pain and the darkness.

"Ares."

I followed the voice in my mind, knowing that she was beckoning me toward her. And wherever I found her, I'd find them.

"Lora," I whispered in reply.

She was still alive.

The animal state crumbled within me, feeling only relief and a love far stronger than any powerful mutant hormone.

As a result, I was back to my human state, and I focused on my Alpha's call, running towards the source—or at least I assumed I was running towards her. I began to question myself after a few minutes, but it didn't stop me.

They needed my help.

They were alive, but alive didn't mean safe. I pushed away the images that crawled into my mind, thoughts making me sick, and pushed myself forwards. I couldn't allow myself to think of the worst-case scenario because it would turn me in the opposite direction.

Eventually, the sound of crying drifted in with the wind, and I approached the fence, looming over the bodies within its shadow and offering them safety from the moon. *If only it had protected them from the night.*

I refused to look at the mutilation around me. I was standing on a battlefield.

"Ares!" This time, Lora's voice was audible to the human ear, no longer using her Alpha abilities to speak to my inner ear.

I turned to face her, my heart pounding as I took in her evolved state, not so much as a scratch on her skin. My hands patted her body, hair, and face, trying to convince myself she was alive and standing there and that she was *really* okay.

She's alive.

She's alive.

She's alive.

I collapsed into her, but no hug was quite tight enough. "You're okay," I whispered into her hair. My heart was beating so fast that I struggled to breathe.

"I'm fine," she reassured me. "Where have you been? We thought that they had taken you, too." Lora's voice was desperate, heartbroken. Her eyes and hair glowed with menacing energy.

"What do you mean? What's going on?" I looked around now, searching for faces.

So many bodies lay around us.

Tye, Zee and Indigo crowded at the gates. Jayleigh stood next to Diego, and my heart dropped to the ground as our eyes met.

"No. They can't—They didn't."

The sobs came before I had confirmation.

I sank to my knees, and Lora collapsed alongside me, pulling me closer. "I'm so sorry, Ares. We'll get him back, I promise."

I wanted to believe her. I *so* desperately wanted to believe her.

But I knew better.

If the Night Walkers had Hail, he was likely already dead.

CHAPTER TWO

ARES

I glanced down at the broken bodies surrounding us. I recognised the puncture wounds, like those the drones had inflicted on Teri in Phase Two.

Only this was far, *far* worse.

Gore. Violent and cruel.

The farmers foamed at the mouth, and blood streamed from their eyes, nose and ears. The bodies lay crumpled around the gates, appearing to have snapped like twigs underfoot; that's how easy it seemed for a Night Walker to kill a human. Where the blood met skin, the tissue bubbled and blistered away as though the liquid that once flowed through the farmers' veins had turned into a highly corrosive chemical. The sight made me queasy.

At a guess, there were fifty or so bodies. Fifty farmers lost battling the Night Walker army. The image scarred my mind as we returned to the barn. I didn't recall the walk, my thoughts of Hail with the Night Walkers overriding my senses. That boy had been through enough already. *Why him?* What had he done to deserve this?

What were they doing to him?

Images of blistered skin and blood clouded my vision. *They wouldn't have taken Hail if they wanted to kill him,* or so I told myself as I placed myself on the bench next to Lora.

Her eyes looked just as void as I felt.

"Hail was gone by the time the sirens woke us. At first, I thought it was the beginning of Phase Three, but then we heard the farmer's screams, so we ran towards them. It was already too late when we reached the gates. They were gone." Lora refused to look at me as she explained. Jayleigh paced the barn whilst the other hybrids retired to bed. My gaze followed her, backwards and forwards, backwards and forwards.

"A few farmers hid within the trees during the attack, and they told us that the… Night Walkers, I think they called them, must have had some mind control over Hail. He seemed to go willingly. I tried to mind jump to Hail but couldn't get to him. It's like there was a shield keeping me out. I considered going after them, but we were so unprepared. How could we fight two

Night Walkers strong enough to take out that many farmers? We know nothing about the enemy at all."

My breath halted.

"There were only two Night Walkers?" My skin was iced over in disbelief. It was true; we were very unprepared.

"But we can't just let him go." Jayleigh slumped next to me on the bench and retrieved her hand knife from her pocket, twirling it against the tips of her fingers.

"We won't. We can't," I agreed.

"So, what do you suggest we do?" Lora questioned, still motionless apart from the shivering of her bottom lip. "Run after them with no plan or knowledge of what we're up against? It sounds like you've both developed a Veno mindset."

"I don't know what I'm suggesting, but I know we can't sit by and let them… Who knows what they'll do?" Jayleigh clenched her jaw and stopped playing with the knife as though her imagination was on overdrive.

"I know." Lora had tears in her eyes, but she blinked them away. "We'll get him back, but we need a little time to get a plan together. It's been a long, tiring day, and I'm sure we'll all be able to think clearer after a couple of hours of sleep. The sun's about to rise, so they can't go too far."

It had been a very long day. None of us would have been any help in a rescue mission in our current state. The adrenaline and desperation were the only things to keep me sitting upright.

Jayleigh retired to her stall, and I considered if now would be an appropriate time to fill Lora in on my generation category. She was still under the impression that I was a Gen. 2, thinking she was ill for having feelings towards me, and I knew it must be adding unnecessary stress.

As I opened my mouth to tell her the news, she dropped her head onto my shoulder and sighed.

"Can it wait until morning, Ares?" she said in defeat.

I stroked her hair, wondering if it was okay to do so. "It's good news, I promise."

"Then I'll better receive it once I've slept a little." She raised her head, and a small, forced smile appeared on her lips.

I thought about kissing her, telling her in fewer words that we were okay, we'd work it out, but I tucked her hair behind her ear instead, brushing her cheek with my finger. "Of course. I'll see you in the morning."

I shut my door and gave Lora the routine goodnight wave through the bars, seeming somewhat nostalgic after not sleeping in the barn for so long. Then I climbed into bed.

My head spun.

I'd panicked enough when Hail killed Beckle and ran off into the woods. Now the feeling had been multiplied ten times over. That had been the night Hail had seen the Night Walker on the other side of the fence.

Could it be the same Night Walker that abducted him? Had she come back for him?

Somehow, the questions numbed my mind enough for me to slip in and out of consciousness. Before I knew it, the sun was starting to shine through the gaps in the barn's wall, bringing a cooler breeze than I was used to.

It had seemed a long time since I last slept in the barn, but it had only been a matter of days. The familiarity of waking in my stall blanketed me in soft comfort until the sleep cleared, and I remembered that the Night Walkers had slipped in during the early hours without waking a soul.

The barn wasn't safe.

Nowhere was safe whilst the Night Walkers roamed the Earth.

Dr. White entered the barn before I could climb out of bed. "Good morning, all." His usual chipper tone had flatlined.

He stopped expectantly at my stall.

"What's going on?" I asked. "Do you have any news on Hail?"

My uncle shook his head *no*. "We're working on it. He's already several miles out, but they've stopped with the sun's rise."

"So, now would be the best time to go after him," I

encouraged.

Dr. White didn't reply to my hopes of a rescue mission. Instead, he unbolted my door and motioned for me to follow. "I'm retrieving you for closer inspection of your mutant state. We've recorded interesting data over the past twenty-four hours, and I'd like to run a few tests."

"Is that necessary? Wouldn't our energy be better spent on Hail?" I said.

"I'm not asking, Ares. Despite having connections within The Farm, you're still a hybrid and a part of the training program. It's not up for debate. Please…" he held his hand out as though to usher me from the stall. "Do not waste any more time."

I rolled my eyes. Marshall had said something similar about not wanting to give me special treatment. Apparently, it meant nothing to either of them that we were family.

I reluctantly complied with my uncle's wishes and left my stall.

Lora smiled reassuringly in my direction as I passed, but I could see the doubt in her eyes as I left the barn.

She'd put everything on the line to save me from my monstrous alter ego. She'd bared her soul—something she usually kept guarded with chains and padlocks—in front of the whole pack, and I prayed that she wouldn't live to regret it. I was sure the others wouldn't care to see her vulnerable side, the person she was around me. But Lora worried about everything. It was her job to stress, and I knew this would be playing on her mind.

The doors to the barn closed behind us, and I once again found myself separated from the pack. Being away from them for too long felt unnatural, so I picked up my pace, forcing my uncle to walk faster.

The icy breeze did nothing to calm me as we walked the path to the silo. I usually relied upon the peace I felt within nature to control my animal state of mind, but something felt off today.

Maybe it was the lack of sleep or the knowledge that the Night Walkers had Hail? The memory of the farmers' bodies strewn across the ground flashed before my eyes, and I fought to push it away.

I had plenty of reasons not to feel my usual self after the events and revelations of the past few days. In some ways, I would be stupid to believe I could still be the same person who entered Phase Two. So much had changed.

Not so many feet crunched the gravel around us as we walked, nobody worked the amber fields, and as we descended in the lift to floor -3, I realised that the facility was in mourning.

The bunker was calmer than it had been the night before.

Farmers stopped their tasks and glanced up as I stepped from the lift into the top-secret compound buried hundreds of feet underground.

Eyes followed as I walked beside Dr. White through the corridor of desks toward the tunnel marked 'Infirmary'.

My pace slowed as I witnessed the glossy walls and tiled floor. Blue fluorescents played with my eyes.

"Why are we here?" I asked as the corridor stretched out before us. The farmers in this part of the bunker swapped their usual gray attire for white coats and gloves in-fitting with the sterile environment.

Dr. White didn't reply. I peered through windows and doors as we walked. What lay beyond the windows? Was this where the experiments took place? Were children undergoing experimentation right now?

I came to an abrupt stop as we reached a glass panel. My uncle swiped his tablet over the reader and entered a password which allowed us entry through the glass door. It automatically retracted for us, a blue hue welcoming us through the floor-to-ceiling windows on either side of the narrow room. It was a bridge of sorts overlooking the warehouse below.

"On this side," Dr. White began, "We breed the animals used to create your hybrid basis. You could call it a zoo, with each tank containing a species compatible for cross-engineering."

I wondered, as I peered from the window to my left, how they managed to get the animals into the warehouse. And there were so many habitats that I couldn't see the far wall. How many miles did the zoo stretch on for, and how many animals did the warehouse hold captive? Hybrids weren't the only animals trapped on The Farm, it seemed.

"And what's on this side?" I asked as I turned to the window behind me, the opposing warehouse seeming just as significant.

"These are the hybrids in hibernation."

My mouth fell open as I witnessed rows upon rows of cylinder tanks, each housing a semi-conscious test subject. "There are so many." I couldn't believe it was real.

"Yes. But these are the last." Dr. White slowly tapped his pen against the board of his folder as he glanced over the machines.

I was partly relieved to hear that children would no longer have to experience what I did, but the war was far from won, so this news surprised me. "Why?"

Dr. White walked to the far end of the bridge and opened the door leading down into the Infirmary. He motioned me through it and explained as we descended the metal spiral steps, the metal clanging and shaking underfoot.

"I told you once that we are not winning the war. The Night Walkers' numbers outweigh the entire human population, and we can't afford to send search parties for refugees and put our people at risk. The groups outside the fence who have survived this long would not risk the journey here and put the support they've built for themselves in jeopardy. By now, I expect The Farm is nothing but a myth to the outside world. The few survivors wouldn't search for something they didn't know existed."

"Why can't we find them? Aren't we safe to travel within the day? I presume that the Night Walkers don't move in daylight, given their title?"

"It is far more complicated than that, Ares." He waved a hand as I stepped from the spiral staircase and onto the polished warehouse floor, signalling that he refused any more questions.

The air was cooler down here, pricking at my cheeks.

"What will happen to Dickward and the Venos who survived yesterday?" I glanced at the nearest tank, the screen confirming that the hybrid inside was destined to be my rival pack.

"We're currently unsure. Phase Two has never ended as it did yesterday."

My uncle's tone worried me. "You can't kill them, especially not after the Night Walker attack last night." I fought for the Venos despite knowing they'd kill me the first chance they got. "If *this* is all we have," I gestured to the hundreds of machines and tanks around us, "Then we need to be careful with our numbers."

After everything I'd seen last night, I doubted it would be enough to bring down the Night Walkers.

"But the Venos are not intelligent enough to fight against the Night Walkers, and it's not for you to say what we should be doing, Ares. The farmers will decide what will happen to Steven and his pack."

I grumbled low in my throat, already tired of the 'not your place' talk, and turned away from him.

My eyes fell to the next tank. Inside was a girl, barely twelve; her body seemed too small for the cocoon she would live in for the next ten years. Suspended in the thick liquid, she moved as though she were running, jumping, fighting. She was nimble, her legs thin and yet to gain the muscle she would have by the time she woke from hibernation. Braided hair floated around behind her, and something about how she moved reminded me of a young Jayleigh.

My heart pinched.

I imagined how my friend would have looked within this machine, tubes up her nose and hair drifting about, like this girl.

It wasn't right. It wasn't natural.

My hand fell upon the glass of her tank, and Dr. White yelled at me, "Do not touch the incubator, Ares!" But it was already too late.

I flinched back as a screen lit up the glass showing what the young Jayleigh was seeing within her simulation. She jumped from one rock to another, the land around her crumbling away and leaving nothing but emptiness. If she missed her target, she would fall to her death.

"They're training," I confirmed what Lora had told me as I watched the screen from a first-person perspective. "Can a hybrid die in hibernation?" I questioned as the girl jumped for the next rock, which seemed smaller than the last.

"No. If Annitah falls, she will restart the challenge and continue to do so until she reaches the end."

"But that's torture… How long can it take?"

"I recall that your record was fifteen days for one challenge." Dr. White cocked an eyebrow in my direction as though he were trying to prove a point.

I shook my head. "Just because we can't remember it doesn't make it any more just."

For a moment, I forgot that I'd also been in a tank like this for fourteen years.

I joined the dots in my mind. "So, this is where you were hiding when Marshall needed you?"

I was curious if I'd get a reply. I already knew my uncle had found refuge beside my hibernating body when my mother died instead of helping Marshall take over The Farm.

"No. You weren't here. It would have been obvious to Marshall if I'd spent so much time in this room. The cameras are always watching the Infirmary."

"Then, where was I?" I hadn't expected my family to go through so much trouble to ensure that Marshall never discovered my identity. He *was* isolated, just as much as I had been.

Dr. White gestured that I follow him through a door near the staircase into another corridor.

"This is where we kept the refugees until they were old enough to start their metamorphosis." He pointed towards each door as we passed. "That leads to the dorms… This one is the classroom, the playroom," And then we reached the last door on the left. "And this… was your room."

CHAPTER THREE

MARSHALL

"Get me out of these wires!" I commanded the woman busy documenting the state of my health.

I began to rip the tubes from my hands and the pads from my arms. "Fuck." They stuck to me like a leach; the idea of it drained the life from me as though they were sucking the blood from my veins. "I'm not ill. I don't need any of this," I said more to myself than to her, but her eyes suggested that she thought otherwise, watching me stumble from the bed and crumble to the floor of the Safe House.

"Sir," she started, but I didn't allow her to say any more.

"I need an update on everything happening on the surface level."

"That is not my area of expertise, Sir." She backed away

slowly, cowering as I picked myself up and smoothed myself over. "I'm aware of that..." I raised my eyebrows at her expectantly.

"Jenna."

"Thank you, Jenna," I scrambled through the cupboards next to the bed in search of my clothes. "But I don't care about your area of expertise. What happened? How many are left?"

The sirens stopped some time ago, I wasn't sure how long, but the sound had blurred into one distinct wail like an endless scream: my scream. I'd been drifting between the conscious state and the drugged peril, where my nightmares came to life.

I recognized that noise only too well.

I'd not heard the sirens in eight years since the night my parents died.

I'd not heard the sirens since the Night Walkers last broke into The Farm.

And now they were back, and I was in the basement with little knowledge of what was happening. And it seemed that Jenna wasn't planning on helping me out.

"Sir, I'm under strict orders to keep you—"

"Let me clear something up for you, Darling." I snatched my grays from the cupboard furthest away from the bed. Daniel would have put them there on purpose. "I run this operation. If I ask you a question, you will provide me with an answer. You will open the door for me if I want to leave this room. If you refuse, I can have you moved to level -2 to sieve flour for the rest of your life. How would you like that, Jenna?"

"I understand, Sir. But you are still—"

She was adamant about her orders, and I respected her for that.

"How many people died in the attack, Jenna?" I snapped.

"Fifty-two, I've heard, Sir, but I'm not sure of much else. I'm just a nurse."

Fifty-Two.

It was more than we could afford to lose, especially after Ares destroyed many drones.

Ares.

My mind spun with new information and emotions as the revelation came. I wanted to be angry with him; this was partially his fault, but the usual fire that occupied my mind whenever I thought about him didn't rage as fiercely. It dwindled, still there but somewhat calming like a flickering flame. I couldn't process what it meant. An emotion I'd never experienced before, and I didn't have a word for it.

I placed it somewhere between familiarity and understanding.

I had a brother.

Sure, he was the biggest nuisance I'd ever come across, but

we were the same flesh and blood; he was *family*.

The word left a hollow in my chest. I no longer knew what it meant to me, but to have a brother in a time like this was rare. It was a treasure.

Ares was an imprint of myself, just as headstrong, just as ruthless. Upon further inspection, we had more similarities than I'd ever realized. If only he could set his high-strung morals aside.

Morals are subjective. Morals can be influenced.

I formed a plan in my mind. There was still a chance to save humanity, and there was still a way to honour Father's wishes. Our family could still save the planet.

"How many animals died?" I asked, my mind spinning with new possibilities.

"None, but I think the Night Walkers took a Titanium."

No… no...

"Who? Which one?"

"I'm not sure, Sir. I don't know—"

"Get out!" I looked back at Jenna, my eyes seeming to show my rage. I figured that she would view it as insanity. "Unless you want to stay for the show?" I began to pull at the strings of my gown.

Jenna blushed slightly and quickly hurried from the room, reminding me somewhat of a field mouse.

I'd seen three field mice in my time. Once, when I was very young, Father had taken me on a rare outing about The Farm, and it was one of my favourite memories of him. The two of us hid behind a fallen tree so as not to scare the mouse as it collected food, and Father told me facts about the small animal. At that moment, I'd categorized it as vermin, just like most animals.

The next couple of times I'd seen field mice, not so long ago, underground, I'd killed them both.

I dressed in my grays and pulled on my boots. "Where is my cap?" I spoke to myself and spun around a little too quickly as I searched. The world blurred in my eyes, and as I steadied myself, my vision landed on the tablet Jenna had left behind.

I was no doctor or nurse, but I knew enough to understand the data displayed there.

"Well, shit."

I needed to find my cap, find Wilson, set up Protocol Six, and then pay a visit to the biggest field mouse I knew.

Oh, and I needed to fit a cup of coffee into that schedule too, sooner rather than later.

ARES

Dr. White unlocked the door with his tablet and motioned me inside.

I didn't enter.

I stared into the box room—my room—but there was no proof that I'd ever lived there at all. The room stood as blank as my memory of it.

It was void of love.

They hadn't bothered to decorate, the walls the same shade of white as the rest of the bunker and the Infirmary, and the bedsheets resembled that of the bed in Dr. White's hospital room.

"Has it always looked like this?" I slowly followed Dr. White inside, searching for proof that it once belonged to a child. *Me.*

"Yes, except we moved your incubator in here whilst you were in hibernation."

It wasn't the answer I had been hoping for; I wanted to hear that the room had once been filled with an abundance of toys, bright colors, and drawings. I tried to imagine that, at some point, I had experienced something other than this grim bleakness.

But it was untrue. I had lived a grayscale life from the moment I was born.

"It looks like a prison cell," I said, the disapproval clear in my voice.

"How would you know what a prison cell looks like?"

"On the TV in the playroom." I pointed back in the way we came but stopped as I realized there was no way I could have remembered that the playroom even had a TV. "It used to play a video about a dog that solved mysteries."

"Interesting." Dr. White studied me. "I wonder if seeing glimpses of your past is awakening parts of the hippocampus that we've shut off… We must run those tests."

He quickly began writing something into his folder.

"Is that all I've ever been?" I questioned, my voice breaking. "A science experiment?"

Dr. White looked genuinely saddened by my response. "Of course not."

"Well, I'm not seeing much proof," I muttered. "My bedroom is in the Infirmary, for crying out loud."

A silence hung between us. I didn't care to hide my anger.

I crossed to the bed and slumped onto it, hoping it would spark a memory of life before hibernation, but nothing else came to me.

"We're in the middle of an apocalypse, Ares. I'm sorry that

your room doesn't quite live up to expectations, but I can assure you that what you missed out on in comforts was made up for in love."

My hands gripped tightly at the sheets, balling them up in my fists and bending my fingernails. My mother may have touched these same sheets as she tucked me in for the night before retiring to her bedroom in the guesthouse. The same sheets I might have once pulled over my head after a nightmare, praying that the thin cotton would save me from whatever monster lurked in the emptiness of my room. "I suppose I'm to take your word for it?"

"Yes!" Dr. White shut me down. "You had it a lot better than Marshall, so I would stop complaining if I were you."

Somehow, I found that difficult to believe. At least Marshall had a certain level of freedom, the ability to go above ground, and I presumed he had a bedroom with windows. And he hadn't been a secret for the first twenty-three years of his life.

I stared at the blank wall before me, wondering how many times I'd done so. My eyes eventually fell upon a small engraving just above the bed's headboard, and I brushed my fingers over it.

"What's this?" I asked as I studied the usual shape.

"I've always wondered the same thing." Dr. White replied. "I assume it was something to do with whatever this room used to be before the war when The Farm was a secret military base. I asked your mother once, but she wasn't sure either."

I pressed it, wondering if it was a button, but nothing happened. I sighed.

"I don't understand... Why did she experiment on me if she loved me as much as you claim? How did I end up like this?"

"It wasn't Samantha's choice." My uncle's voice was stern. He squinted his eyes closed and pinched the bridge of his nose between his thumb and index finger.

"What—What do you mean it wasn't her choice? Was it my father's choice? Did he force her to experiment on me?"

"That's enough." He opened the door wider and held his hand out, demanding I follow.

"Why won't you tell me? I deserve to know the truth."

"Some things are better left buried, Ares. Trust me when I say that you're not ready yet." His tone was cold, warning not to push any further.

I wasn't used to seeing this side of Dr. White, and I couldn't say that I liked it. But he was now under pressure to run The Farm whilst Marshall recovered, and the last thing he needed was me pushing him. I had seen first-hand what the stress could lead to.

I backed off.

"Why are you showing me this?" I asked. "I thought that you would be busy doing… leadership stuff." I didn't quite know what to call it.

"I've left Wilson in charge for now. I thought that you would want to see this. I know how curious your mind is, and after all the commotion of the last few days, I don't know... I just wanted to show you the world that your mother created. Without her, we'd have all been dead many years ago."

I looked back into the room as he closed the door, imagining all the times he'd hidden beside me. Was showing me this his way of proving that he cared?

Like hiding me in the Safe House whilst the Night Walkers attacked.

"Thank you," I whispered, even though I was still annoyed that he was keeping things from me.

"You're welcome." He nodded once. We stood outside the door for a moment, neither of us knowing what to say.

"So, you wanted to run some tests—"

"Let me show you the Biome."

We spoke at the same time.

I paused. All I *really* wanted was to return to the barn. I'd already been away too long and needed to speak to Lora. But I had no idea what a Biome was, and I guessed it held importance for Dr. White to suggest it. Naturally, my curiosity won out. I followed him back the way we came and then through too many corridors to count. I quickly learned that level -3 was a maze. We eventually entered a small room, and he waited for me to close the door before sealing it behind me, waiting ten seconds, and then releasing the one before us.

I stepped into a new world.

"You've got to be kidding," I whispered, finding a well-developed rainforest within the dome. The trees towered above us, a small stream trickled through the centre, and a wooden bridge connected the paths on either side. I began questioning whether it was real or a fragment of my imagination. A gentle breeze tickled the skin of my cheeks. "What… How? It's so warm. How is this possible?"

Dr. White smiled in response. "I knew you'd like it. Your mother used to bring you here as a child so that you'd get a sense of the world above. You used to help her plant the trees, play on the rope swings, pick the bananas and harvest coffee beans. It was your playground and a small project you both shared."

This rainforest had been my escape and the only connection I'd had with nature until I woke from hibernation.

My smile faded. I had always stayed in the world of level -3. I'd never seen the sun or felt the wind against my skin, only the artificial lamp that beamed down on us and whatever created the rustling of the trees. If the doctor's words were true, the only experience I'd had with nature were those memories built within this manmade paradise.

Despite the vastness of the Biome, I suddenly felt claustrophobic.

"No..." I backed slowly against the smooth bark of a towering palm and held onto it for support. "I can't do this."

Dr. White saw the panic within me and hurried me out of the Biome, locking the door and sealing the vacuum with haste. "That's enough for one day." He tried to play cool, but I sensed a nervousness within him.

He was scared, worried that I might lose control and he'd become reacquainted with my animal alter ego. His hand slowly slipped into his lab coat pocket, and I knew he was locating the taser. "We need to get you to the lab for those tests," he said coolly.

"It's okay, Doc. I'm in control." I leaned against the shiny surface of the wall behind me.

He fumbled with the second door as he spoke. "I'm sure you are, but we can't risk your heart rate rising too quickly."

My panic faded as we rushed back through the corridors until we reached a hospital room like his on level -1. I sat on the bed, and several farmers entered the room to poke and prod at my skin with apparatus.

"Is this all necessary?" I asked the woman who removed the plaster from my neck. The knife wound had healed overnight, and I wished my emotional damage would heal just as fast.

Dr. White nodded. "Quite. We consistently monitor your daily levels via the tech built into your clothes. We've recorded some unusual data over the past few days, and as you're a Gen. 3, we'd like to study it further. It's just as new to us as it is to you, although it's nothing to be concerned about."

I nodded, but I doubted if Dr. White was being honest. I didn't interrupt as they finished up, packed everything away, and led me back to the lift where a figure awaited us, leaning against the wall with arms folded across their chest.

"Uncle Daniel," Marshall welcomed Dr. White with a slight gruffness. "Ares." His tone was enough insight into how he felt about me abandoning him in the Safe House.

"You should be resting, Marshall," Dr. White said. "I told the nurse not to let you go."

Marshall rested a hand on Dr. White's shoulder. It would have seemed a friendly gesture if not followed by his next words, "You forget the hierarchy, Uncle. You know I don't act kindly to acts of terrorism, and I could have you killed for overthrowing the system."

"Stop with the dramatic outbursts. You need to rest—"

"What I *need*," Marshall interrupted, tilting his cap back to study me without moving his head, "is to speak to my brother. Alone."

For a moment, I forgot that he was talking about me. It was going to take time for me to come to terms with the fact that I was related to this piece of crap.

Neither of us replied, but I shared a worried look with my uncle.

"We were just about to head back—" I started. I *really* wanted to see Lora. The thought of telling her my news, seeing the joy on her face, and holding her in my arms made my heart ache in a way I'd never experienced. I'd known longing, and I had known lust. But this was something else entirely: a dying plant on a riverbank, starving for water.

"You should go." Dr. White turned to me suddenly. "It might do you both some good."

I wanted to nudge my elbow into his ribs so hard it might break a few. *Save me*, I thought, *don't encourage it.*

"Are you sure?" My voice was doubtful. In my experience, no event where Marshall was present had ever been 'good'.

"Of course." Dr. White offered Marshall a closed-mouthed smile, and I knew I was missing something.

I regretfully followed as Marshall walked away, turning back to call Dr. White a traitor as we neared the corner of the tunnel, but he'd already vanished into the sea of other farmers.I was left alone with the one person I despised most.

CHAPTER FOUR

ARES

"How old are you?" Marshall asked, bringing my attention back to the situation I was in and away from worrying about Hail.

"Twenty-three," I replied.

"Figures," Marshall said, more to himself than to me. "They sent me out to Wilson's camp whilst Mother was pregnant. I thought it was a chance to experience life outside The Farm and build my skills, but they sent me away to hide you. No wonder Mother seemed so distracted when I returned."

I hadn't been paying attention to where Marshall was taking me until he swiped his tablet and led me into an impressive room split across two floors. Screens and monitors filled an entire wall like small windows to the different areas of The Farm. This was how Marshall witnessed the world above, detached from it, as though the people on the screen were merely there for entertainment and not real people at all.

I understood now how he so easily hated and gave orders to end lives when all he experienced was this one-dimensional view.

He thought he knew us from what he saw on the screens, but the cameras only captured part of the picture, part of the story and who we were.

Marshall thought he understood me because he'd followed me through these electronic windows, but he was about to learn that I was more than a figure on his screen.

"Welcome to the Observatorium," he muttered as though it were more of a standard requirement. I followed as he weaved up the ramp and leaned against the only desk on the upper floor.

The ground floor was occupied by farmers at computers, many of them typing or watching the moving mosaic. Some turned to stare at me.

"Get back to work!" Marshall yelled at them, catching me off-guard. I tried not to flinch. "They've been monitoring you for weeks. I guess it must be like having a celebrity in the room."

"I'm glad you're just as kind to them as you are to us," I said, trying for a lighter mood, but my brother didn't know how to take a joke. "What am I doing here, Marshall?"

He frowned and slumped into his chair, then hiked his feet onto the desk, sighing as though it released a world of pain from within. "I don't know. What are any of us doing here?"

I stared.

He was keeping me from Lora for no reason at all. He was talking to me instead of planning a rescue mission for Hail.

The bruise around his neck had turned purple overnight, and I considered replacing my hand over the mark I'd left and finishing the job I'd failed to complete last night.

I wasn't a killer and didn't encourage violence, but Marshall brought out a side of me I couldn't control. He enticed the animal state with minimal persuasion.

"You can start by apologizing for stabbing me," I suggested.

"You strangled me first," he pointed out between sips from his flask.

"Because you ordered Dickward to kill me."

"Yes. And you tied me to a tree."

I huffed. We would be here hours if I listed everything he'd done to piss me off over the past few weeks.

"You know what? I'm going to be the better man because

evidently, you don't have the manners or decency to do so..." I ground my teeth together. "I'm sorry."

Marshall nodded and then spun on his seat to face the wall of screens. "Apology accepted."

"That was your cue to say it back."

Marshall shrugged. "I won't lie to you, Ares. I'm not like Daniel. So no, I won't say it back because I'm not sorry."

I shook my head. "I don't understand."

"Do you know how much trouble you've caused over the past few weeks?" He tilted his head and faced me again. "You deserved everything you got. Hybrids who refuse to mutate should not be on the program. Hybrids who find ways to work around the rules don't deserve a place here." He pointed towards the black screens on the far left. "You see those? You did that the night you and your girlfriend decided to leave camp and save Tye. You took down too many of our defences, leaving us vulnerable. Drones are our eyes within The Farm and around the fence, so the Night Walker attack was your fault too. Just as much as mine. I want you to know that. Actions always have consequences, so consider when sacrifices are necessary next time. You can't be selfish in this world and get away with it." Sweat began to break out on his forehead, and I wondered what had happened to his cap.

"I don't see how saving a life was a selfish act. If you hadn't put Tye in danger first, then we'd never have destroyed the drones. If you brought me here to make me feel guilty, then it will not work, Marshall. I stand by what I did."

"I brought you here to slap some sense into you!" He stood, and I suddenly became very aware of how dangerous this situation could become. Marshall was the most unpredictable person I knew. "If I die, the responsibilities of leading The Farm will fall to you. That's the *only* reason I haven't killed you for what you did yesterday."

My mouth was a desert, my tongue scratched at my sandpaper gums as I spoke, "What about Dr. White, or Tim, or—"

"There is nobody else, Ares. There's a reason our parents left The Farm to me, not Daniel." *Our parents.* "Everybody has a part to play. They're all experts in their field and taking them out of their roles to lead The Farm would leave a massive gap in the system. It can only be us."

I nodded in understanding but felt a weight drag my heart. For as long as I could remember, I'd wanted to find the leader of The Farm and ask him to change his methods, but I had never wanted to *be* the leader of The Farm.

Marshall rocked slowly on his chair, and I pictured sitting in his place one day. It was a dizzying, stomach-churning thought.

Distracting myself, I looked to the screens, finding those

which showed the Titanium barn. It was empty. A few screens to the right, the Venos sat silently on benches. The camera below showed my fellow Titaniums huddled together in the library, watching a video Tim played on his tablet.

I could see the whole farm from here, whether on ground level or within the bunker. The only room I couldn't find was my own; the Infirmary's cameras left a blind spot where I knew my door should be.

"You were in this room the day our parents died?" I seemed to recall bits and pieces of his conversation with Dr. White yesterday, but I'd tried to block out the memory as much as possible. "You saw it all?"

Marshall seemed void of emotion as he replied, "Father locked me in here whilst he ran out to save Mother. I watched the Night Walker destroy them both."

"That must have been traumatic," I tried to sympathize. I couldn't imagine what he'd gone through that night.

Marshall began to smile, and the smile turned into a laugh, and I stood clueless as to what was so funny as the sound bounced from the white walls. The farmers within the Observatorium paused to look at us. It wasn't a pleasant sound because Marshall wasn't a pleasant person. There was a hefty dose of bitterness within the hysteria.

"You're just like them. You can't therapize me, Ares."

My head shook in defence. "I wasn't trying to—"

"You probably do it without even realizing." His face fell flat, and a snarl replaced his crazy smile. "Don't ever do it again."

"Why? What are you so afraid of?"

Marshall glared.

I was pushing him, and I knew it. It's what I did best.

"Let me show you something." He turned to his computer, pulling up a 'Camera 72' file. He clicked through a few more folders until he found what he was searching for.

The video began to play, showing figures huddled around the lake. I recognized the woman from the photograph in my pocket, which Dr. White had given me, his twin, my mother.

"Shut it off!" I ordered once I realized what I was seeing, and dread filled my veins. Marshall really was sick.

"No, Ares. You need to see what we're up against to feel that sense of hopelessness and revenge. You need to know why we are fighting this war."

"I already know. This video won't prove anything." My hands fumbled to take over the mouse and close the video down, but Marshall held his taser out in warning.

Neither of us knew if the electric device would work on me now, as it hadn't the night previous when I'd been in my mutated state. My body seemed to absorb the shocks. But I was in my human state now and wasn't willing to test it. If I went out, I'd be out until Marshall was ready to wake me, and I had no idea how long he'd keep me unconscious just to spite me.

"Shut up and watch it!" he commanded. "Or I'll make you watch it in your sleep for the next week."

I didn't doubt that he had the science or technology to make that possible, so I watched the monitor and told myself that it was nothing more than a film. I didn't know the people, which wasn't a lie.

I told myself they weren't my parents, just Samantha and Joe. Strangers, two people on a one-dimensional screen.

Camera 72 focused on the bank next to the lake, not far from the Titanium barn. Samantha was standing on the bank. Her face was stern, focused, and somewhat panicked. She used the tablet on her arm to communicate with somebody whilst a woman walked into the frame. She stood motionless; her red eyes fixated on Samantha.

I wanted to call out to her, to tell her to turn or run, but I knew how stupid it would appear. This video was eight years old, and no outburst of mine would help the woman on the screen.

In a moment, the red-eyed woman had Samantha wrapped in her arms, one hand smothering her face, the other gripping her shoulder.

"Did the video skip?" I asked, my voice so quiet I wasn't sure if Marshall heard it.

He didn't reply but continued to watch as a man walked into the frame. I didn't repeat my question.

That must be Joe, I thought. He was broad like Marshall, with the same copper hair and piercing eyes. But his curls reminded me of my own, and I tried desperately to disconnect myself from the image of my father because I knew the nature of what was about to happen.

Samantha was calling to Joe, crying from within the red-eyed woman's grasp. The Night Walker looked at him; suddenly, it was as though my father couldn't move. He stopped his advancement, and his body shook as though he were sobbing but unable to let the screams out.

He watched as the Night Walker dug her teeth in and tore a chunk from Samantha's neck, but he couldn't move to save my mother; he couldn't even scream for the Night Walker to stop.

Samantha's blood began to soak the collar of her white coat, and then her body fell limp. The Night Walker dropped her to the ground in a slump.

"No!" I yelled out. "Marshall, turn it off. I understand. I do. Please, stop this—"

"Watch it, or we'll cancel Hail's rescue party," Marshall said.

I stopped my disruption.

Hail is with these monsters right now…

I swallowed back my regret and bit my tongue to distract myself from the emotional pain. I'd take physical pain over this any day.

My eyes landed back on the Night Walker on the screen. Her focus was solely on Joe. He moved somewhat unnaturally as though he was fighting against his skin as he stepped towards my mother's crumpled body. He reached towards Samantha and dragged her by the hair towards the lake before proceeding to submerge her until she bled out or drowned, whichever came first.

A part of me drowned alongside her. I could feel the lake in my throat, the water choking me. It released itself from my body in the form of tears.

After Joe killed his wife and stood helplessly watching her floating body, the Night Walker rid him of his suffering by swiftly beheading him with brute strength.

The head splashed into the water, where it remained as she picked up my parents' corpses and turned to face the drone. My heart picked up speed.

I knew her face.

I recognized the Night Walker. The woman from my dream in the cell near the Safe House.

The woman with the answers.

I tried to form words to tell Marshall I remembered her, but my sobs made the sentence inaudible.

And then the red-eyed woman ran out of frame with the bodies in her arms.

Marshall clicked the mouse to close the file as if it were one of Tim's training videos and then spun in his chair to face me.

I wiped my eyes and tried to process what I'd just seen without replaying any of it in my mind.

"So now you know what we're up against," he said.

Red flashed before my eyes. The color sinking into my mother's white coat, the color of the Night Walker's eyes, the color that slowly crept into my vision as I tried to calm my mutant alter ego.

"They're… vampires." It was all I was able to process.

"Vampires are myths." Marshall shook his head, seeming repulsed by my conclusion. "Night Walkers are merciless, intelligent, blood-sucking monsters."

"Where did she take them?" My voice sounded frail. "Their bodies?"

Marshall shrugged. "I don't know. She escaped The Farm, taking down a quarter of the farmers and my—our…" he corrected himself, "parents' bodies with her. But we have a headstone for them in the graveyard, if that's what you're asking."

"And the head…?"

I'd swam in that lake. I'd almost drowned in that lake, too.

"Father's head is buried there, yes."

My mind was restless. *Vampires...* My skin was ice.

"Well," Marshall stood abruptly, turned, and took another swig from his flask. "We'd better get you back to the pack."

"You show me that and then expect me to return to my day as though nothing has happened?" My voice was higher in pitch than I was used to. "Are you crazy? Don't answer that. Of course, you're crazy. You're out of your goddamn mind—"

Marshall began to laugh once more, then he stumbled, and slumped against his desk whilst holding a hand over his chest.

"Marshall?" I asked, wondering if this was another of his strange lessons.

He waved me off, "It's just the drugs that Daniel forced into me. He's trying to flush my system or something. It's doing a number on me. Get me back to the hospital," he commanded and lunged his body in my direction. I quickly caught hold of him, wrapping his arm around my shoulders as he struggled to walk.

"Need a hand?" A voice appeared behind me as I headed for the door; Greenman, the hoverer who liked to spy on our training.

I'd forgotten that he existed.

"Please." I nodded. "Which way to the hospital?" I questioned as we left the Observatorium, and Greenman took Marshall's left arm.

"This way." He veered us back towards the bunker. "I'm sorry, we haven't been formally introduced. I'm Wilson," he called over Marshall's head.

"Ah, so you *do* talk. I'm Ares, but you already knew that, right?" I shifted Marshall under my weight. "What do you do here? Other than watch hybrids train with that creepy expression on your face."

I couldn't see Wilson's mouth, but I heard a laugh from his direction. "I wasn't aware, but thank you for pointing it out, Ares. I was the leader of the Northern Camp, but Night Walkers overran it. The Farm was the only place we knew to go, so I gathered the survivors and made our way here. Your Farther used to work with my mother before the war."

"Less talking, more walking!" Marshall yelled from between us. It alerted the other farmers as we entered the bunker, where Dr. White waited for me. He rushed forwards and called for assistance on his tablet.

"What happened?" the doctor asked.

"One minute, he was forcing me to watch the video of our parents' death, and the next, he was demanding to be taken to the hospital."

Another farmer thankfully took my place in Marshall's armpit, and they carried him away. "Nice to formally meet you, Wilson," I called as he disappeared. He held his thumb up in reply.

"He did what?" It took a while for Dr. White to register my words. "How dare he—"

"She was a vampire," I interrupted as the door to the lift closed. It seemed my body was waiting for privacy because as soon as we began to move, the reality of everything that had happened over the past twenty-four hours overwhelmed me. "Night Walkers are vampires, aren't they? And now they've got Hail, and he's going to die the same horrible way that my parents did, and we're wasting time planning a rescue mission instead of actually rescuing him—" it spilt from me in uncontrollable sobs.

"Breathe, Ares." My uncle hesitated before awkwardly placing a hand on my shoulder, and he was probably weighing his chances of surviving if I mutated in this small box. Keeping me calm was in his best interest.

The lift slowed, and the air shifted before the door opened. Winter welcomed us, and I inhaled as much of the icy breeze as my lungs could take. "Do you think they're planning to turn Hail into one of them?" I questioned and shuddered.

Dr. White didn't get the chance to reply through the sound of yet another siren.

CHAPTER FIVE

LORA

Focus.

My mind wandered from Tim's tutorial once more.

But where was Ares? He'd been gone too long.

Where was Hail? At a guess, twenty-something miles away. The Alpha connection remained by a thread. If he put any more distance between us, he'd break away, lost to me forever.

Focus, Lora.

This was important.

We sat in the library, watching the screen as Tim played a video of a past Alpha who had presumably died many years ago for us to be standing here today. The Alpha was like me, conducting a brilliant beam of light as the energy exploded from within him. It was refreshing to see it from another's perspective and fully appreciate it. The power was magnificent, but then he did something unexpected, pulling the energy through the palms of his hands. It sparked like mini strikes of lightning, astounding. My jaw fell open, and I quickly closed it before anyone saw it.

The energy bounced through his fingers as the Alpha contained the ball of lightning, glowing white, lighting up his face. Once he was sure he was in control of the energy, he shifted his focus to his surroundings, chose a target, and launched the electricity into a nearby tree. The branches disintegrated into dust.

My hybrids gasped in awe as they witnessed the power and control of the other Alpha.

"Phase Three will teach you to harness the energy within yourself. To accomplish this, you must be able to evolve." Tim began to explain. "Using the energy in this way can temporarily paralyze and disarm a Night Walker. You're all aware of how powerful a Night Walker can be after last night's events, so..." Tim paused as though distracted by the memory of the night before.

Hail, my heart called out.

"Every one of you can accomplish this, not just an Alpha, although Gen. 1s tend to be a little stronger."

My eyes skittered back towards the door.

We'd been in here for almost half an hour now.

On the tablet, the hybrid began to demonstrate how to push the energy from his being through his fingertips.

My mind fell back to Hail.

If only he'd known this before the Night Walkers took him.

"Lora?" Tim interrupted my thoughts. I hadn't noticed him pause the video, and now everyone was staring in my direction. "Everything okay?"

I swallowed hard.

"Of course."

"You seem distracted."

"She's missing her boyfriend," Tye mocked.

There it was.

I knew the pack would have something to say about my emotional breakthrough yesterday. It had been a moment of hopelessness, and now they would never see me the same again. I'd lost their respect.

Love had made me vulnerable.

Ares had made me vulnerable.

I couldn't let my pack view me this way.

I hit my elbow between Tye's shoulder blades before he could process what was happening, slamming his head into the table as he fell forwards. I gripped my fingers into his afro and held his ear close to my face to ensure he fully understood my message. "Don't *ever* mock me. Jealousy is an ugly trait, Tye, and I don't care for it."

Tye held his bleeding nose in shock as I let him go.

The pack remained silent.

I fixed my hair behind my ears.

Tim hovered behind his desk, holding the remote and ready to taser us unconscious if we didn't simmer down. I backed away and nodded towards him in reassurance.

It was under control. *I* was in control. Just.

I glanced back towards the door.

Where is Ares?

My heart fluttered at the thought of him, and my mind spun a web of questions.

This was too much all at once.

I could feel myself slipping out of the darkness and into a colorful world where love *fixed* problems instead of causing them. I'd opened myself to that possibility during Phase Two because I felt stronger around Ares. He had brought me back from the numb land I'd once called home and made me feel more than the stress of the war and the responsibility of the pack.

He was like my battery, breathing life into me with his touch. I needed him now, and I needed the comfort I found within his arms and the happiness and reassurance I felt from just being near him.

I was becoming reliant on Ares, which was more dangerous than anything I'd ever encountered because I didn't know what to do if I lost him. I couldn't face the desperation I'd felt that night of the drone attack again. He'd been so distant. He'd come so close to death I'd felt the energy fade from within him. And I knew then that I'd struggle to live if it was not by his side.

I couldn't lose him.

Yet, I knew that I had to leave him.

There was no other way.

"The Night Walker attack was a surprise to us all." Tim nodded. "I can understand why you're all feeling on edge."

His words caught me off guard. "On edge?" I repeated, my tone blunt, eyebrows raising. "What will happen to Hail? What are the Night Walkers capable of, Tim? After everything that's happened, I think we deserve to know."

"I'm not allowed to share that kind of information." He leaned his elbows onto the table and scratched his fingers over his chin. "But you're right… It's not as though Marshall's in charge now. I can reason with Dan." He spoke the last words under his breath.

"So… What will they do to him?"

Tim pulled out a stool and suggested we do the same. "It's difficult to know. Not many come across a Night Walker and live to tell the tale. They're fast, feed on human blood, and can control our minds. I'm not sure why they want Hail, but at a guess, I think they'll try to turn him into one of their own."

"So, we're going to go after him. Tim? Tell me there are plans in place for emergencies like this. We can't let them turn him! We can't-" My anger was rising. I drew in a deep breath and lowered my voice. "We don't have time to sit here and learn magic tricks. We need to find him. We need to rescue Hail."

"There are plans in place, Lora." Tim remained calm, but I didn't believe him.

I swallowed the panic rising within me.

After killing so many hybrids for trying to leave in the past, the farmers would let the enemy walk in, pick off one of our strongest and turn him into one of their own.

I wouldn't allow it.

But Ares isn't back yet. I have to say goodbye.

Tim refused to answer any more of my questions until the farmers filed in, leading us back to the barn.

Tye still held onto his bleeding nose. Jayleigh looked at me as if she knew exactly what I was thinking whilst Zee and Indigo laughed amongst themselves. Diego stayed silent but watchful, as per usual.

Ares was still nowhere to be seen.

And suddenly, I realized that might be a good thing because he would try to stop me if he were here. And if he couldn't stop me, he'd try to come with me.

And he'd get himself killed.

My mind was at war with my heart as I considered my options. Every cell in my body longed to wait for Ares; to see his freckles wrinkle and eyes sparkle as he smiled; to be embraced by the smell of wild mint, his signature scent; to feel his fingers brush my cheek for one last time.

But I couldn't risk it.

I couldn't allow him to put himself in danger for me again. I'd almost lost him the last time.

I could only take the hybrids who could evolve, those the Night Walkers couldn't control. Ares would be safer here with Jayleigh for support, and he could continue his training whilst we were away.

As we returned to the barn, I headed straight to my stall and took a moment to compose myself, holding my breath.

I couldn't waste any more time. It was coming up to midday, and Hail was too far. We needed to make the most of the daylight. I sat on my bed, held a breath, and squeezed my thumbs tightly as a harsh reminder of what I'd been through and everything I'd already come back from. I would come back from this, too.

I slowly released my breath and headed in Jayleigh's direction.

"You're going after Hail, aren't you?" she whispered.

I nodded once in confirmation, keeping my voice low. "Tell Ares that I'm sorry."

"Of course. Taking him along would be a suicide mission."

I released my shoulders in relief, thankful that she understood. "Am I doing the right thing?" I asked. I once resented Jayleigh for her ability to empathize, but now I needed her support.

"Right in every sense of the word. If Tim's theory is true and the Night Walkers are planning on turning Hail into one of their own, then we're all screwed. Whatever the farmers are planning is taking too long. We need to act now."

She confirmed everything my mind was struggling to put into words. I only seemed able to hold two thoughts in my mind at that moment: *Where is Ares? Where is Hail?*

"Will you hold Tye back?" I said.

Jayleigh accepted the challenge with a smile. "I thought you'd never ask."

And then, I headed towards Indigo and Zee to fill them in on my plan. They agreed to the mission with little persuasion.

A beam of white light erupted from within as I evolved,

energy rushing through me and restoring life to my body. I'd never tire of that feeling, like magic in my veins. I was reborn.

I smashed my way through my stall's withering wooden wall, knowing that the farmers wouldn't expect us to create a back entrance. It would buy us a little time, if nothing else.

Once I was out of the barn, an evolved Zee and Indigo followed, and we headed for the gates. I took one last look back. Jayleigh flipped Tye around, sending her foot into his nose as he tried to follow, reopening the wound I'd created earlier.

Then I tore my eyes away.

My heart ached more than my muscles ever had. No training would have prepared me to leave them behind, and no nightmare could have prepared me to leave Ares.

The pack will be fine, I convinced myself. I'll be back before they have time to miss me.

We made our way around the lake, the energy surging through me, the strength pushing me forward.

The adrenaline and nerves created static energy, which seemed to spark from me as we reached the gates. I claimed it.

There was no room for error.

No room for doubt.

I prepared myself as the pair came to a halt behind me. I'd been training my whole life for this. I pushed all emotions aside;

I pushed Ares aside. I knew there could be no room for distraction on the other side of the fence, and love *was* a distraction, although I'd recently learnt that it could be so much more.

I used the pain and guilt to fuel the fire within me.

Until I returned, I couldn't afford to be Lora, only the Alpha of the Titanium pack.

I closed off my thoughts and tuned in on the static energy around me. It danced on my skin like lightning within a storm.

"Stay here," I mind jumped to Indigo and Zee.

They followed my orders, and the farmers turned to face me as I plunged my body ten feet into the air and landed beside them atop the gate tower.

"I don't want to fight you," I offered them an out, holding my hands out in surrender. I didn't know why, but they sparked white and blue like the Alpha I'd seen on the screen earlier.

Both humans began to shoot.

I held my hands out instinctively, protecting my face from the tranquilizers.

But they never reached me, dropping from the blue static barrier I'd managed to create from the energy that swelled within. I looked down at my hands momentarily in astonishment.

How? I've never been able to control my energy before.

Yet, I'd managed to build a forcefield, which crumbled as I stared.

I didn't stop for too long to question it, knowing I was short on time. I pulled the guns from the farmers, using their surprise to my advantage and proceeded to crank the gate open via the lever.

The farmers charged forwards, and I swiftly pushed them aside, not wanting to hurt them. We'd lost enough people today already.

Once the gate was high enough, Zee and Indigo slid underneath before I quickly dropped it down again. The gate-tower farmers began climbing to their feet as the alarm blared. That was my queue.

I plummeted to the ground on the foreign side of the fence.

The air felt sharp against my skin.

The siren rang too loud in my ears.

Finally.

The sensation swept over me like a rush of icy water. I hadn't known it, but I'd been longing for this. My body had been craving a release.

As I landed, I threw my knuckles into the dirt, leaving a small crater in my wake. The pain charged the energy inside.

I took one step into the wilderness of the world beyond

The Farm's boundaries. And then another.

I was ready.

CHAPTER SIX

HAIL

I dreamt of clouds in red and blue.

Sometimes the clouds turned into trees, rabbits, and spirals which made me dizzy, and abandoned buildings.

Sometimes the clouds cleared, and I stared into a pair of eyes.

Red eyes.

And then the fog took over, and the dreams came back to me.

Sometimes I could smell rain. Sometimes I could smell pie. And sometimes the sweetness changed into something so metallic I could taste it. I knew that smell. It was death. I remembered the smell of blood from the day I'd killed Beckle with my bare hands.

And then the red eyes were back, and the clouds returned.

Sometimes there was running water. Sometimes I could hear Donnah's voice as though she were sitting next to me. She sang to me, an angel, and stroked the hairs on my arm with her fingertips as she always used to. Sometimes I could hear other voices.

They said, "We're on track."

"We're waiting for nightfall."

"The Alpha has followed."

And then the red eyes were back, and the fog took over once more.

ARES

The siren echoed around the valley; birds fled the forest; water rattled on the lake's surface.

"It's different to the siren from last night," I noticed, but Dr. White was talking to somebody through his tablet and didn't reply. Through the blaring, I picked out the words 'gates', 'evolved', and 'gone'.

The siren's two-pitched wail dragged and blurred together

into a mind-numbing hum. My heart picked up, and sweat broke out across my skin.

Something was wrong.

It was not the same as the previous night, yet I couldn't quite work out what was different.

And then Dr. White tasered me into unconsciousness.

I awoke sometime later, on the sofa in the common room of level -1 next to Jayleigh, Tye, and Diego.

Dried blood covered Tye's nose with no evidence of injury. Diego was still out cold, and Jayleigh looked at me apologetically.

Why was Tye bleeding? Had there been a fight? Where was Lora?

"What happened?" I questioned. "Where are the others? Did the Night Walkers come back? Lora. Is she? Has she..." my words turned into sobs as I imagined the Night Walkers dragging her away as they had with Hail the night previous.

"Lora's fine." Jayleigh rested a hand on my arm awkwardly. "She's gone after Hail with Zee and Indigo."

The sobs stuck in the back of my throat, and I choked on my panic. "She's done *what*? Without us? What—Why? Why would she do that?"

"Breathe, Ares, it's okay." She patted my arm as though trying to calm a dog in a storm.

"It's not okay!" I yelled. "How can any of this be okay? She left us behind!"

"To protect us."

I shook my head and tore my arm away from her.

Lora had looked at me with such desperation that morning. It had worried me as Dr. White pulled me from the barn, but I hadn't realized the consequences until now. "No. She's running away. She's running from me. It's the only thing that makes sense." Only nothing made sense anymore. *Lora's left me.* "She's the one that initiated the relationship between us! We promised to fight for each other, and now she's left me, and I don't know if I'll ever see her again." My voice started to raise in pitch. "I didn't get to tell her that she's not ill, it's okay for us to be together. But she couldn't wait to hear me out, couldn't she? Oh, no!"

"I know that it's a shock." Jayleigh's tone was calm in contrast to my own. "But I honestly believe she left us here for our own good. She took Indigo and Zee because they can evolve, and she left everyone else so that we wouldn't fall victim to the Night Walkers' mind games."

"We could have mutated," I spat. "Night Walkers can't control us in our animal state."

"Ares, we can't even control ourselves in our animal state, especially you." She tried for a laugh and passed me a bottle of water. "Here, sip this."

I did as she asked, but I wasn't happy about it. I snatched the bottle, flicked the lid away, and then my eyes landed on Tye.

"What happened to you?" I studied his nose. There was no wound to suggest that the blood was his, so either it was somebody else's, or he'd already healed.

Tye glared, but he didn't reply.

He turned on the sofa and faced Diego, who was now awake, thanks to my yelling. Neither of them spoke, although Diego smirked at the image of Tye's face.

"Lora beat the shit out of him," Jayleigh mouthed. "And then I knocked him out."

My eyebrows raised. I wanted to smile. I really did. The image I built in my head was perfect, and any other time I would have laughed until my lungs gave out, but I couldn't bring myself to feel anything past the horror of Lora leaving us behind.

A couple of minutes passed, and we sat silently on the oval sofa. Farmers lined the stairs and blocked off the tunnels which branched from the common room, and they watched us in the same way I watched the fish swim backwards and forwards within their tank.

"They're holding us here until they get Lora back," I realized. "They're worried that we'll try to follow."

Jayleigh rolled her eyes. "God forbid they lose their precious Alpha. If only they'd acted so quickly to find Hail, we wouldn't be in this situation."

"Do you think she'll find him?" I asked the question that had been playing on my mind for the past few minutes.

"Of course."

Worry and doubt started to creep in. I wiped the palms of my hands on my thermals as questions buzzed around in my mind. What would happen if they didn't reach Hail before sundown? Or better yet, what would happen if they *did?*

I couldn't bear to think about Lora, Indigo and Zee fighting the Night Walkers.

Marshall's video from Camera 72 caught up with me, and I reimagined the vampire delving her teeth into my mother's neck. Only this time, it wasn't my mother but Lora.

I closed my eyes and leaned my head onto my hands, slowly rocking backwards and forwards… back and forwards…

"They don't know what they're up against. They're not prepared," I whispered through my fingers.

"They can evolve, so the Night Walkers can't control them. They'll work out the rest."

I dropped my hands to my lap as though they carried the world's weight. "The Night Walkers are vampires, Jayleigh, real-life vampires. They killed my parents."

Jayleigh snapped her mouth shut and looked at the empty table before us. "I'm sorry, that's…"

"Yeah… I know." I shook my head and sighed. "This just doesn't feel right."

"You're anxious and tired. Try to take deep, slow breaths. Calm the nerves."

I'd heard that too often. Breathing wasn't helping, but I tried to do as she said.

"How long have we been down here?" I tried to change the subject, wiping the sweat from my forehead on the back of my arm. Was the air usually this thick?

Jayleigh shrugged. "I've been awake for an hour, maybe more. It's hard to tell without any daylight."

I glanced around the room for the hundredth time.

"Psst… Hey," I called to the nearest farmer. "What's the time?"

The farmer seemed to look straight through me, acting as though I didn't exist. I huffed.

I missed Katie. She would have told me the time.

I tapped my foot against the leg of the coffee table repeatedly and took several sips of water.

Tye turned back to glare at me but said nothing.

I tapped my foot louder.

Whatever happened between him and Lora seemed to have

finally knocked his confidence. I could almost see the word 'Nerd' forming in his eyes, bulging from him, although he chose to bite it back.

My mind drifted back to Lora.

Why had she punched Tye?

How far away was she now?

The sweat dripped down my face and ran along my jawline.

Did she feel guilty for leaving us behind?

My stomach churned again.

"This *really* isn't right," I whispered to Jayleigh, rising to stretch my legs. "Something's…"

I spun, the world seeming to tilt off its axis, and I reached forwards to steady myself.

"Ares?" Jayleigh panicked and stood to assist me. Only the same dizziness claimed her, too.

We both fell back into our positions on the sofa as chaos seemed to erupt around us.

Tye slumped onto the floor.

The farmers activated, rushing to check on us. Diego yelled out in pain.

My heart stammered.

I lifted my hand, witnessing three images begin to contort within each other.

Bile rose in my throat, and I quickly turned away from the

commotion. I'd not yet eaten, so nothing came up as I retched.

Pain. My whole body ached.

My head pounded as the darkness closed in.

All I could think about was Lora.

She was gone.

CHAPTER SEVEN

ARES

The light was blinding and artificial, creating a blue haze around me.

"Ares, can you hear me?" Dr. White's voice appeared distant, as though I were hearing him through a solid wall.

"Vitals are steady," another voice appeared.

"Ares?" the doctor repeated.

I nodded slowly.

It hurt.

My whole body felt like a thousand needles pierced my skin.

"What did you do to me?" I asked, my voice raspy.

Dr. White came into focus as he leaned over me, a mask covering his face and a needle in his hand. "We saved you. All of you."

I didn't understand.

"Are you a qualified surgeon?" I asked as the man I didn't recognize moved away with an interesting tool.

"I am," he replied. "I oversee all of the engineering here."

"What do you mean, engineering? Have you been experimenting on me again? How old am I this time? How long have I been asleep?" My mind spun with questions. It was exhausting.

"It's not what you think, Ares. You've only been asleep for fifty-three minutes. You passed out in the common room alongside your friends."

I tried to sit, observing the theatre. "Where are they? What have you done to us?"

"Heart-rate raising." This one was a woman's voice, placed somewhere behind me.

"Ares, you need to calm down. I will answer your questions, but not until you relax." Dr. White rested a hand on my arm.

"I'll relax once I'm off this bed and away from him." I nodded towards the surgeon. I was unsure if my words formed correctly or if they slurred together.

"You can go." My uncle ushered them away.

The surgeon nodded and evacuated the room, followed by

the woman and several other figures standing around the room.

Dr. White offered me a hand from the bed, and I leaned on him for support, using my other hand to ensure that the back of my gown didn't create a draft or a view.

"Where are the others?" I asked again as I sat in the chair.

"They're next door. I will take you to them in a moment."

I touched my chest. A sharp pain shot through my body so fast that it surprised me.

"What's going on? What happened?"

Dr. White let out a long breath as he carefully planned his words. "We didn't go after Hail because we knew that he would die before he reached the Night Walkers' nest, and the Night Walkers wouldn't be able to turn him if he was already dead."

He... what?

I didn't like how emotionless his voice sounded. Maybe he was tired, but it didn't stop me from comparing him to Marshall. My uncle had been in charge for less than twenty-four hours, and he'd already started talking about sacrificing my friends.

I tried to prolong my anger, needing to hear my uncle out with a clear head, although everything remained fuzzy from the surgery.

"I don't understand. Why will he die before reaching the Night Walkers' nest?"

Nest. I imagined red-eyed beings swarming an abandoned building, hiding in the shadows it contained like spiders. They set their traps and lured in their prey. An uncontrolled shiver crawled up my spine. My body shook and the pain in my chest intensified.

"A hybrid cannot be far from their Alpha, Ares. Once they surpass a certain distance, the spiritual connection is lost, and the hybrid's body will start to shut down. Lora was unaware of this before she left. It's why we acted so quickly to get her back. You were dying. Being so far away from your Alpha was killing all of you."

I paused, remembering the sensation that had swept over my body, leaving me a ghost in my own skin. "And you didn't think it was important to tell Lora this? That she could kill us by leaving us?"

"She should never have wanted to leave her pack, Ares. It's uncommon for an Alpha. There was no need for us to tell her."

"So, what? You disconnected us from Lora?" I tried to make sense of what he was saying. My heart dropped as the realization left me feeling empty. "You couldn't stop her, so you separated us from her so that the distance didn't kill us?"

Dr. White ground his teeth together and tapped his pen onto his folder. "Not quite. The Alpha connection can never be broken. You would die if we tried. We humans don't, *can't* understand it, but we're not just talking about science here. We live in a world where magic is very much real, and the connection that binds you seems to sway more to the magic side. But we do know how to *create* the Alpha bond."

His silence led me to believe that I had missed something. I was still slow from the sedation, and I stared back at him as I tried to work it out, watching his pen tap against the paper folder and wondering if it held the answers I was looking for. Eventually, he realized that I wasn't understanding.

"Your Gen. 3 hybrid basis allowed us to develop. We transferred the pack E Alpha hormones to you so you can substitute in Lora's absence. A Beta, if you will, second in command. We've managed to bind you to the Titaniums left on The Farm."

I was suddenly glad to be sitting down. Once again, the room began to spin.

A Beta... second in command...

My mind hummed.

I gripped my fingernails into the chair's fabric, hoping it would steady me.

Did the farmers think that this was a good idea? I wasn't confident enough to lead a pack; I barely got *myself* through challenges, never mind the other Titaniums.

Dr. White waited for me to look at him before continuing,

and when I did, I saw three of him. "But your body tends to absorb abnormalities, like the drone venom, which should have been enough to kill you, and the taser that Marshall attempted to use last night. The animal side of you swallows any foreign sensation, so, likely, this alteration won't last for long."

"What are you trying to tell me?" I massaged my temples. Was my skull shrinking?

"The Alpha bond that Tye, Jayleigh, and Diego share with you *will* fade over time due to your Gen. 3 tendencies, and once it does, it will be unfixable. This operation will not work again."

"So, the farmers need to hurry up and find Lora before my animal alter ego ingests my new hormones and destroys us all?" I summarized.

"No, Ares," Dr. White corrected. "You and the rest of the pack must leave The Farm to find Lora. It's the only chance you have of surviving."

CHAPTER EIGHT

ARES

"I'm not ready for this. I've never wanted any part of this war, and I don't want to be responsible for anyone dying out there. You can't leave this on my shoulders!"

Dr. White handed me a bottle of water. "I know it's a lot all at once, but there is *no* alternative. You are the only hope that they have. Lora isn't coming back until she has found Hail, and if our people are out there searching for her after dark, then it's doubtful they'll return."

"But I'm not a leader." I took the bottle, wondering why everybody was so insistent on hydrating me. Water wouldn't fix my problems. I tipped it over my head, pushed back my hair, and rubbed my eyes. "I'm the guy who runs at first sight of danger. That is what I'm good at. That is what I do."

"Ares." My uncle reached forward to place a hand on my shoulder but hesitated, realizing that it was wet. He tapped it quickly. "You are capable. You just need to believe in yourself. Think back on all the challenges you have already overcome. Sure, you took an alternate approach, but you got through. You sacrificed yourself for Lora and Tye and stood up against Steven in the final battle yesterday. They all seem like decisions a good leader would make."

I stared at him.

I wanted to tell him that all the reasons he'd just given had been for my gain, but it was unusual for somebody to speak about me positively, and I didn't want to change my uncle's opinion of me.

He seemed to believe that I could do this. And if the substitute leader of The Farm thought that I could be the substitute leader of the Titanium pack, then *maybe* I ought to at least give it a try.

It wasn't like there was any other alternative.

"Now, go and tell your pack what is going on." He pointed towards the door.

I nodded and rose from the chair, feeling a slight chill. "Can I change my clothes first?" I asked. "I don't think they'll want to listen to a leader dressed in a hospital robe with his butt hanging out. It doesn't give the strongest impression."

Dr. White smiled and pulled my clothes from the draw. My uncle left the room and returned soon after I'd finished dressing.

"This is for you." He held a tablet in his hands. "We have tracking devices in each Titanium's sleeve so you can see where Lora's group is and where Hail is."

I located each of their markers within the map. Lora, Indigo and Zee were halfway between The Farm and Hail.

"Lora would have found this useful. She's out there tracking Hail's scent."

"It would have been useful, yes," he agreed. "Once you reach Lora, you must return straight away. You aren't to go anywhere near the Night Walker's nest, outnumbered and unprepared."

I was about to tell him that I didn't plan on meeting with any vampires, but I also didn't like the idea of leaving Hail in their nest. That was not part of my mission and, therefore, not my decision to make. All I had to do was get pack Beta to Lora before my animal state destroyed our Alpha bond, and then Lora could decide the rest. "Okay."

"Go and see your pack. I'll meet you in the corridor in three minutes."

"Okay," I repeated, fastening the tablet around my forearm as the farmers wore it, placing additional batteries in the pockets of my cargos, and then I opened the door.

I didn't know what to expect from the hybrids. I almost expected them to rebel against the idea of me standing in as a substitute Alpha— a Beta. But it seemed that my bond was just as strong as Lora's.

For now.

The pack stared at me, and I stared back at them through new eyes. Because that's what the sixth sense was like; feeling the connection that bonded the four of us as though it was something I could see or touch.

"So, I have some news." I started, and my words died as I recognized the expression on their face.

"What the… shit, man?" Tye managed to say.

Diego shrugged as he leaned against the wall.

Jayleigh smiled. "I'm gonna start calling you Mom."

"That won't be necessary." I laughed.

"I still want to hate you," Tye continued. "But I can't."

"That's a good thing, right?" I questioned as my own body confirmed it. I looked at Tye; the usual bitter feeling had mellowed into something soft. I wanted to protect him and see him smile instead of panic because panicking was exactly what he was doing. I could sense the worry within him.

"Hmm," he didn't sound convinced. "We'll see."

"It's only temporary. We'll go back to hating each other

before you know it because my animal hormones are hell-bent on killing us all and will slowly destroy this new Alpha bond. So, we're going to find Lora before that happens." The pack remained silent. "Did I mention that we'll die if we don't find Lora soon?"

Jayleigh was the first to process the news. "So, shall we get moving? I don't think we should waste any more time."

I nodded and pointed towards the doors. "Dr. White is waiting for us."

"Can I still call you Nerd?" Tye questioned as he walked next to me. "I kind of feel like it's too disrespectful. It doesn't seem right anymore."

"Call me whatever you like, Tye." I sighed. "I have more stressful things to focus on."

"Like leading us through Night Walker infested waters on a time limit?" he suggested. "If we run into a Night Walker, we die. If we don't make it to Lora in time, we die. If we-"

"Yes, exactly. Hearing it out loud isn't helping." I ran my hands against the fabric of my clothes. Was it warm in here?

"How much time do we have?" Diego asked. I wished I could appear just as collected as he removed a stray hair from his sleeve and dropped it to the ground, seemingly unfazed by whatever our future had in store.

"I have no idea." I shook my head, thinking about the night

I'd attacked the drones. The venom paralyzed me for a few hours, so I just hoped my body would take longer to absorb this foreign matter. "I don't think we have long."

Dr. White waited in the corridor as expected and hurried towards the bunker as soon as we emerged. We fell into line behind him, and the doctor overloaded us with information.

"Never underestimate a Night Walker. They're intelligent beings who enjoy playing mind games. Of course, you should always try to mutate or evolve if you encounter one; otherwise, it will compel your mind and kill you. They are incredibly fast, just as fast as an evolved hybrid, yet you can paralyze them for a short time if you can project your energy towards them, as Tim was trying to teach you earlier."

I had no idea what he was talking about, but I assumed it had something to do with whatever they'd been watching on the screen in the library whilst I was with Marshall in the Observatorium.

We entered the bunker. Pack Beta, *my pack*, gawked at its magnificence. Several farmers stopped to watch as we passed through and headed for the corridor titled 'Weaponry'.

"In here." He guided us into a large room stocked with shelves. As soon as I noticed what the cabinets contained, I looked at Jayleigh, her face lighting up with glee.

"Now I finally have an answer to Hail's question. I love this room so much more than pizza." I swear there was a tear in her eye as she ran her hands over the daggers.

"The only way to kill a Night Walker is with a titanium dagger through the heart," Dr. White informed as he pulled one from the cabinet, "so you will all need one. You are free to choose whichever takes your fancy, although I must stress that we are short on time, so please be quick in making your selection."

I opened the cabinet nearest, testing out the weight of each dagger. Each was a different shape, size, and design. The artistry was precise, perfect.

I opted for one with a comfortable, solid titanium handle and a cross-guard which reminded me of a bat wing, fitting for the occasion.

"Are we done?" Dr. White urged us on.

I looked around to find Jayleigh admiring a double-ended dagger with flowers carved into the grip, Diego eyeing up a retractable weapon, and Tye opting for what I could only describe as a pointy grey stick.

"These backpacks contain the essentials." Dr. White held them out for us to collect. "And the daggers will fit into the pocket at your gastrocnemius— your calf," he explained. "Keep them on your person at all times. And now, if you'll follow me, I will escort you back to the lift." He turned away, leaving us to fumble with our belongings and trail after him. He was back to reciting information as though it were spilling out of him. I wondered how long he'd been waiting to tell us about the vampires and if my parents decided it best to keep us in the dark about their behaviours. Now my uncle had limited time to feed us everything we needed to know.

"The Night Walkers cannot stand in direct sunlight. The radiation burns their skin, which also happens when an evolved hybrid projects its energy. It is enough to hurt them but not kill them. You *must* use your dagger to kill them. Always aim for the heart and remember to retract the weapon from the body. You will have to become resourceful if you lose your weapon in battle. I presume you all still carry your hand knife from Phase Two?"

We nodded as we reached the lift. I'd since changed my clothes, but my knife was to my new cargos.

"That knife will not work. It must be solid titanium."

Typical. I tried to take note of the information, but the nerves clouded my senses. It was happening so quickly.

"If you need me, Ares, I'm just a call away. Usc your tablet to contact me, come day or night."

"Thank you, Dr. White." I nodded as we waited for the lift. I wasn't sure if I'd ever see my uncle again, and the urge to hug him swept over me, but I held myself back. Goodbyes were final; this wasn't final, only a short, deadly, and unpredictable vacation. "For everything."

The pack loaded into the lift, but Dr. White kept me back.

"Of course." He nodded briskly and held onto my shoulders, gripping them tightly, scared I might vanish like the rest of our family. "You'll have to make tough decisions out there, but remember who you are, remember why you're here and remember what your favourite uncle told you from day one."

The surprise numbed my body.

"But I don't remember Flynn, Uncle Daniel." The joke left me before I could assess its relevance in this situation. Now was not the time.

Dr. White's eyes squinted as he smiled and lifted his glasses to wipe his tears with a handkerchief. "You twerp…"

I didn't know what a twerp was, but I knew that he said it in good humor.

"For the greater good," I recalled his words, and he nodded. His eyes gave away a raw emotion; if I didn't know any better, I'd have said it was pride.

I felt lifted to the sky as he smiled.

"Follow your heart, Ares. It hasn't led you wrong so far."

"I will," I tried to reassure him, although I was unsure of myself, as he guided me into the lift and pressed the button which would take us to the world above. "I'm sorry I got angry earlier," I said. The bitterness couldn't linger until I returned.

"It's water under the bridge, Ares. I'll see you all when you return." He composed himself quickly and waved us off as the doors closed. "For the greater good!" he repeated the words.

The doors sealed, and the lift lurched into action.

My uncle's words echoed around us.

"I can't believe this is happening," Jayleigh whispered and started to re-braid her hair into a tight plait down her back, tucking away any loose strands. It was the first time I'd ever seen her look rattled.

"Me either," I agreed. "But it's going to be okay. We'll find Lora, and we'll head straight back."

Tye scoffed. "You've just been downgraded from Nerd to Fool. You can't honestly think it'll be *that* easy."

"No." I closed my eyes. "Of course, I don't. I was trying to be optimistic."

"Try *realistic*, Fool."

"I see the Alpha bond has already dimmed." I rolled my eyes. "You don't seem to have a problem calling me names anymore."

"I still don't feel comfortable with the name-calling, but you seem to need reminding."

"That's enough, Tye," I warned. "Let's get one thing

straight. We won't survive out there unless we all work as a team. One unit. I'll be happy to leave you behind if you're going to cause problems." We all knew what leaving him behind would mean, and Tye didn't reply as the door opened, and we evacuated the lift. "I'm going to assume that your silence is an agreement to my conditions."

Tye nodded once.

I released a large breath.

It's happening. We're leaving The Farm.

And Lora was already out there, in danger. "If anything hurts her. If anything so much as touches her…" I let my words die out.

"You'll what? Tell it off and make it stand in the naughty corner?" Tye couldn't stop himself.

"No," I said in all seriousness. My jaw clenched at the thought of a Night Walker finding Lora before we could. I had to blink the image away, heat searing through my veins. "I'll kill them."

I surprised myself as the words left my lips, but if there was one thing I'd learned in the past few weeks, it was that I had to do everything within my power to ensure the survival of humankind. I couldn't let my worries blind me from what was at stake. If I refused to mutate—if I ignored all the warnings—this generation might be the last. I had to do what was right, and if giving way to my animal alter ego was the solution, then so be it.

"I'll kill them," I repeated.

"Now, *this* is an Ares I can get on board with." Jayleigh looked at me as though I were Diego, giving me a slight raise of her eyebrows. "Where have you been hiding, Mr. Dark Ares?" she drooled.

I felt highly uncomfortable with the thought of her starting to gain feelings towards me.

It's just the Alpha Effect. The new hormones blind her, and the feelings will fade soon enough, I reasoned with myself. Jayleigh was my closest friend, and the thought of there being anything more between us just felt wrong.

"On that note..." I pointed along the path, put on my bravest voice and said, "To the gates!"

Pack Beta stared. Tye mouthed the word 'Nerd' whilst Jayleigh muttered something about 'Dark Ares' being good whilst it lasted, but I drowned it out as white noise filled my ears.

This is really happening.

I lost control of my breathing, and my heart began to stutter.

How did Lora cope with so much pressure? I was sure the anxiety would kill me long before any Night Walker could.

Stop thinking. Act.

I broke into a run, heading for the gatehouse, and the pack followed behind out of courtesy. Jayleigh and Tye could have outrun me if they'd wanted to, and Diego's weight from the bulk of his muscle was the only thing to hold him back.

The nerves overwhelmed us all.

I could sense it in the air around us.

I wondered if my insecurities seemed evident to them or if, like Lora, they could only sense assurance.

Who was I kidding?

I'd never live up to Lora. Having me as an Alpha was probably the root of Pack Beta's nerves, the guy who jumped at the smallest of noises and the guy who ran from danger, the guy now tasked with leading a group outside the fence.

I would have been nervous, too, if I were them.

My heart raced faster as we closed the distance to the gates.

The fence came into view, and The Farm's boundary was the limit of my comfort zone. My self-belief faded the closer we came to the parameter.

I wanted to turn around.

What I *really* wanted was to return to the barn and curl up into bed with Lora by my side.

We slowed as the fence towered over us.

I shouted to the guards, but the sound of a vehicle

distracted me. It was a truck approaching with speed, and it grew louder as I turned back to face the old track.

Had we forgotten something? Was Dr. White following to make sure we left safely?

The truck came into view as a farmer within the gate tower shouted, "Are you ready?"

"Just one second," I replied.

The pack looked at me in question. I was just prolonging the torture.

The vehicle halted beside us, and Katie hopped out of the driver's seat. She smiled apologetically in my direction, which I only assumed meant one thing, before crossing to the passenger side and opening the door.

I groaned as Marshall stepped out. This was the last thing we needed.

"What do you want?" I sighed. Was it too much to ask that he'd come to say goodbye?

"I heard that you were leaving," he started.

"I didn't think you'd care."

"I don't."

I sighed again. I shouldn't have waited for the truck... "Then why the hell are you here? You look like crap." Whatever Dr. White had been flushing his system with appeared to have aged him ten years.

"I'm here to make you a deal," he replied.

That spiked my attention. I looked at the pack for their input, but they met me with blank expressions. "What kind of deal?"

"The truck, and Rachel to drive it."

Rachel? I looked at her, feeling cheated. I don't know why I was so surprised that Marshall knew her real name, but she still looked more like a Katie to me.

"What do you want in return for the truck and… Rachel?" I wondered if she'd given Marshall permission to bargain her off like this.

Marshall squinted through the afternoon sun and jerked his head towards the gate. I hadn't prepared for him to say, "I want you to take me with you."

CHAPTER NINE

ARES

"Why in hell would you want to come with us?" Jayleigh asked the words we'd all been thinking.

"You've got to be kidding," Tye joined in.

Marshall ignored them and instead waited for me to say something. But I had no words.

It was bad enough that I had to leave The Farm, never mind leading a pack. Adding Marshall into the equation just seemed somewhat suicidal for all of us. I wanted to tell him that the idea was ridiculous. I wanted to see the disapproval on his face when, for the first time, he realized that I had *his* fate in *my* hands, and I was able to tell him no. Yet, something held me back.

"Who will run The Farm if you go?" I asked. He'd already

made it clear that he disapproved of Dr White standing in.

Marshall shrugged. "Uncle Daniel, Wilson, Tim. I don't care anymore. I want out. I want to help find Lora, Indigo, and Zee."

I didn't believe it for one second. "There's wanting out, and then there's leaving the safety of The Farm, Marshall. Are you sure you're in the right mind frame to make decisions like this?"

My brother sighed, stepping away from the truck he had previously slouched against and proving that he was well enough to carry his own weight.

"Of course, I'm well enough," he shot. "I'm not stupid, Ares. I'm doing this to help you."

That was yet to be determined. Marshall wanted to leave The Farm, knowing he had no defence against the Night Walkers. It sounded stupid to me.

"We can get you to Lora a hell of a lot faster with the truck, and once you're all together, we'll have the chance to get Hail back, but without Rachel and me? You guys will most likely die. Lora will eventually return to her human state and become so overwhelmed with grief and guilt that she'll get herself killed too. Face it. You need me."

I shook my head. "No. We don't need you, only your truck."

"It's programmed for farmers. We couldn't risk a hybrid using it to escape The Farm."

"We have a farmer." I nodded towards Katie. "We don't need you."

"Unfortunately, Rachel is under my protection. I would be considered a highly irresponsible boss to put her under so much stress and danger to leave The Farm alone with a group of hybrids. She is simply accompanying me on my mission."

"When did you start caring about being a responsible boss?" He'd not been pleasant to the farmers in the Observatorium this morning.

I could see his patience wearing thin, and I knew we were wasting time.

I needed to decide.

"My combat skills are phenomenal. I trained the farmers after my time in Wilson's camp up north, and—no offence—I feel that you could use my expertise out there." He tried to sell himself.

"What do you think?" I questioned the pack as I turned away from Marshall.

Tye raised his eyebrows in horror. "Wow, the whole family has lost their goddamn mind." He wiped his hand down his face as he walked away.

It was a possibility.

"Am I? Losing my mind?" I turned to Jayleigh for her input.

She shrugged. "Using the truck would be much faster than travelling by foot and safer. But I don't trust Marshall. He's definitely got an ulterior motive here."

"Of course he does. He's Marshall. So, the real question is if we want to risk finding out what the ulterior motive is…"

I looked towards Diego, who held his hands out in surrender. "I only met this guy yesterday. I have no opinion." Then he added, "But if he steps one foot out of line, I will not hesitate to kill him, whether he's your brother or not."

"That's fair." I nodded. "I tried to kill him yesterday too. So, we're in favor of the truck, three to one?"

"In favor of the truck." Jayleigh nodded. "Just a shame we couldn't take it without Marshall."

"Amen to that."

I turned back to tell him the news, not quite believing the words were leaving my mouth. "Fine."

"Fine?" He laughed. "I'm doing you a favor, I expected a little more than *fine*. But whatever." He turned back towards the vehicle and held the door open for me to jump into the passenger seat. "Well? What the fuck are you waiting for—"

"Under three conditions," I interrupted him. "Condition one: if you piss us off, we will leave you in a ditch. Condition two: you're no longer in control. Forget all about your rules. From here on, what I say goes. And condition three: always stay where we can see you."

Marshall didn't pause to consider the terms of my agreement. Instead, he jumped into the front of the truck and closed the door behind him.

He smiled through the window and raised his flask in cheers as I opened the back door for the hybrids to load in. At least he was listening for now.

"I don't like this," Tye grumbled.

"I don't think any of us do," I replied. "But we need to get to Lora as soon as we can. We really need this truck. I promise to cut him off as soon as he makes one wrong move. I learnt my lesson yesterday. Marshall doesn't deserve second chances."

"Can I be the one to kill him?" Tye asked. "He's killed more of my friends than I can count on one hand."

"Yeah. Sure. So long as you hurry up and climb in. Everyone seems to be forgetting that we're on a very tight schedule here."

I ushered him in as though it wasn't me to hold them back in the first place.

He slid onto the bench on the left. I followed, pulling the door closed and signalling to the guard in the gate tower that we were ready to leave.

The gates were ten feet tall, made of metal, and only retracted when the farmers pulled a lever. The mechanism began to clunk and clank into action, the sound echoing throughout the valley and shaking the ground around us as the truck pulled forward.

At least Marshall's interruption had momentarily distracted me from the nerves of crossing into the outer world. I trapped my hands between my legs to hide how they were shaking.

Confidence, Ares, I reminded myself. Fear is just a trick of the mind.

I tried to believe it as we crossed the threshold into the unknown.

It was a good sign that after fifteen minutes of driving, we were yet to see another soul, human or otherwise.

Did Night Walkers have souls? I doubted it. The vampire I'd seen on the camera in the Observatorium seemed to lack any sign of humanity as she'd killed my parents.

"How far?" Marshall questioned. He had been unusually quiet until now.

"They're still a fair distance away, but we're closing in on them.

"They had almost a four-hour head start, and they'll be

moving fast as they're in their evolved state, but they won't be able to hold it much longer," Marshall contributed. "The two newer hybrids will lose control of the state as they tire, and once they do, it'll make it easier for us to catch up."

And more unlikely they'll reach Hail before sundown.

I watched their pins move north— in Hail's direction, whose pin stayed secure in one place.

I hoped it meant the Night Walkers were waiting out the sun and not that Hail was injured. It was easy for my mind to flick over different possibilities knowing how cruel the Night Walkers could be.

A cold breeze crept up my spine at the thought, and I quickly shifted my attention out of the window. It didn't look so different to life within The Farm's boundaries, and it was almost too easy to imagine that we were still safely tucked behind the fence.

"Where did they come from?" I asked Marshall, who turned in his seat to glare at me.

He didn't reply, but his nostrils widened.

"Katie, pull over. Marshall's getting out."

The truck slowed but didn't stop.

"No, I'm not," Marshall interjected. "Keep driving, Rachel. I'll tell them what they want to know."

Katie looked at me for direction, and I nodded.

"The Night Walkers," I pushed. "Where did they come from?"

"They didn't come from anywhere. They've been around, stealing people away in the middle of the night since there were humans to feed on. They were just whispers in the wind then. A shadow in a dark alleyway. The cause of a missing person or an unexplainable murder. Night Walkers have always hunted us; we just didn't know it."

"So, what changed? Why now? What caused the apocalypse?" I questioned.

"At some point down the line, they started working in groups rather than individually. The threat was there for years before we decided to do anything about it. Maybe if we'd listened to the theorists instead of casting them aside, we'd have found a way to hold the Night Walkers off. But humankind has never been a species to listen to problems other than their own, not until the problem affects them directly, by which time it's already too late. Maybe we'd have stood a better chance in this war if we'd listened to the warnings, seen the signs, and done something about it before the damage became too great. Yet here *we* are, the last chance of saving humankind from becoming vamp food. We've prepared our whole lives, and now we're risking our lives for the sake of a helpless, selfish species."

Silence took over the truck.

Marshall sucked at his teeth as though he'd just bitten into a lemon, leaving a bitter taste in his mouth.

"I think humankind is worth saving," I said finally. Unlike Marshall, I knew what a privilege it was to be human, and I knew it was something to be cherished and proud of. I understood this because I also knew how it felt not to be human. The side of me which stirred more restless each day was a creature of death and destruction, and it too was a selfish being—an uncaring animal.

And in contrast, my human state understood that the small details, the ability to *appreciate*, made humankind beautiful. That's what stood us apart from the other species on the planet. Although, it seemed somewhere down the line that our kind had lost their way a little if what Marshall said was correct. There must have been some truth to his words for him to act so passionately about the subject.

I directed Katie/Rachel through the lanes as we put more and more distance between ourselves and The Farm. Somehow, my nerves began to fade as I realized that the world wasn't as I'd imagined. It wasn't burned or destroyed; if anything, the lustrous land around us was thriving. So long as we had daylight, we'd be safe. We just had to keep away from the shadows.

Instantly, my eyes drifted towards every inch of darkness within the area, scanning for movement. They were out there, and they were watching us.

I leaned into the wall of the truck and took a deep breath. As the air filled my nostrils, I recognized the scents around me for the first time. They weren't new, just amplified at a rate I had never experienced—the other hybrids.

I had been so focused on my nerves and my newfound responsibilities that I hadn't stopped to notice my Alpha abilities develop. I closed my eyes, letting the sensation grow, and when I focused, I could feel the energy radiating from the other hybrids, almost as though I could sense the invisible connection between us.

Their energy registered with mine as though they were a part of myself, an odd sensation which left me feeling a strange form of happiness, despite the crazy situation.

I relaxed into it.

This was how it felt to belong to something bigger than myself.

My eyes remained closed. I focused further and further.

I found peace.

Embraced by the warmth of the constant exchange of energy, I didn't realize that I had started to drift off until I felt Jayleigh poking at my arm, trying to make sense of the map on my tablet.

"Yeah, we should have turned left several minutes ago," she replied to Katie.

"Shit!" Marshall slammed a hand into the chunk of the car before him and then turned back to yell at me. "Wake the fuck up, Princess. Or give the bloody map to somebody else."

Jayleigh continued to prod the tablet. "Ares? Wake up, Buddy. I know you've been through a lot in the past twenty-four hours, but we need you to fight the sleep for a little longer."

"I wasn't asleep." I shook my head through half-closed eyes. "Oh, crap. Where are we?"

The fading light through the window proved my couple of seconds of shut-eye had been longer than I'd anticipated.

"What's going on?"

The sun started to set behind the rooftops of long-abandoned buildings strewn with graffiti and overgrown plants. We'd reached a town.

Or what little remained of it.

The tall buildings hung shadows into the street, littered with dust-covered cars and weeds. The plants had escaped through cracks in the tarmac, slowly dying off in the cold weather and lying squashed on the ground as though something had recently trampled over them.

My skin crawled at the possibility of the Night Walkers

lingering behind the smashed windows, watching us. I glanced towards the nearest buildings, old shop fronts and offices, with no evidence of glass debris around the sills. This town hadn't seen life in a long time.

I wondered what had happened to the people who once lived here. Were they dead? Had they been turned into Night Walkers too?

"We need to find a place to set up camp. We're not going to reach Lora's pack before sundown." My heart picked up the pace at Marshall's words, and the severity of the situation sunk in.

"We're spending the night out here? With the Night Walkers?" Tye sounded winded.

"Why can't we keep driving?" I asked.

Marshall shook his head. "They'll hear us, and it'll attract every Night Walker in a two-mile radius. I'm not sure if you've noticed, but nature's only sound out here. We might as well paint targets on our backs."

"Fine. Then we'll sleep in the truck?" I suggested. "Hide it in a good spot, one person watching through the front window and another watching through the back? At least we'll have that extra barrier of protection."

Nobody opposed the idea, so we found a place to park the vehicle, tucked between a five-story building which had once been flats and an old cafe called Jiggle's. The sign had faded in the sunlight, and the door hung on one hinge.

Jayleigh and Katie offered to take the first shift, promising to wake us at the first sign of trouble. I wondered if the trouble would be a disturbance outside the truck or inside; Marshall was still on edge, and I didn't trust him.

"I need a piss," he said.

"I think somebody should-"

He cut me off, "I can take a piss by myself, Ares. But thank you for your concern." He opened the door, climbed out, and then turned back to add, "On second thought, maybe we should all try now before the sun sets. We all remember what happened to Teri when she went out after dark to take a shit."

He walked away whilst tugging on his zipper.

We stared after him, not knowing what to do or say in response. My heart raced at the carelessness of his words. Teri was a part of our pack, a friend, a sister, and Marshall had tricked her into leaving the safety of the camp during the night. He'd killed her through his electronic drones, which replicated a Night Walker attack.

So that's why Teri left camp…

The drones the farmers had made to replicate Night Walkers must have called her name and enticed her from the camp's boundaries. Tye had also been affected by the drones' hypnotic abilities while he was still in his human state. I recalled how he'd scrambled towards them as they whispered his name.

It was starting to make sense to me; the strange teachings of the farmers and their methods, even down to making us bathe together in the cave pools because privacy didn't seem like much of an option outside the fence.

We evacuated the truck whilst it was still safe to do so. I didn't want to risk what happened to Teri happening again.

Marshall is the reason she crossed the boundary. Marshall gave the order to have her killed.

My jaw clenched as I imagined him sitting on his plastic throne, watching out over the world of screens. Two simple words were all that he needed to end that poor girl's life. And he wasn't sorry. He didn't lose any sleep over what he'd done.

And why?

Because she couldn't swim?

Because she slowed the pack down?

Every inch of me was begging to give in to the animal state. The rage swarmed through my veins.

Deep breaths. He is your brother. He just needs help.

Talking to myself wasn't doing anything to calm me. Marshall turned, a smug pout on his lips. I wanted to smack it clean off, but Katie's scream broke through my senses.

Panic brought me back to the present, and I quickly circled

the truck to find her face down in a puddle, scrambling to stand. I couldn't process what was happening.

The pack were still further down the alleyway. I could almost sense that they were behind me, yet I still turned back to count them.

Surely enough, they were all there, so who were the two beings inside the truck?

The vehicle revved into motion and sped away, taking with it our only hope of a safe night outside The Farm's boundaries.

CHAPTER TEN

ARES

Thankfully, we'd taken the backpacks out of habit. During training, we'd carried our rucksacks for miles, almost as though they had become a part of our bodies. So at least we weren't at a complete loss. I tried to focus on that positive to distract me from the fact that we'd have to spend the night within the town.

And the reminder that we were not alone.

We needed to find somewhere safe— if such a word still existed— to set up camp.

Unlike Phase Two, there was no red paint to symbolize an area where the Night Walkers couldn't reach us. We had to create our own safe zone.

My first instinct was to climb.

We needed height, clear exits to guard, and a visual of the

surrounding streets.

We needed a rooftop.

I took it upon myself to become familiar with the neighbouring buildings, starting with Jiggle's.

Jayleigh followed behind, her shoes crunching against the dying weeds underfoot. "Well, this isn't ideal at all," she whispered as we put distance between ourselves and Marshall. "We brought him along for the truck. And now the truck is gone, and Marshall's still here."

"I'm less worried about Crazy out there," I nodded in Marshall's direction. "And more worried about the crazies hiding in the shadows."

My gaze landed on the crumbling petrol station across the road, and my heart began to race, knowing they were out there and waiting for the sun to sink behind the horizon.

The sky already matched the colour of Jayleigh's cheeks.

We didn't have much time.

I swung the door open a little wider, and Jiggle's bell jingled upon entry. My body froze up. The Night Walkers couldn't venture into the sun, but they could hide in abandoned buildings and wait for daylight to pass. If they used this old coffee shop as a home, I'd surely just woken them.

I quickly pulled my dagger from my ankle pocket and held it before me to be safe.

My sharp actions panicked Jayleigh. She quickly zipped into attack mode and threw her double-sided dagger into the room ahead.

I wasn't sure what she'd seen, but I was glad to have her next to me.

"Crap!" I held my weapon with both hands, trying to steady my shaking.

Has she killed it?

We stalked forward slowly, heading for the still figure in the opposite room. I expected the unexpected, waiting for something to jump out at me or grab me from behind. I could hear my heartbeat as it echoed through my ears.

The room was dark, but I could see just enough to make out a silhouette pinned against the far wall with Jayleigh's dagger through its center. Perfect aiming.

My hands began to cramp, my knuckles turning yellow.

We reached the archway and peered in.

I sighed in relief as I understood what I saw for the first time and loosened my grip on my dagger. It still didn't mean we were safe, though.

"Congratulations," I whispered, "you successfully killed an armchair."

She nudged an elbow into my ribs. "You were making me nervous!"

My eyebrows quirked as I held a hand over the spot she'd just bruised. "Well, I do seem to have that effect on the females."

Jayleigh didn't respond. Clearly, now wasn't the time for my nervous humor. She turned to examine the room. "Reckon they have any food?" she said as she ducked behind the counter.

My eyes were glancing at every corner of the room.

"Nope," I replied. "Maybe a few disintegrated croissants."

She rummaged for a few minutes, and I searched my backpack for a torch. The light was fading quickly now, and Jiggle's Coffee Lounge was sparse of windows, save for the two large panes of glass accompanying the door. The room suddenly appeared dark.

I turned on the torch and pointed it towards Jayleigh as she let out an *"Ah-ha!"* small box of unopened oat biscuits in her hand. "Best before November 2073," she stated. "Only a couple of years out of date. What do you reckon?"

"Worth a try," I suggested, but I didn't hold my hopes up. We had food in our backpacks so that wasn't a problem. We just had to find somewhere safe to sleep for the night.

Jayleigh threw them at me with a shrug of her shoulders. I dropped them into my backpack as commotion began to break out. It sounded like it was coming from the alleyway.

For a moment, we shared a look and tried to figure out

what we were hearing, both of us overcome with dread. My duty was to go out and help, but my body didn't agree.

I tried to ignore the part of me that desperately wanted to cower away from the danger. I was responsible for the people outside. I was an Alpha now, and I needed to start behaving like one.

I gripped my thumbs between my fingers as I'd seen Lora do so many times before, hoping that it would provide some form of confidence or, if nothing else, help me feel a little closer to Lora.

It didn't work.

I turned for the door as Jayleigh began to run back.

"Where are you going?" I couldn't believe my eyes. She'd never run from a fight.

"My dagger!" Jayleigh yelled back to me; the weapon still stuck amongst the springs of the armchair.

I held my breath. I couldn't wait for her. They needed me out there.

The bell rang again as I reopened the door and leaped into the fight. My mind began to race as I prepared myself for mutating. The Night Walkers couldn't claim me then. I'd be stronger. I wouldn't be able to control my actions, but neither would the Night Walkers, and they were the greater evil.

I rounded the corner to the street where the truck had sat

just minutes ago.

But what I found in the alleyway stopped me in my tracks.

Under the orange blaze of the evening sky, I saw two grown men grappling, seemingly oblivious to the dangers around them.

"You've got to be kidding me!" I couldn't believe what I saw as I ran towards the fight. "What the hell are you thinking!" I squeezed myself between Tye and Marshall as they wrestled.

Marshall stepped back, but Tye wasn't giving up so easily. "It's all your fault!" he was yelling.

Marshall laughed and turned around to grab something on the floor. An old broom, the bristles deformed and the base rotten. He snapped it over his knee and used the handle as a staff, swinging it over his shoulders. "Are you sure you want a piece of this?" He tormented Tye.

"You killed Beckle. You killed Teri. And Torn, Shyla, Donnah, Jenson, Zayne, and so many others I can't keep count." Tye's eyes filled with rage, and his eyebrows twisted. "It's time you paid."

"I didn't kill Beckle." Marshall smiled, toying with Tye, "Hail killed Beckle. I just watched it. And so did you and him." Marshall pointed towards me.

"Pack it in, Marshall," I warned. My patience was starting to wear thin. Tye edged forward, so I corrected myself, "...both of you! This little spat is putting us all in danger. Every Night Walker in town will have heard this, you idiots."

"Let's leave him as a sacrifice," Tye suggested. "He's here because we needed the truck, and now the truck is gone."

"We're not sacrificing anyone!" I yelled as Jayleigh screamed.

We all froze.

I assumed that Jayleigh had retrieved her dagger and followed me outside, but she was nowhere to be seen.

I broke into a run, preferring to be inside with Jayleigh and a Night Walker than out here with these two airheads.

I entered Jiggle's once more, Diego hot on my heels. Jayleigh was in the room at the back, rolling somebody over a table. Her moves were erratic and unplanned, unlike the Jayleigh I was used to.

My mind fell blank.

I didn't process what I was doing or moving at all. I just knew that I couldn't let her die. I couldn't experience this world without her.

Before I could understand what was happening, the Night Walker threw Jayleigh to the ground, pinning her arms to the side. My body was already hurdling forwards, unable to think of anything except the trouble that my closest friend was in. The Night Walker showed its teeth.

Jayleigh.

Dear God… Jayleigh.

But I was too late to help.

CHAPTER ELEVEN

ARES

Jayleigh plummeted her feet against the Night Walker's chest, sending him stumbling backwards, losing his footing, and tripping into the armchair.

The dagger, thankfully, was still stuck into the back of the chair, and it impaled him as he fell into it. I couldn't help but watch as the blade reappeared straight through his chest. Blood oozed across his shirt. His red eyes landed on me, and a frown covered his face before his skin fazed over in gray. He slumped. His body looked as though it had been decomposing for weeks.

"Now I understand what Hail meant about the smell." Diego held a hand over his nose before heading towards Jayleigh to ensure she was okay.

I sensed her shift in energy before I turned to face her, eyes glowing and a wicked smile on her face. *How has she evolved?* She stalked passed Diego, who stood dumbfounded, and leaned over the Night Walker. "That's right." She pulled the Night Walker's body from the chair and threw it to the floor, "Sit down, Bitch."

Jayleigh turned around quickly, yanking her weapon from the armchair and throwing the dagger again.

Katie and Tye stood at the entrance, the weapon flying between them and planting itself directly into the chest of a red-eyed woman outside the building.

The pair released a large breath as though they had been drowning and resurfaced for air.

Jayleigh ran forwards to retrieve the dagger as the Night Walker's skin faded of colour. And then she paused.

My eyes followed her beyond the smashed windows of the coffee shop.

"Everybody, upstairs. Now!" I ordered, witnessing a slow-moving crowd of red-eyed beings gather outside. We needed to get to higher ground for a better view of what we were up against.

I stood at the bottom of the stairs and waved everybody up as though I were reeling them in.

"There are too many out there," Jayleigh informed me as

she trailed the rest of the pack. "I can stay and fight them off, and it'll give you guys a better chance of escaping."

"I will *not* allow you to do that." I shook my head in disbelief. "I appreciate the offer, but I'd rather keep my pack alive, thanks—"

She began to argue that this would help the pack, so I interjected.

"The whole pack, Jayleigh. I can't lose you."

"Wow. Sorry, Lora." Her voice was dripping with sarcasm. I was beginning to see that evolving not only enhanced a hybrid's abilities but their personality too. "Let's go, Mom."

My fear overpowered the urge to roll my eyes, not the fear of violence or death as I'd experienced before—violence was necessary if I wanted to survive. I was becoming okay with that for the sake of the others around me. Death was the only sure thing left in this world. I'd come close to it during my initiation. I'd drank in the darkness and prepared myself for it all to come to an abrupt halt. But I'd never experienced this before—the fear of letting others down.

This was about more than fitting in. I no longer worried about what the pack thought of me and how it might affect our relationship. These people were *relying* on me, and I needed to get them to safety, one way or another. Suddenly, I experienced the same fleeting feeling I'd seen in Lora's eyes so many times.

It was like the walls were closing in, and we'd all crush if I didn't find a way to escape. Not just me but everyone.

I closed the door once I reached the room at the top of the stairs, but I knew this wasn't the escape I was looking for. The walls were still closing in. We were still in danger.

Jayleigh pushed a cabinet before the door to stop the Night Walkers from following, and I made for the window, looking down to the shadows within shadows.

Marshall appeared next to me, still holding his broom handle in one hand, and a torch in the other. "What can you see?"

"Three in the window of the petrol station." I pointed to the steady silhouettes. "The building across from us is riddling with them, two in the red car, and that's not including the group that followed us into the coffee shop. You can't see them?"

Marshall shrugged. "I'm a puny human, Ares. Hybrids have a slight advantage seeing in the dark."

I huffed at his choice of words. Marshall was many things, but puny was not one of them.

"Still a far cry from what the Night Walkers can see, though," Tye interrupted.

I looked back and forth between the pair, wondering who had won their argument in the alleyway. "Have you two kissed and made up yet?"

They looked at each other and then walked to separate ends of the room.

"What are they waiting for?" I asked Jayleigh and Diego. There was no sound from the staircase on the other side of the wall, so I assumed the Night Walkers hadn't followed us.

"Orders?" Jayleigh suggested.

A chill crawled across my skin.

It hadn't crossed my mind that they could have a dictator. Just how complex was their community?

I shivered.

The idea of them having a community almost made them seem more humane, and that was a disturbing thought.

I glared down at the group in the petrol station.

The moment felt timeless, as though it could have been one or one-hundred seconds. I knew for sure that we couldn't trust them. Even from this distance, I could feel them enticing me, calling me forwards.

Whispering my name.

I wished I could evolve the same way the others could.

If only focusing on the Alpha sixth sense that bound me to the pack was enough to trigger it, like it was for Lora. There had never been a worse time to be a Gen. 3. Becoming angry made me mutate—much like the other hybrids—but feeling love or pride brought me back to my human state instead of helping me to evolve, so I knew that the new Alpha hormones wouldn't help me here.

Why do I have to be different? I asked myself the question that had played on my mind even before I knew I was a Gen. 3.

Everything would have been easier if my mother had made me a Gen. 2 like the others.

As much as I hated to admit it, part of me resented her for it. She didn't want me to fit in, and there had to be a reason. She *must* have had alternate plans for me.

"What do you suggest we do?" Jayleigh questioned, and I tore my eyes away from the Night Walker closest to the door. "When they charge into action, they'll be up those stairs so fast that cabinet won't stand a chance."

I scanned the small, square room, occupied by nothing more than a bookshelf, a desk, and a swivel chair which Marshall had claimed as his own, hiking one leg up onto the sill.

Plenty of windows.

I crossed to the opposite side of the room, knocking Marshall's feet in the process. He scowled but said nothing, which was a first.

The five-story building sat next to us, the narrow alleyway separating the two. "Horizontal rope of doom?"

Jayleigh appeared next to me once more. "The power

lines?" she questioned.

"Electric's permanently out." I shrugged casually to hide the growing panic inside. "Reckon it'll hold our weight?"

I turned slowly to face Marshall, whistling quietly to himself as he pulled open the drawers within the desk and examined its contents.

"There's only one way to find out," I replied.

"You've got to be kidding." Marshall didn't take to the plan. "That power line isn't going to hold us. The bracket is rusty. We may as well jump into a pit of Night Walkers."

"That's why we're sending you out there first." I offered. "You were *so* eager to join us on this mission, so make yourself useful. Especially now we no longer have the truck."

He cleared his throat. He was biting back a response, and I couldn't help but smile as I watched him consider his options—or lack thereof. "Rachel," he called Katie forward. "You go."

Katie looked at me with her eyebrows arched, her eyes darting between my brother and me.

"No, Marshall," I interrupted. "Remember condition number two?"

He glared as he recalled my rules. "You're in charge," he huffed like a sulking child, and Katie's shoulders sank in relief.

"Fine."

I urged him forwards.

He slid the window open and slowly leaned out to grab the cable, tugging on it once and then retracting himself. "Nope. Not sturdy enough," he confirmed. "I don't think that you require me to climb out the window to prove it."

"Hmm… I think that we do." I nodded along with the other hybrids in the room. "Remember our agreement."

"Are you sure you want me to go first?" he stalled. "Your own brother? Why not somebody that you don't care for? Like Tye? It would be good to get him out of the picture, right? No more rivalry for Lora's love. Or Rachel? You don't even know —"

The door interrupted his speech as it slammed against the cabinet. The Night Walkers were moving. They'd received their orders, got the all-clear, and now they were coming to claim us as they'd claimed Hail.

"Fuck it. I'm going." Marshall scrambled out the window with haste as the Night Walkers continued to break into the room.

Not fast enough.

I wanted to push him. I'd never considered how fast hybrids moved compared to humans until I watched my brother escape, legs hitting the wall on the way out. I could only imagine how slow it must have seemed to Jayleigh, still in her evolved state, glancing between Marshall and the door.

Hurry up, Marshall, I thought.

Once he had a firm hold of the cable, he slowly but shakily lowered himself over the alleyway, crossing to the neighbouring building and dropping onto the fire escape. The metal clanged upon impact. "Piece of cake," he called across to us in confirmation. "I don't know what you snowflakes were so worried about!"

My eyes drifted behind him, worried that more Night Walkers lingered on that side of the alleyway, but inside, the building seemed motionless.

I urged Katie forwards next. If she died, it would be up to me to babysit Marshall, which was not an option, and she was the next highest at risk.

Katie was nimble, unlike Marshall, who had so much muscle he could barely cross his arms in front of his chest. She moved like a cat—if cats could cross a wire upside-down.

One by one, I watched pack Beta make it safely across and climb to the roof via the fire escape steps. Eventually, Jayleigh and I remained within the Night Walker-infested building, and I urged her to go next.

"But—"

"Nope," I stopped her. "I can always mutate if I need to.

I'm sure my animal alter ego would love to take down a few Night Walkers just as much as yours."

She scowled but didn't argue. That was the greatest thing about Gen. 2s. They followed their Alpha's orders without question.

Jayleigh looked unamused as she climbed from the window, traversing along the cord.

The pushing of the door grew more ferocious. The bracket began to groan as she reached the halfway mark. My heart picked up the pace.

A Night Walker's arm reached through the expanding gap, attempting to move the cabinet that wedged the door closed.

I turned back to the window as the bracket creaked again and then entirely lost its grasp on the wall.

"Jayleigh!" I panicked and leaped forwards to catch it, my stomach hitting the windowsill so fast it knocked the air from my lungs, but it was for nothing. My fingers snatched and missed. The cable dropped from reach.

Jayleigh swung the remainder of the distance and leapt towards the fire escape on a much lower level. She rolled onto the platform with grace and control and turned back to me, shaking her head. "You should have gone first."

I gritted my teeth, one word spinning around in my mind over and over. *Crap.*

Now I was stuck.

Crap… Crap!

The Night Walkers were almost in. I could see a shoulder squeezing through the gap as they rammed against the door.

There had to be another way out. I scanned the alleyway for anything that could help.

But there was nothing.

The door pounded as multiple bodies slammed against it. The cabinet budged several inches forwards.

A cold sweat clung to my skin.

I thought of yesterday's fight with Dickward. The fear. Watching him shift into his mutated form and charge towards me. The fight or flight decision, choosing to stop and fight.

I had defeated the enemy Alpha with little effort because of my animal alter ego.

I had beaten one inhuman being before. I could do it again.

Or I could leap out of the window.

My mutant self couldn't feel pain. Dickward had squashed me, yet I'd felt nothing.

I could jump.

Do something, Ares. Anything.

My body didn't move.

The fear claimed me once again.

The cabinet flew into the back wall as the door burst open, and three Night Walkers stalked into the room, stopping before me with their eyes burning holes into my soul.

CHAPTER TWELVE

ARES

'Ares.'

The sound echoed around me as though it were a trance, not seeming to come from the male's mouth at all. It was a tangible object, brushing over my skin, dancing through the wisps of hair on my arms, and settling within the base of my neck.

My body wore a coat of ice.

I felt lightheaded. Woozy.

They were going to take over my mind, as they had done to Hail. Were they going to take me back to their nest too? Or did they plan on killing me?

I couldn't let that happen. The pack would die if I died.

Lora was still too far.

Oh, Lora…

I couldn't die without saying goodbye, without telling her that I'm a Gen. 3, without confessing that I'd only lived this long because of the hope she fuelled within me. The thought of never seeing Lora again hurt more than the possibility of my life being vacuumed from my body by the undead creatures before me.

I wanted to feel the heat of her cheeks and experience the taunting glare of her silver eyes. I'd once hated that expression. But as the Night Walkers stalked into the room, I'd have given anything to be confused by Lora just one last time.

Then fight, I scolded myself.

The fury appeared in a burst of flames.

I was angry at *myself*. Angry that I'd allowed myself to fall into this situation, to put the people I cared about at risk. I was mad that I'd spent so much time worrying about my morals, putting my fear of violence before my training, that I didn't know how to evolve in my time of need.

I was angry for how selfish I'd been.

Mutate.

My body lurched into action. Summoning the inner animal always came easily, but controlling it was the struggle.

I threw myself from the room as the hormones began to run wild in my veins. I couldn't allow my alter-ego to attack.

There was too much at risk.

My fingertips grabbed at the window frame as I propelled all my weight forwards, leaping through the air with my arms scrambling out around me in an attempt to keep balance. I clawed at the railing of the fire escape where the pack had found safety moments ago, but I didn't make it.

My fingertips brushed the cool metal of the stairs for barely a second, and then they searched again, desperately trying to find something to grasp onto.

My body fell, gravity pulling me down, winter slicing at my skin.

The gravel welcomed me. Finally, something solid and stable.

The air left my body in a winded gasp, but I couldn't feel the pain in my mutated state. The adrenaline clouded my senses. The energy fuelled my anger and prepared me for the fight which was sure to follow.

Ignoring the metallic taste which filled my mouth, I fought my body as it tried to wipe the blood away.

I was bait, sitting alone in an abandoned alleyway and unable to fully control my actions, and I was bleeding.

My head snapped back. My ears searched for the approaching Night Walkers.

I saw shadows within shadows.

Everything remained still until something dropped behind me.

My animal alter ego didn't miss a beat. I'd been expecting the attack, and I moved without thought.

The only thing running through my mind was *survive… survive… do whatever it takes.*

So, I did what I needed to.

I didn't turn to face the monster behind me as I propelled my body into action, hoping to catch them by surprise. My erratic movements were interrupted by a strong, steady fist to the temple, perfectly placed. Calculated. Premeditated.

The dizziness came first, and then darkness crept into the corners of my vision. It oozed over the alleyway like spilled ink until everything—the bricks, the creature in front of me, the night sky—was painted black.

"Goodnight, Ares," Jayleigh laughed as my body slumped to her feet.

I was staring at the stars long before I realized what was happening. They first appeared as beams of light breaking through the fuzziness, and I watched them as they played hide-and-seek with the clouds, feeling content for the first time in a long time.

I couldn't remember why I was lying on a roof, glancing up into the vastness of space, but I appreciated the moment of silence through the commotion of the world around me. It reminded me of how significantly small I was—a fragile being on a minuscule planet.

If I focused hard enough, I could feel the world spin on its axis.

Or was that just the headache?

I reached a hand to my temple, bruised.

"You attacked me." Jayleigh slumped to the floor next to me, and I tried to sit up, but the stars were moving, and they seemed impossibly bright now.

"I thought you were a Night Walker. I was trying to protect myself," I grumbled through the pain. "You gave me a concussion."

I could almost hear her shoulders shrug. "I didn't have much of a choice. You would have tried your luck with any of the Night Walkers, and you would have lost, resulting in the rest of us dying alongside you. And I couldn't have talked you down. I saw how that went for Lora in Phase Two, and I didn't fancy myself a broken arm."

"Thank you," I said. There was truth in her words, although it was hard for me to admit. I was unpredictable in my animal state. And I'd thought Jayleigh was a Night Walker, which is why I'd attacked. It was proof I'd have tried to fight my way through the undead army that swarmed the town. "You shouldn't have to risk yourself for me. I'm sorry I put you in that position."

"Yeah, well, the Night Walkers retreated to their former positions as soon as you hit the ground. Whatever orders they'd received when they barged into Jiggles must have been retracted. The only danger I was putting myself in when I came to save you was... you."

I swallowed hard.

We needed to get to Lora. I was a danger to my own pack, and that wasn't fair to them. They needed a leader who they could trust to make the right decisions and not be a danger to them. And I needed time I didn't have. I needed to work out what exactly made me different from the Gen. 2s to find a way to evolve, something I couldn't do with all this going on around me.

The group started settling, pulling items from their backpacks and sprawling across the roof. Diego had constructed a small shelter against the wall opposite me, like those we'd used in Phase Two.

I made nest next to Jayleigh, who'd retired to her human state and rummaged through my bag for the oat biscuits she'd found in Jiggle's before the attack.

"So, you finally found something worth evolving for." I nudged her as she usually did to me. If only killing Night Walkers could be enough to make me evolve, but I didn't enjoy how I felt when I was in danger. I didn't feel the same thrill Jayleigh did coming face to face with the undead monsters.

"Kicking a Night Walker's butt." She nodded and smiled so brightly it could have lit up the night. "What a buzz."

"The girl who fell in love with killing monsters." I laughed. "I'm not sure whether I should feel scared of you, you know, after seeing you so pumped to end a life."

"A Night Walker life." She pointed her stale oat biscuit at me, and a few crumbs flew to my lap. "They're technically already dead, so…"

"I found it very attractive." Diego appeared beside me as I wiped the crumbs away. He leaned against the roof wall as though unfazed by the drop on the other side, his eyebrows pulled together to shadow his eyes from the moon, and I found myself trying to copy his expression, although I didn't know why.

"Really?" Jayleigh faced me and fake swooned before turning back to Diego—the hybrid she'd referred to as 'The Beast' on multiple occasions. "You're coming on a little strong there, Pal. At least take me to dinner first." She nibbled down on her biscuit without breaking his eye contact.

Diego shook his head in defeat and walked away, muttering something to himself in Spanish.

I gave her a questionable look.

"Got to keep him on his toes." She shrugged. She'd been all over the guy like a rash since the day he joined the pack. I couldn't believe she was throwing away this opportunity, especially considering that Diego rarely showed interest in anything. There was no understanding Jayleigh; I'd come to realize.

"So, how was it? Evolving?" I moved the conversation forwards.

Her eyes challenged the stars as she recalled the feeling. "It was just as amazing as Hail said it would be."

We paused at the mention of Hail's name, and Jayleigh's smile faded.

I looked at the tablet on my arm, knowing what I'd find now the sun had vanished, but it didn't stop my heart from dropping to my stomach. The feeling made me queasy. The tiny purple pin traversed across the screen, heading towards the coastline. Further from us. Further from Lora and Pack Alpha.

"He's moving." I felt confined, even though I was the freest I'd ever been. I wasn't hidden within the underground world of Level -3 as I'd been in my childhood, and I was not contained within the fence of The Farm, yet, on this roof in the middle of the vast, open world, I felt more trapped than ever. We were helpless on this roof. "And… Lora's pack has stopped."

I tried to reassure myself that Lora had made camp for the night just as we had and that it had nothing to do with the Night Walkers. If only I could sense them as I could Jayleigh, Diego and Tye to know that they were okay. Could Lora still feel us, despite the distance? Could she read my worry and guilt? Did she know how I longed to be near her again? To hold her in my arms and never let go. My body craved the scent of her hair as though it were a sedative to calm the unsettled feeling inside.

"I miss them," Jayleigh mumbled.

"Me too," I said. My voice appeared void of emotion, scared to show Jayleigh how vulnerable I felt without Lora nearby. I could be strong for them.

"Hail would be so angry if he knew that Lora left to save him. He's always been an every-man-for-himself kind of guy." Jayleigh tried to make light of the situation.

"That's why I liked him," Marshall pipped up from further along the rooftop, rubbing his gloved hands to keep them warm. "Nothing going on upstairs, but at least he knew when sacrifices had to be made."

He blew air into his hands as his eyes landed on me, remaining for longer than I was comfortable with, and I knew he was reminding me of our conversation in the Observatorium.

"Nobody asked you," I shot back. "And Hail is still alive, don't refer to him in the past tense as though he's already dead." I pointed to his pin on my tablet, now a mile or so further than it had been the last time I checked.

"They're going to try to harness his powers, Ares. He's not going to be one of you for much longer."

Marshall leaned back on his elbow, plucked a couple of round, brown objects from a bag, threw them into the air, and caught them in his mouth. I didn't want to consider that what he said was probably the truth, the horror of it created a hole in my chest, so I diverted my focus and rummaged through my backpack for gloves. The November night's temperature had dropped to near freezing, a vast difference from what we had experienced a few days prior. Winter had arrived.

Once I pulled the gloves on, I stood, plucked out the fireproof mat and set up an area to boil the oats. We each had a compact paper log to burn, a torch, a large water bottle, a limited food supply, and a thermal sleeping bag.

"Where's yours?" I asked Marshall and Katie.

"In the truck," Marshall's nostrils flared as he spoke. I held back the sigh.

"You two can share mine," I suggested, but Katie looked

like it was the worst news I could have given her.

"I'd rather freeze," she whispered.

"What did you just say?" Marshall turned to face her. "What's wrong with sharing my sleeping bag?"

Katie remained silent, but Marshall pressed for an answer.

"You're my boss, Sir. I think it may be a little inappropriate."

"You don't trust me? Is that it? Worried that I'll—"

"That'll do, Marshall!" I scowled at him. He just didn't know when to stop. "Katie, if you'd rather pitch in with Jayleigh, I'm sure she wouldn't mind?" I suggested. I had planned to kip with her, but I didn't trust Marshall either.

"Of course," Jayleigh agreed.

Katie seemed hesitant in both directions. "I don't mean this to offend anyone," she started, "but since I arrived at The Farm, I've been taught not to trust the animals—hybrids," she corrected herself.

I scowled in Marshall's direction. He'd scared her into hating us.

"We don't want to hurt you, Katie."

I held my hands in surrender whilst, in the background, Marshall asked, "Who the hell is Katie? Why do you keep calling her that?"

I tried to hold Katie's attention. "We're all on the same side here. The enemy is down there." I pointed towards Jiggle's. "Why don't you take a sleeping bag to yourself? Jayleigh can bunk with one of the guys, and I'll squeeze in with Marshall?" I gritted my teeth as I finished the sentence, but I couldn't force Tye or Diego into sharing with my brother. It really would be a squeeze.

Katie nodded slowly. "Thank you."

"Of course."

Jayleigh winked at me as though I'd done her a favour and Diego stared blank faced as she approached him and linked his arm. "Hey, bunk buddy."

Diego continued with his Spanish swears.

Marshall glared at me, obviously unhappy with the idea. I wondered if he'd ever had to share anything in his life or if this would be a new experience.

He spat something on the ground.

"What's that?" I questioned. "What are you eating?"

His eyes dragged back to my face.

"Coffee beans." I wasn't the only one to stare as he repeated his earlier process of throwing small objects into the air and catching them in his mouth. "And no, I don't eat them. I'm not a psycho… I suck them," he said as though it made the situation less weird.

"You suck… coffee beans?" I added it to the list of things

wrong with my brother. No wonder his breath always smelt so bad.

"Not usually," he replied. "I have a strong caffeine addiction, and my flask is empty, so this was my only solution. I brought them with me from The Farm. I keep them in my pocket."

"Of course you do… You don't have a sleeping bag, but at least you remembered your useless coffee beans."

"They're not useless. It's a tactical move," Marshall's tone was sharp as he tried to defend himself from the strange looks we were shooting in his direction. "Addiction kills part of the brain, so I figured it might help should a Night Walker ever try to highjack my mind."

"It won't help." I shook my head. "You're killing off the wrong part of the brain."

I wasn't sure how exactly I knew this.

Marshall shrugged. "Anything's worth a try for a defenceless human like me." Bitter. And for a second, I was almost convinced that Marshall was jealous of us. I quickly dismissed the thought. Marshall hated hybrids. That was common knowledge, although I was yet to figure out why. "At least it keeps me happy for a short amount of time. It's the small pleasures, eh?"

Silence filled the air as Marshall sucked more beans.

"What a barrel of laughs," Jayleigh commented finally. "I'm so glad we brought him along." She turned and began to set up her sleeping area.

"Hey," I grabbed Katie's arm as she followed suit, taking the sleeping bag from me and turning to the corner of the roof, the furthest point from the group she could possibly get. "I want you to feel comfortable with us, we must be a team out here, and I know it's not in your nature to trust us, but you can. If I'm in charge, you will be considered a pack member, okay? I'm so sorry that you've we've dragged you into all this."

She gave me a small smile. "It's not your fault. It's just going to take a while for me to get used to the change in dynamics."

I smiled at her choice of words, "Okay, cool. I'm afraid we have watery porridge for dinner. I'm not sure what you farmers are used to eating."

"We live on blended sludge. Porridge will be nice for a change, finally a little texture." She nodded as she walked to the far corner of the roof to set up her sleeping area.

My eyes landed back on my brother, and I wondered how I could be related to such a Prick.

"There's no way we're both going to fit in here." Marshall held a sleeping bag to the sky. "What is this? A sleeve?" He stuck his arm into it.

"We will." I tried to keep a positive mindset; I'd need it to get through the night with Marshall. "It might be a squeeze, but when there's a will, there's a way… even if it means we have to spoon."

Marshall's jaw clenched as his eyes landed on me. "If you dare, I will throw you over the edge of the building."

"Sheesh. Learn to take a joke, Marshall." I held my hands up and walked away to start the fire.

Ten minutes later, the water simmered over the flame, oats boiling away, and I peered over the roof's edge to examine our Night Walker situation. Jayleigh had been right about them; they'd become idle again for whatever reason.

A group had returned to the petrol station, peering up at our roof but not looking like they had any intention of moving soon. The couple in the red car slowly climbed out, closed the door, and paused. The pack gathered around me to witness what was going on the ground below.

"The truck," Tye whispered.

I heard it, too, a couple of seconds later. The vehicle stolen from us was roaming around town in the dark of night.

I shook my head.

I was new to this post-apocalyptic world, but even I knew that driving through a Night Walker-infested town at this time was a bad idea.

The Night Walker couple, who had now climbed out of the car, moved forwards as though I were watching them in slow motion.

"What are they doing?" I whispered.

"Tracking. They're locating the truck."

"But it's miles away."

"Just wait and see," Marshall whispered back.

I recalled the footage Marshall had forced me to watch from Camera 72. The Night Walker that had killed our parents acted the same way as she compelled their minds, and then she took off at such a speed that the drone's camera couldn't pick it up.

The truck grew louder and closer. Headlights illuminated a street at the far end of town.

It was as though they were trying to get themselves killed.

And then the Night Walkers took off, running faster than any human could move.

I wanted to scream.

Even though these people had stolen our truck, they didn't deserve to die violently. The noise that gargled in my throat was placed somewhere between turmoil and despair.

I held back the sob. It was already too late.

The sound of tires screeching across the cracked tarmac flooded the town, followed by distant yelling. The remaining

Night Walkers in the surrounding buildings fled the area, heading towards the truck.

More lights flashed from a few streets across, the commotion growing louder as more people joined the fight.

"What's going on?" I asked. "Why are they being so reckless?"

"They're human, Ares. They're tired of this life." Marshall shrugged. "Unlike us, they don't have The Farm to return to. Every night is a challenge, questioning if they'll live to see the sunrise or if they'll finally fall victim to the Night Walkers. They're tired of living in fear, so they're doing something about it."

"But they're all going to die!" I tried to hold my voice to a whisper.

"Well, sometimes the fear of living outweighs the fear of death."

"That's stupid." I shook my head and covered my ears to hide the sound of human slaughter. But I knew there was truth in Marshall's words. I'd experienced demons of my creation. On my darkest days within The Farm, I'd taunted Marshall and hoped he'd actually pull the trigger on his gun because I felt that was the easiest path for me. But I had been wrong. There was always another path. I just couldn't see it at the time.

My path was finding Lora.

And I was the path that the humans needed but could not see.

"We need to go and help them." My voice shook as the words left my lips.

Everybody turned to face me, each showing a look of disapproval through the sound of screaming.

"This isn't our battle." Marshall shook his head. "Necessary sacrifices," he reminded me. "...for the greater good."

"You sound like Dr. White."

"No, it was Mom's saying. He took it from her after she died."

"I don't care whose saying it is. Those people down there need our help. The more time we waste, the more lives this world will lose."

I began to walk towards the fire escape, figuring it would be safer than using the stairwell within the building. I dropped the ladder. My fingers brushed the metal as a hand caught my arm.

"Ares." Jayleigh's eyes were pleading. "I understand, I do. But think about what you're doing. Think about what you're asking of *us*. You're impulsive and passionate, but right now, you're also being damn right stupid."

I paused in my tracks.

"Do you think Lora would make these same decisions if she stood in your place?"

The screams were starting to dwindle. The suffering was almost over.

We were already too late.

I swallowed.

"She would put the safety of the pack before anything else."

"And right now, we're safe." Jayleigh took the ladder from me and retracted it so nobody on the lower levels could climb up to us. "I agree with Marshall, for once. This isn't our battle. We need to save our energy to reach Lora and save Hail. *Then* we can consider helping the humans once we're all together again."

"You're right." I sighed through gritted teeth. "It's all so new… I think that being outside of The Farm is making me think irrationally." I clenched my shaking hands and, for the first time, admitted something I'd been holding deep within. "I'm scared, Jayleigh." Saying the words released a world of tension from my shoulders, and I instantly felt lighter.

She lingered, her arm still on the ladder as though she were debating a friendly hug; God knows I needed one, but Jayleigh wasn't the hugging type, so instead, she bit her lower lip and nodded. "Yeah, I know. Me too." She patted my shoulder, hoping it would offer the comfort I needed. "I would question the sanity of anyone who claimed they're not a little nervous by our situation."

"I'm glad you're here." I rested my hand over hers, glad I had her to talk sense. "I'd be losing my mind without you."

"Well, I'd quite literally die without you, so I win," she tried for a joke, and it just about cracked the tension. A small smile crossed my face. "Just promise me something, Ares..."

"Of course." I squeezed her hand.

"When this is all over..." she started, "please brush up on your cooking skills... I can smell the porridge burning from here."

I'd forgotten all about dinner. "Crap."

She laughed at my effort as I rushed to the pan over the fire. The oats had burned from the lack of stirring, but none of us cared. We ate in silence, formed a small shelter in the centre of the roof, and as the fire slowly faded to embers, Marshall took it upon himself to teach us a few tricks with the dagger.

At least there was one advantage for bringing him along after all.

"Flick your wrist," he directed me as I flipped the oversized knife, fire reflecting in the blade. Jayleigh naturally got it right the first time, and Tye ignored every word that Marshall spoke. He glared at him across the roof with his dagger gripped tightly in his hands.

The night grew as cold as Tye's mood as we retired to bed.

"We should take shifts," I suggested, my breath creating clouds as I spoke. "An hour each. I'll take the first. Marshall can take the second, then Katie, Diego, Tye and Jayleigh."

"For the last time, her name is Rachel." Marshall's nose flared.

"I prefer Katie." Rachel nodded at me, and I wondered if it was true or if she was saying it to spite Marshall. Either way, it put a smile on my face.

Marshall sighed as he climbed into our sleeping bag and shuffled around to find a comfortable position.

It didn't take long for the pack to fall asleep, used to harsh conditions and the understanding that everything might change by the time they woke.

I watched over the town as everybody dreamt. The Night Walkers were yet to return from the massacre, and I prayed that they had moved on—so long as they stayed away from Lora's pack and Hail. I watched Hail's pin move across the map. I stared at pack Alpha's idle pins for so long that my eyes started to blur. *If only I could see her…*

Marshall shuffled around, grunting and huffing through everybody else's snores.

"Maybe you should have taken the first shift." I was leaning against the wall, flipping the dagger as I spoke.

He sighed. "Well, now there's no chance of me sleeping."

"Don't act like you were drifting off. You've not stopped fidgeting in the last twenty minutes."

I heard Marshall unzip the sleeping bag, a shuffle as he climbed out and wrapped it around himself, and then he walked across the roof towards me.

"It must be near freezing." His teeth rattled.

I was suddenly highly thankful for the hybrid clothing, keeping us somewhat warm in these harsh conditions.

I'd been trying to perfect the dagger trick Marshall had taught us, flipping it between my fingers and jabbing the handle. The titanium slipped between my fingers each time. Closer, but not perfect. I continued to focus on it as I asked, "What are you doing here, Marshall? Really?"

Marshall frowned, bewildered. "I told you, I'm here to help you. To guide you through life outside The Farm and get you to Lora sooner, so my years of effort don't go wasted."

"But that's the thing," I said. "The only time you've ever left The Farm is when Mother was pregnant with me. You said you went to Wilson's camp for a year. And then you came straight back. So, what help can you actually provide now that the truck is lost?"

Marshall puffed his chest, standing straighter, the sleeping back rustling like thin paper. He appeared defensive. "Whilst in Wilson's camp, I learned everything I'd need to survive in the outside world. So now I'm here to pass that information on. Who do you think taught Tim and Sally how to fight? I've worked my life away with endless research and overseen the missions of previous hybrids. I won't let you all die and waste the resources and time I've spent on you."

"Watch it, Marshall. You're beginning to sound like you care about us."

He scoffed, "I care about my purpose and *your* purpose and what I believe this pack is capable of. Trust me. I could never care about anything more than the war and my mission."

My eyes lingered on him, the scar on his forehead and the tired, bluish-purple hue which hollowed the space between his nose and eyes.

He'd given everything to his cause over the years, risking his health and life. My gaze dropped to my handprint around his neck, just visible under the blanket. Was it so crazy to trust his words were true? That he was here to help us and return to his plan for the war and defeating the Night Walkers?

As his eyes drifted across the landscape, crumbling buildings, overgrown plants, and shattered dreams, I wondered if it was his mission or somebody else's. What kind of person would Marshall have been if he'd had a normal life?

Or a life like the rest of us, at least.

He'd witnessed violence and death his whole life. Our

father had encouraged it. *He cares about one thing more than the war,* I concluded.

"I don't believe you," I said, testing him.

He shivered under the blanket, wrapping it tighter as he copied my stance against the wall. "I don't care what you believe."

My eyes rolled on their own accord. "See, that is why we don't trust you. You can't be a part of this team if you refuse to act like a team player."

Marshall sighed again and began to walk away, muttering. "Why do I even bother?"

I steadied the dagger in my gloved fingers.

There was no changing the fact that Marshall was stuck with us, truck or not. The pack might have written my brother off, but I still had a lot to learn from him.

"Hey," I called out, not wanting to miss the opportunity to talk without prying eyes and ears. "Can you tell me about Father?"

There was a long pause, and then Marshall dragged his feet to a halt, turning back reluctantly.

I continued, "I understand if you want the extra half-hour shut eye before your shift, but all I've ever heard about our dad is what Dr. White has told me… Which isn't a lot. I'll put the dagger away if that is making you nervous. Actually, I'm going to put it away to save my own nerves. The last time we were alone with a weapon, it didn't go too well, did it?"

A scowl dragged at Marshall's face. "Your voice gives me a headache."

"That's probably just the caffeine killing your brain. You really should really consider laying off the coffee."

I watched his jaw twitch, and eventually, he gave in and returned to the wall. "I'm going to regret this," he said under his breath, forgetting that I could hear it.

CHAPTER THIRTEEN

MARSHALL

I should have walked away. I should have returned to my section of the roof and at least pretended to sleep. I could have wrapped the sleeping bag tighter and soaked in the last of the heat from the fire.

But Ares wanted to talk about Father.

Nobody *ever* wanted to talk about Father.

So, I found my body turning and walking back to him. *Un-fucking-forgivable,* I knew I'd pay the price later.

My feet were so numb I could barely feel my toes like I had bricks at the end of my shoes. The skin would be blue and purple if I removed a sock.

But it was nothing I hadn't experienced before.

Julia's voice echoed in my mind, telling me to 'grow the

fuck up'. Travelling to the North as a child had been a culture shock. I trained alongside the other boys while the girls focused on less physical activities like in Father's history books.

It was surprising to see how quickly the two groups had adapted to the pressure; and how actions that The Farm would have punished were encouraged at the Northern Camp.

They had a mindset of brutality, and at the ripe age of nine, I'd licked it up like strawberry jam.

Life there suited me well.

Returning to The Farm after a whole year was a slap to the face.

Father wasn't aware of the differences between the two safe zones, and he didn't realize that the environment in the North was harsher, with stricter policies. Being there changed the way I approached situations.

I challenged.

I attacked first.

I stood up for what I believed in.

"Father had his demons," I replied to Ares' question after a lifetime of reliving everything I'd been through. I pulled the sleeping bag tight, hoping he wouldn't witness my shivering. "He'd seen a lot during his time in the military, and I'm not sure if he'd been the right person to run The Farm, but he was the only one with enough experience."

"What do you mean? Why wasn't he—"

"Shut it, Princess." I rolled my neck back and closed my eyes. *This* was what pure exhaustion felt like. "One question at a time. No interruptions."

Ares raised his hands in surrender, his sarcasm evident in his words as he said, "Jeez, sorry."

I shifted my weight from one foot to the next, marching slowly to keep the blood pumping. The smell of the world freezing around me burned at my sinuses, and it was a familiar sensation.

That, I realized, is what my life felt like, freezing and burning all at once. My body was in a constant state of tearing towards opposite ends of a spectrum. I was trying to keep myself together. I needed to find a happy medium, but I wasn't sure if I'd ever been happy. I was failing miserably on both sides of the scale.

I covered my nose through the blanket, jealous of how unfazed Ares seemed by the temperature.

He was oblivious to most things, not just the cold. I'd noticed before how he bypassed situations without a blink of an eye. He was one of the most ignorant animals I'd ever met.

But he was a Gen. 3. Unprecedented. Unpredictable, and it made him the most dangerous hybrid of all.

My heart recoiled, and rage simmered within. Uncle Daniel

had been stupid to keep such vital information from me. What made it worse was that he knew how fucking wrong it was. He'd cowered in the corner of the room as the explanation left his lips; whether he was making space for me to throw objects around or genuinely concerned for his safety was a different matter. I wasn't sure if anything *had* hit him, but my fists had not.

That had been my first instinct. I'd wanted to knock some sense into his skull.

It didn't matter that Mother had asked to keep Ares' identity a secret, and it didn't matter that he was my brother.

For Ares' safety, I should have known about his true genetics.

Daniel still refused to tell me, even after I'd ripped the flimsy folder from his hands. I'd figured he'd kept his notes on paper instead of a tablet so I couldn't access his records, but I'd never imagined how deep the secrets ran. I never suspected he was hiding a brother from me.

The papers had flown out across the room, taking the last of my sanity with them. They dispersed under tables and wedged against the apparatus. The hospital room Wilson had carried to after my episode with Ares in the Observatorium wasn't the tidiest of rooms. I'd scrambled to find my brother's doctoral notes as though Daniel's tornado of a sigh would pick the papers up and send them flying again. After a short while of studying my odd behaviour, Daniel announced that what I wanted could not be found there. Still, he'd refused to tell me any more than that, instead changing the subject to the above-ground situation.

Lora had escaped, and he was sending Ares to go after her.

I'd decided at that moment that I was leaving The Farm too. I saw an opportunity, and I took it.

I looked at Ares now, wondering if I'd made the right choice. Probably not, but I was past caring at this point. So much so that I didn't bother to filter my following words.

"I hated you because you remind me of Father."

"What?"

"That's a question, Ares..." But I knew that my brother would have questions. Who wouldn't? Ares looked as though he wanted to cry, but I couldn't understand why. "I told you not to ask questions."

"Crap. Sorry," he choked on his words.

Fragile hybrid, I thought. Ares made up for his lack of sensory input with emotion. The boy was a mess.

"Father was just as stubborn as you, always thinking he knew best—"

"You're not so different, you know," he interrupted.

"Yeah? That explains why I butted heads with Father most

of the time."

Ares frowned. "I thought you were close to Dad?"

I shuffled again, this time out of discomfort rather than the cold. I certainly should have gone back to bed. It was getting too personal.

"Being close to somebody doesn't always mean you get along. You can spend time with somebody and still dislike them. I mean, look at us." Ares blew air through his nose in response. "And you can disagree with people and still want to please them. Father and I were both strong-minded beings with different views and approaches, and that caused a rift in our relationship."

"Do you wish you'd acted differently now..." he studied me, wondering how far he could push, "now that it's too late to change it?"

Defeat. I glared. "*I wish* you'd stop asking questions."

"Oh, come on, Marshall," he whined like a child, "how are we ever supposed to trust you if we don't know you? How can we help each other if you refuse to let us in?"

It was too much for one day. My head was spinning, and I needed to grab the coffee beans to make it through my shift.

Surely Ares' shift must be coming to an end soon, I prayed.

But then... I wasn't sure if I wanted to spend the hour alone with my thoughts. At least Ares took my mind off everything else happening, however uncomfortable the conversation made me.

"If you want to get to know me, maybe try asking the lighter stuff first instead of counselling me."

"Okay…" he nodded and glanced up to the stars. "What's your favorite type of animal?"

"The Venos," I replied with little thought before realizing he wasn't talking about categories of hybrid.

He gave me a worried look, which reminded me so much of Mother that it hurt, and paused.

"Woah. Hold on." He held his hands out in defence. "You prefer Venos over us? I know Dickward was like your pet or something. But honestly? They're vicious, inhumane—" he stopped ranting suddenly, and his eyes narrowed. "Oh, actually… No, I totally see it. You'd be a Veno if you were a hybrid."

"What's that supposed to mean?"

"You'd fit right in."

I wasn't sure whether to take his statement as a compliment, but the tone suggested that he didn't mean it as one. "You don't think I'm smart enough to be a Titanium? I could be a Titanium; I'll have you know."

"I don't think you *feel* enough to be a Titanium."

"I feel!" I bit back too eagerly, annoyed that he'd come to

such a conclusion from the little information he knew about me. "Forget it. I wouldn't want to be a Titanium anyway."

Ares had more to say, but he held it back. For that, I was grateful.

"What's your favorite color?" he asked eventually.

Black.

Eternal darkness.

The color of silence.

"Yellow," I lied.

Ares stared at the stars a little longer. Then his eyes scanned me. I felt judged and didn't like it; the only people with the right to judge me were dead.

"Really?" He looked sceptical, and something on my face must have given me away. "Why?"

"Do I need a reason?"

Ares shrugged. "I guess not."

He was expecting me to return the question, but I didn't care what his answer would be. It was a childish question, and it reminded me of my learning days in the infirmary, where the kids would spend their time counting to one-hundred and learning to spell their names.

Meanwhile, I was drawing maps of The Farm and the underground levels. I'd recall Father's lessons from the previous evening and wonder what mood he'd be in that night. I'd watch the other children, knowing that none of them would remember me after their hibernation. I didn't join in with their games; I watched and completed more extra-curricular work, wishing I could be one of them just for a day.

Poor little Marshall, I mocked as I recalled the memories and realized my brother's eyes were still on me, waiting for me to return his question.

"Have you ever played I-spy, Ares?" I wrapped the sleeping bag over my head, sighing as it relieved the draft around my neck.

"I doubt it," he scoffed.

"I'll go first. You'll pick it up."

And he did. Ares was a speedy learner. It was no surprise that he'd tested as a Titanium, although Mother would never have allowed him to proceed as a Veno.

Ares' shift blurred into mine and the moon shifted in the sky. I noticed things about my brother that I could never pick out on the screens of the Observatorium; the way Ares scrunched his nose like Mother when he laughed, and he laughed a lot for somebody in such a stressful position.

Despite the age of his body, his mind was still young. Younger than I'd realized, at least. I almost felt guilty for the way I'd treated him. But he'd survived it all, and it had made him stronger, so I concluded that I'd done him a favor.

We played the game of The Farm's child refugees until Ares woke Rachel and passed her the tablet. She proceeded to the wall, wrapping her sleeping bag around her in a similar fashion as I had, and barely looked me in the eye as I bid her goodnight.

Rude.

Somehow, both Ares and I squeezed into the sleeping bag, and I was quietly thankful to have him next to me. His body heat was a saviour.

"If you so much as touch me in the night," I said, "I'm kicking you out."

"Oh, come on. There's nothing wrong with a cuddle."

I glared in his direction, but I couldn't see a thing.

"Fine… Fine." He shuffled beside me. "I get it."

I turned away and coughed, wondering how good Ares' eyesight *really* was in the dark.

"Don't catch a cold, Marshall. We'll leave you behind if you try to hold us back," he joked.

I coughed again, exaggerating it this time and wiping my mouth on my sleeve. "You only wish you could get rid of me that easily."

"It's true. You're a pain in the ass. Goodnight, Marshall."

He wriggled about some more as though the ground wasn't comfortable enough for him.

I'd treated them too kindly to give the animals a bed during their training. Father hadn't allowed the animals a bed.

"'Night, Princess."

CHAPTER FOURTEEN

HAIL

The dreams of blue and red were making me sick.

I couldn't breathe.

My body was stuck, but it moved.

Something changed after a few moments of real life. The dizziness stopped, and my back pressed against something solid, the spots in my vision clearing enough for me to make out things I recognized.

Stars, the moon, trees. I counted them one by one to calm my nerves. These were three things I'd seen before, which meant that life outside the fence couldn't be so different to life on The Farm. I was not on The Farm because it smelled different here. It smelled like death.

Now and then, somebody passed by.

Red eyes landed on me.

"She's late." A male voice came from the shadows, and my eyes darted to find the source. All they saw was more red and blue haziness. But I knew that voice. It was the *thing* that took me from the barn. I'd barely had time to process what was happening as it called out to me, stopping me from running.

I'd tried to call the others for help, but she'd asked me to follow, and my body moved, only stopping when she told me to. I didn't scream as she plunged her teeth into my neck and a feeling so hot and painful swept over me. It was like how the energy flowed through my veins whilst I was in my evolved state, but it drained me instead of giving me power. The dreams started then, and I couldn't work out what was real and what was happening in my mind.

I'd seen Donnah dancing in an empty field to the sound of screaming, carried by the wind. I blinked, and she was gone.

The voice called my name, and red eyes met mine as I turned towards it, the colours swirling in my vision. Then I was lifted from the ground, and time seemed to start and stop. It stuttered with my heartbeat.

Everything was a mess of blue and red clouds for a long time.

Had it been minutes? Days?

"She'll be here," a second voice replied to the first, much

closer than I expected. Fear shot through me, and the blue haze deepened. This was the woman I'd seen outside the fence a few weeks ago... She'd come back for me. "It's all going to plan," she said a little while later as footsteps approached. "The pack follows."

"All of them?" The new voice asked.

"Yes. They brought Marshall and Rachel, too." *The man knew their names, too.*

"Perfect. Get Hail into place and alert the others." The new voice replied.

"Yes, my Queen."

"Let the trials begin. I'll meet you on the other side." The new voice vanished with a rush of wind.

And with that, we were moving again. I was lifted into the sky, or so it felt. My stomach churned, and I almost spewed.

Or maybe the conversation I'd overheard made my stomach sick, not the movement…

The pack follows.

And those creatures had planned it all.

It was a trap. *Trials.*

I needed to warn the others, but I could do nothing because Donnah was singing to me once again, and I'd happily have lived in her song.

She's back. Donnah's back, and this time I won't let her go.

The stars turned red.

She looks beautiful.

CHAPTER FIFTEEN

ARES

Jayleigh woke us to the sound of metal on metal. "Wake up, Losers." She clanged her dagger against her hand knife.

I sat slowly and rubbed my eyes, confused as to why the sleeping bag seemed restricted. I looked down to find Marshall glaring at me, his teeth chattering.

"Good morning." I ran a hand through my hair. "Did you sleep well?"

"Don't speak to me." He clambered from the bed and wrapped his arms around his body. "Shitting hell. No wonder I'm so fucking cold!"

Beyond the tapered shelter, a layer of snow had coated the ground, an inch thick and pearly white. The sky remained thick with clouds, pink in colour and still shedding themselves around us.

"We should get a move on," I spoke to the pack, looking at each member in turn. The strange warmth I'd experienced yesterday had faded significantly overnight. My Alpha hormones were dwindling.

Panic surged through me. Where was Lora? How close was she? Had she already continued her mission to find Hail? Was she okay?

Jayleigh noticed the expression on my face and held the tablet out for me to examine. My heart leapt. Something was wrong. Jayleigh's eyes said it all.

I almost didn't look, afraid of what I'd find on the map. Only, it wasn't the map that I found on the screen, but a small image of a phone and an envelope which expanded to reveal the words:

Ares.

Please return my call as soon as you are able.

-White

I frowned at the simplicity of the message and turned it towards Marshall, who let out a *"humph"* before turning to check his own tablet.

"What about Lora, pack Alpha, and Hail?" I asked.

Jayleigh shrugged. "The map went off when Dr. White called, and I've not been able to get the map back on the screen since."

My heart hammered. "But everyone was okay last time you checked?"

"Ares, calm down. They're all fine. Hail stopped, though, somewhere up the coastline. They managed to cover a hell of a distance overnight."

But his pin was still there, which meant he was still alive. That was something, at least.

"How do I call Dr. White?" I asked Marshall.

"Tap on the phone. Isn't that obvious?"

I did as he said, and the ringing sound echoed around the roof.

Dr. White answered on the second call.

"Ares," he stated my name, his voice apprehensive.

"Hi, yes… Hello, Dr. White." I held my arm to my ear to ensure the mic would pick up my voice. Marshall moved my arm away from the tablet to a more appropriate distance. "Is everything okay? I just received your message."

Dr. White sounded concerned. "All is fine here, Ares, thank you. It's you that I'm worried about."

"We survived the night, don't worry. We ran into a few Night Walkers, but we sorted it. Jayleigh evolved and killed the ones that caused a threat. The others didn't seem too bothered—"

"Yes. I'm aware that you're alive, Ares. I'm still receiving the data from your clothing. In fact, that's the reason for my call. I have your results."

I frowned, unsure of what he was talking about. "What results? The data from my clothes?"

"Results of the tests we ran before Lora escaped. I've been comparing it to the data we recorded."

Of course.

I'd forgotten all about them and hadn't realized they were so important. My uncle had played them off as a simple check-up.

Dr. White seemed hesitant, and the longer I waited for his news, the more impatient I became. "Okay…" I urged.

"Your animal hormones are rising, Ares, even whilst you're in your human state."

I stared at the tablet, waiting for his words to make sense. Rising? As in increasing?

Marshall spun towards me, seeming to understand what this meant. "At what rate?" he interrupted the doctor.

"Ah, Marshall. I'll catch up with you once I've spoken to Ares."

"How fast, Daniel?" The stern manner of Marshall's tone

worried me.

"Well, that's the thing… It spikes every time Ares mutates, but the levels never return to normal when he switches back to his human state. They're increasing at a higher percentage each time."

Marshall's face was solid and unreadable. He looked at me through eyes of stone.

"I don't understand," I pushed, although it was a lie. I understood perfectly, but I didn't want to believe it.

"Ares, you lose more of your humanity every time you mutate, and the animal gains more control. If you continue mutating, you will eventually lose your human state and will effectively *become* your animal state," my uncle explained.

Sirens erupted in my mind. I swallowed back the anger.

Tears threatened my eyes.

"So, the more I mutate, the more humanity I lose."

I looked at my hands, wondering how much of my humanity I'd already lost in the five times I'd mutated.

Were these the same hands to pull me up the rope of doom? Were they the same hands to dislodge the carrot Jayleigh had choked on? Were they even the same hands to hold Lora's? Did these fingers remember the skin of her cheek or the way her hair felt?

Or were these the hands I'd wrapped around Dr. White's

throat? The hands that had broken Lora's arm and almost killed Marshall.

Were they the hands of a man or a monster?

I was crying because I needed an outlet for my anger.

I'd tried so hard not to mutate, and they'd punished me and told me it was selfish, that I would die outside the fence if I didn't learn to control the animal inside.

But somehow, I'd known.

Maybe that was a Gen. 3's sixth sense, my intuition. All along, mutating felt wrong until I accepted and welcomed it and convinced myself that I could learn to control it like the others.

But I'd never be able to control it.

The mutant would become me.

It had already started. My mind flickered over the violent thoughts I'd experienced over the past few days. Things I would never have dreamt of saying this time last month.

It was true.

It had already started to change me, and I'd not even realized it.

So, I cried.

This was a death sentence.

"I'm outside the gates," I said finally. "I need to mutate so the Night Walkers can't compel me, but I can't mutate without losing a piece of my humanity."

Marshall kicked one of the backpacks, and it flew across the roof, landing in the snow. "What the hell did she do to you?" He asked quietly, referring to our mother's experiment.

I shook my head and tried to calm my tears. "I have no idea."

"We're working on a hormone stabilizer," Dr. White tried his best to sound optimistic. "But there's no saying whether or not it will work."

I nodded, although Dr. White couldn't see my response. "Okay." I wiped my eyes.

"It's not too late, Ares. There's still time. The best way to preserve your humanity is to stay human, and only mutate if you must. Now, if you'd pass me over to Marshall, I'd like a word."

Marshall looked less than amused as I unconnected the device from its holder and passed it over. My brother walked to the fire escape to talk to Dr. White, turning the loudspeaker off to stop us from overhearing their conversation.

Jayleigh stood next to me, not saying anything.

Everyone had overheard the call. They knew that I would slowly but surely lose control of my body and turn into something that couldn't be contained.

I wanted to make a joke, play it off as though the words hadn't affected me, and the tears had just been from shock. But deep down, the truth swirled as thick as blood.

I was slipping.

The mutant was growing stronger, and as a result, the Alpha hormones keeping pack Beta alive were fading faster and faster.

We packed our belongings and ate the oats Jayleigh had prepared during her night shift.

Marshall was still talking to Dr. White. I was surprised he'd continued the conversation, expecting him to hang up on my uncle just seconds in.

I walked towards Marshall, who sat on the ladder two stories down the fire escape.

"No. Of course, I haven't told him! And I certainly can't now. Not after you just dropped that bombshell." Marshall whispered aggressively into the tablet. I paused in my tracks, hoping to hear more, but the snow gave me away as it fell from the fire escape and alerted Marshall of my approach.

His head snapped in my direction, and he quickly ended the call. "Goodbye, Daniel."

Marshall began to climb back to the roof, and I recovered myself, trying to act as though I hadn't overheard a thing. "We're all packed up," I called down to him. "I was just coming to let you know we've left some oats for you."

Marshall shoved the tablet into my chest as he reached the

roof.

"Everything okay?" I questioned.

"Sunshine and rainbows." He snatched the oats and stalked through the snow, kicking at a snowdrift in the corner.

I put the tablet back on my wrist and tried to recall bringing up the map.

Initially, I assumed I'd done something wrong because the pins were not where I expected them.

Hail had travelled double the distance within the night, now resting somewhere along the coast, as Jayleigh had warned.

But that's not what confused me.

Jayleigh peered over my shoulder as she witnessed my shocked expression. "What's up?" she asked.

I didn't reply.

I pointed to the pins representing pack Alpha, now moving away from Hail and back towards us.

And there were no longer three pins.

Just two.

CHAPTER SIXTEEN

LORA

I didn't expect to leave the pack for this long.

Hail had travelled further than I'd initially anticipated, and before long, it was a question of whether to turn back on wasted efforts and rethink our plan or grit our teeth and dig in our heels.

The pack are safe and can manage another day or two without you. Hail needs you, I reminded myself.

I pushed Indigo and Zee beyond their limits, but we all knew the consequences of falling behind. We had to reach Hail before the Night Walkers turned him into one of their own.

We were roughly ten miles out when I started to feel it; the Alpha bond was dragging me back, slowing me, forcing me to stop. But I couldn't. Not without Hail.

The pack will be safe on The Farm without me, but Hail is far from safe.

Eventually, the pressure eased, or I became immune to it. We travelled as far as we could before darkness fell, and the hopeful sky retired to one of darkness and desperation.

We'd exhausted ourselves.

We hunted our dinner using the last of the energy our evolved state permitted and found shelter in an abandoned warehouse; its windows smashed and an icy breeze seeping in. The three of us huddled into a corner of the room, instantly falling asleep, despite the harsh conditions.

I awoke several hours later feeling as though somebody had ripped out my internal organs or something to that effect.

My animal alter ego must have stopped me from feeling it whilst I was in my evolved state, channeling the pain into power.

Only now could I feel it.

Only now did I realize that something was horribly wrong.

"Lora?" Indigo woke to the sound of my rasped panting. "What is it? What's going on?"

I tightly gripped my thumbs and squeezed harder and harder.

It was so cold. So empty.

"It's the others," I managed to say through the pain.

Indigo woke Zee then, and they watched in horror as I crumpled in on myself, holding my arms and curling my legs to my chest. I lay in the foetal position as my heart shattered like broken glass, impaling me from the inside out.

I'd been heartbroken before—tortured, even— but I'd never experienced anything like this.

"Are they okay?" Indigo laced her voice with worry.

"I can't tell, the connection is ruptured somehow."

"Is it the Night Walkers?" Indigo asked.

I shook my head. "It's different to what I feel with Hail…" it hurt to breathe, "He's distant and faded, but the pack— Something is blocking me from them. I can sense them, but I can't *feel* them. We need to go back."

"It's still dark outside. What about the Night Walkers?"

"The noise I'll make if this pain gets any worse will draw them all in. We'll be sitting ducks."

Indigo and Zee shared a look before complying.

"And you're sure that going back will help?" Zee asked, doubting my judgement. I was making a critical decision under duress, and she had the right to question me.

"I don't know." I shook my head. "But they need our help."

They guided me to my feet, my legs threatening to buckle at any moment. I knew what they were thinking; I'd wasted our energy yesterday. To turn around and retrace our steps now was excruciating.

But this was important, necessary.

The pack was in danger.

I summoned the last of my strength and focused on the pair before me, absorbed by the warmth and familiarity of the Alpha bond in its fullest capacity, how it should feel.

The energy broke through the pain in my chest. The warehouse lit up in a marvelous white light as my inner animal came to life within me, wrapped in chains. I felt her stir but held her back. She was just as uncomfortable with the situation as I was, yet she healed the pain within and beckoned me forwards.

Evolving didn't require me to mutate first, as it had in my early days. I'd quickly learned to control my mutant state during the Alpha Arena, and once I had found something to love, I then mastered the evolved state. I could flick between the three states at will, but I never had a need to mutate. The mutant inside was sleeping. She breathed life into me, healed me, and pushed me, but she was never a problem.

Instantly, the pain began to fade. How long had my mutant been hiding the rupture in the Alpha bond?

I circled the warehouse to give Indigo and Zee a moment of privacy, stretching out my legs and calming the feeling in my chest.

The night was quiet, save for the snow flurrying in the wind like hundreds of passing butterflies. I worried that it might cloud any sound from further afield.

I held my palm outwards, catching the snowflakes in my hand.

Energy pulsated through my veins, and I captured it, channeling it towards my fingertips. There was no visible difference to my skin, but the snowflakes began to glow.

I pushed the energy further, hoping to watch it spark from my fingers as it had when we'd escaped The Farm, but the power lingered and dwindled, and then I lost control of it, and it returned to its habit of circulating my body. I was doing something wrong.

Maybe I was too tired to project the energy now? Maybe my body was too busy hiding the pain my human state would still be experiencing. Or perhaps I didn't fully understand how to project the energy.

It didn't matter. The fact that I could not pull the electricity from my being would be a problem as we advanced.

"All clear," I told Indigo and Zee by mind jumping. *"Time to go."*

They appeared next to me in seconds, although I could sense their reluctance. They'd managed to evolve again in the time I'd been outside. Thankfully, their bodies had rested enough over the past couple of hours to allow it, but I know they wouldn't be able to hold it for much longer. They were new to evolving, and they hadn't built the endurance that I had.

We began the journey back towards The Farm, weaving through the trees of the forest. The snow was sparse in the canopy of the ferns, the ground soft underfoot. It smelt like damp pines, earthy and full.

"It's a cold one," Indigo spoke, using her evolved Titanium abilities. We'd spent so much time in our evolved state yesterday that the pair had managed to pick it up during our journey.

"It's going to get even colder once we're out of the forest," I warned.

We couldn't stay within the trees, for there were too many places to hide.

After a few minutes, we broke into the bitterness of the storm. The snow circled us. It was dizzying.

My heart never steadied. Not even the first sign of sunrise could calm the fear inside.

The snow was too heavy—the clouds too thick. The harsh weather conditions compromised the sunrise.

We ran through too many fields and abandoned villages to count. Eventually, we had no choice but to enter another forest. Going around would take too much time.

My worry for the pack lit a new fire, but I could see Indigo and Zee's light slowly fading. Their pace slowed. The connection between the three of us dimmed like the moon giving way to daylight. It was still there, but the vibrance was challenged.

"I'm not sure I can hold my evolved state much longer," Zee's words crept into my mind.

"It's almost dawn, and then it'll be safe to return to our human states," I urged.

She didn't argue.

Thirty seconds later, I heard a body slump to the ground.

Indigo. We both lurched forwards to study her condition, turning her over to face us. She was okay, just exhausted.

"Indigo!" Zee yelled through the dark.

No…

I held a hand over my mouth even though I hadn't been the one to make the sound. My heartbeat echoed in my ears. I darted around, expecting to see figures looming in the shadows. I'd heard Hail's tales of the red-eyed beings which smelled of death, and I was yet to experience what it felt like to be in the presence of a Night Walker. I'd been asleep when Hail had been taken from the barn—unless the Night Walkers had taken over our minds, too, and left us unable to remember it.

"How far?" Zee asked.

I closed my eyes, imagining the Alpha bond like a series of wires connecting each of us. I zoned in on the pack, and for the first time, I noticed they were significantly closer than expected.

"They're not on The Farm," I replied with dread. My stomach lurched and spun and threatened to regurgitate the squirrel we'd eaten last night. *"Just a few more miles."*

It should have been good news; music to my ears. It should have played like a symphony in my mind; it wasn't long before being reunited with my family and figuring out what was so dangerously wrong. But instead, all I could hear was drawn-out bass and sharp intakes of a scattered violin. It haunted my ears.

Why aren't they safe on The Farm?

And then, within the silence of the snow, we heard it.

'Crack'.

The snap of a twig.

Zee's eyes glowed brighter.

My heart raced faster.

They were here.

"Allora…"

The sound silenced the world of my mind.

The voice was colder than the winter morning. It successfully executed the task in which the temperature had failed; it froze me in place. Just a whisper in the trees, yet, the sound wrapped itself around me, stealing my breath in one last exhale of condensed water droplets, appearing as a cloud of steam in the morning light.

It knows my name.

"Get her to safety," Zee cut through my panic, seeming not to hear the voice.

Had I imagined it? Was it the exhaustion creeping in?

I shook my head. *"We can find a way—"*

"There is no other way, Lora. I knew the shit I was getting into when I followed you. I'm the one who yelled and alerted the Night Walkers of our whereabouts." There was a finality about Zee's words that I couldn't yet process. My mind was still thinking about the voice. It knew my name. My full name. How was that possible? *"You are the future of the pack. You can't stay to fight, it's too risky, and you know it."*

"What?" The tone of her words sunk in and cut through the ice of my mind. And suddenly, everything was back to its usual speed, and I realized exactly what she was trying to tell me *"I'm not leaving you behind, Zee. Nobody is expendable."*

Her eyes flashed with sadness. *"If you die, the whole world will suffer the consequences. Everybody is expendable when it comes to saving you."*

"But—"

"It's too late to change my mind. You can't save me, but you can still save her." Zee dropped Indigo into my arms, tears threatening her eyes. She kissed Indigo once. Light, sweet. Not at all how I

would expect a lover to say goodbye. I hoped the touch would wake Indigo from her unconscious state, but she didn't stir, utterly unaware of what was happening around her. She didn't deserve this, to lose Zee without the chance to say goodbye. Indigo could sometimes be annoying, but she was kind-hearted and optimistic. She deserved a future with Zee. They *both* deserved a future together.

"Zee—" I tried one last time.

But we both knew that it was too late.

The Night Walker's voice hadn't been a fragment of my imagination.

I could feel their eyes on us, waiting.

Zee's eyes begged me to let her go. She slowly backed away from me, and I wanted to hug or thank her, but all I could do was stare and wonder how I'd managed to destroy two lives in a matter of minutes. *"What if they try to turn you into one of them?"* I asked, mortified at the image slowly unfolding in my mind.

Zee shook her head. *"I won't let it come to that."* She pulled her knife from her pocket and pointed it towards her neck.

There was a moment of snow-filled silence as Zee looked towards Indigo for one last time. I knew she was speaking to her mind; I could feel Indigo's spirit lift through the Alpha bond.

"Will you tell her I love her when she wakes up?" Zee's voice was

faint in my mind now as she summoned enough energy to save the two of us from the impending Night Walker attack.

"She knows. She heard you." I nodded, tears falling now. *"Zee, it never should have come to this. I'm so sorry."*

"I'm not." The hybrid backed into the forest, full of whispers and wandering eyes. *"I can't imagine a better way to die than protecting the ones I love."*

I was still crying when Indigo woke.

The sun dyed the clouds cherry blossom, and the snow fell around us like petals in the wind. It was calmer now.

"What's going on?" Indigo asked as I placed her next to the river, letting the water fill the silence for a while. "Why are you crying? Where's Zee?"

I shook my head, unable to answer. Indigo deserved to know what happened. I owed it to Zee to tell her the story, how she gave her life to save the both of us. But no words formed.

I dipped my hands into the freezing stream and splashed the tears from my face. If not for my evolved state, my skin would have felt numb at the touch of the water, reflecting the growing feeling within me.

Indigo's silver eyes dropped as she registered my silence and what it meant, squinting as she struggled to come to terms with the news. She did not cry. Instead, her eyes flared with anger.

"I'm so sorry—" I started, but Indigo wouldn't let me finish.

"No," she silenced me with her finger to the sky. Her face remained unreadable as she climbed from the ground and stumbled around in the snow. "This is *your* fault." She stabbed her finger at me and then proceeded to walk away in the direction we'd just come.

I opened my mouth to reply, but nothing I could have said would have made a difference. No words could make it better. No superpower could turn back time.

Nothing could change the fact that Zee sacrificed herself for us, and I'd let her…

My heart was heavy.

Her screams still echoed through my ears.

I'd been close enough to hear them, distant enough to pretend I imagined it.

But then came the sensation that always swept over me as I lost a hybrid. No matter if I was in my evolved state, this was a pain even the mutant couldn't subdue, a burning heat that swept over my body three times over before settling in my chest and lighting my heart on fire.

I'd felt it with all the Titaniums who'd passed. Sometimes, like Zee, it was instant, but the weaker hybrids tended to take a little more time to break away. The longer the delay from the hybrid's death to the break in the Alpha bond, the more it hurt.

Physical pain was manageable. Emotional suffering? A little less so. But spiritual damage only healed with time. The feeling of one soul disconnecting from another would always haunt me, each broken bond leaving a hole in my heart.

The rest of the pack would soon join Zee if we didn't move quickly. I could sense my bond with the Titaniums growing weaker, meaning they were in more and more danger with each passing minute.

We were wasting time.

I was still in my evolved state as I followed Indigo and swept her over my arms, kicking and screaming.

Thankfully it was light now, the sun barely visible through the snow clouds. The Night Walkers would have to wait until evening before they could attack again, meaning we could make as much noise as we wanted. But our time was limited.

"It's okay to be mad at me," I said. "But don't let the others suffer because of it. They're still in danger, Indi. They need our help. And Hail needs our help."

Indigo wriggled in my arms, still too weak to fight herself free. "You let her go! Why won't you let me?"

"I didn't want to, but we had no other choice." My tone was colder than I intended, but urgency swarmed me.

Why had the pack left The Farm? Why was the Alpha bond fading?

I took a deep breath before continuing, opting for an empathetic tone. I knew what she was going through. Sure, my circumstances had been considerably different in the Alpha Arena, but I knew the pain of losing a loved one. I relived the guilt and suffering as I said, "You have every right to hate me."

She didn't reply, but she stopped fighting against me as I carried us towards the pack. This conversation was far from over. Indigo would want to know how exactly Zee died. I'd have to tell her she'd sacrificed herself, drawing blood with her knife for the Night Walkers to feast upon.

I wasn't sure how Night Walkers turned a being into one of their own, but I assumed that draining a human's blood wasn't the way to do it.

I prayed it wasn't.

For Indigo to see Zee as a Night Walker would be just as heart-wrenching as this moment. I couldn't begin to imagine how it would feel to see Ares with red eyes, smelling of death and destruction. My blood boiled. Could that be what happened to the Alpha bond?

Was I too late?

Had the Night Walkers already turned them?

Could I still spiritually sense them because they

weren't *technically* dead?

Did it feel different because they weren't the same species?

I wiped the questions from my mind, each one building a new layer of worry. Unfortunately, the mutant inside couldn't help my human tendencies to overthink unless I unleashed the animal from her chains and let her take over. But mutating wasn't the correct option.

I needed to keep my entities under control.

Stay positive.

Ares had taught me to appreciate the smaller things I would often overlook, so instead of letting the panic take over, I turned my attention to my surroundings.

I'd only ever seen snow once before, in my first year as Alpha. In those days, I was fuelled by my demons and working to prevent history from repeating itself. I'd closed off from the hybrids around me, appearing unapproachable and stern. But I'd felt broken. I'd played my part well and tricked everybody into believing I was sure and confident in my decisions, but how could I be?

How could I trust myself when I knew what I was capable of?

How could I trust anybody when everyone I'd met had tried to kill me?

Ares had seen through my mask, and it scared me because

nobody had ever seen me for *me* until he came along.

"Ares," I called out to him as we entered a town. My body felt weak at the thought of seeing him. I needed to know that he was okay. The Alpha bond was a web, each silken strand stretched and fraying, and Ares' was the weakest of all. I knew he was close, but he felt so… *so* distant.

Was he injured? Dying?

I compared the feeling to what I'd felt with Zee an hour prior. Was it the connection slowly burning away?

No.

It was more complex than that.

We passed through a maze of streets, getting closer to the pack. The anticipation was unbearable, and it squeezed my lungs.

We turned a corner. I lost balance on my feet, skidding on the ice, and we ploughed into the snow. Indigo complained, but I didn't let her distract me. I couldn't let her; my mind was elsewhere.

Dread swarmed around me. It was a darkness I couldn't comprehend.

It was getting closer, enclosing in on us.

I hurried into an alleyway, placing Indigo onto the ground and cursing at the prints we'd left. There was no way of hiding when our tracks would lead the darkness towards us.

"Stay here and keep quiet," I ordered Indigo. *"Something's out there. I'm going to check it out."*

I didn't think Indigo planned on moving far as she curled herself into a ball and sobbed.

My first instinct was to comfort her, but I didn't have the time, nor would she have wanted my sympathy.

I retraced my steps back towards the darkness.

It led me towards a truck with open doors and smashed windows.

At first, the vehicle didn't strike me as unusual, appearing no different than the others I'd seen on this side of the fence, but then I saw the number plate on the back, which identified it as one of The Farm's. As my panic grew, my hair and eyes glowed brighter in the shards of broken glass.

This was their truck. I picked up the pack's scent on the back seats.

I searched for blood but found none.

What happened to them?

It was apparent that somebody had ambushed the truck. The battered state of it was proof.

Inside was a bag with a farmer's tablet plugged into a port in the centre of the dash, surrounded by several buttons and switches. I presumed that it was charging.

The ambushers left behind the most valuable item, and if

somebody had tried to steal the truck, they'd done a poor job.

If the Night Walkers had attacked, they'd taken the pack alive.

The dread within me intensified.

The darkness was closing in.

My eyes lifted from the truck to something further down the street. It beaconed me in, enticing me towards it.

I recognized the feeling, but it differed from how I'd remembered. Something had shifted, and it felt very, *very* wrong.

I focused in, but the animal fought me. She didn't want me to feel the pain that would come with the knowledge. She didn't want me to understand the darkness or what it meant.

But I cast the animal aside. I needed to know what I was experiencing, and I needed to understand what had happened to my pack.

I returned to my human state to feel whatever my alter ego was trying to protect me from.

And that's when I made sense of it all.

Not the truck; that didn't matter.

The darkness was something else entirely.

Somebody else.

Ares.

I focused once more on our connection and screamed out in pain. It scolded like touching a hot iron rod. My skin felt blistered, and my heart couldn't take it. My mutant had been right to shield me from this.

Ares' aura was painted black.

He was growing stronger, unlike any Gen. 2 I'd ever met. And he was gaining control of my pack. It was like facing another Gen. 1 in the Alpha Arena. Only this time, he was *stealing* my family.

He'd claimed them.

My heart shattered.

I should never have left The Farm, I realized. *I should never have left him.*

Because I'd lost Zee in my efforts to save Hail, and now Ares and the rest of the pack were slipping between my fingers.

He thought that he could take them? He thought I would hand them over, when they were everything I was and everything I'd fought for?

My insides turned into liquid gold as he rounded the corner and ran towards me, smiling as though he had no idea what he'd done, blind to the spiritual shift between us.

Despite it all, I had to remind myself that this wasn't the same Ares I'd left on The Farm.

He looked the same, *handsome as hell.*

He acted the same, *goofy in the best of ways.*

I *felt* the same when our eyes met.

Yet, he'd claimed my pack, and that was something I could never forgive.

He'd already stolen my heart. I wouldn't let him take my family, too.

CHAPTER SEVENTEEN

ARES

Lora waited for us at the end of the street, a beacon of hope in a cold, wild world.

Our eyes met, and my body surged forwards, overcome with relief, worry, and love.

She didn't smile, as I expected she would. Her body slumped slightly. She looked exhausted.

It wasn't how I'd imagined our reunion. I thought she might copy my actions and run towards me, the two of us melting to the ground as we embraced, promising never to leave each other again.

Instead, Lora met me with *that* glare. The one she used when she was conflicted by her emotions and how to act. I hadn't seen it for a while and wasn't pleased to see it return.

I pounded through the snow, my feet kicking out to the sides to keep my balance. The last thing I needed was to slip over in front of everyone.

"Lora, thank God!" I reached out to her to wrap her dainty body in my arms, to reassure myself that I didn't imagine it and she was really here.

I'd have kissed her if the others weren't watching.

I'd have pulled her close and never let go.

Lora frowned as my arm moved towards her, eyes meeting mine briefly.

"Don't touch me," she hissed.

I cringed. "It's okay, Lora. Dr. White explained everything. I'm not a Gen—" I moved my hand towards her shoulder to reassure her, but she cut off my words and flipped me over as she had done in training so many times. I landed with a 'humph'*; the* wind knocked out of me, and shock took over my body. For a moment, I lay there wondering what was going on, and then I rolled around in the snow, trying to escape her reach as she attempted to pin me into the ground.

"What have you done?" she yelled at me. "You think that you can take them just because I left?"

Oh, she's mad.

The snow did nothing to help as I climbed from the ground. "Lora, what are you—"

She charged towards me again, her fist narrowly gliding past the skin of my cheek.

"I won't fight you, Lora!" How had it come to this? What was I missing? Was there another reason Lora had left The Farm? Did she *really* want to fight?

"There can only be one Alpha, Ares. If you want them, you'll have to kill me first."

"Want them?" I could barely speak through my surprise. I couldn't wait to get *rid* of them and the responsibility they carried. "Take them back, please. I don't want to be an Alpha."

She lunged forwards, sending the both of us tumbling to the ground. Her fists hammered down hard, and I tried to block them.

"Lora, stop!" I prayed. "It's a misunderstanding!"

Her knuckles made contact with my lip, and the pain woke something within me. Seconds later, the copper taste of blood filled my mouth.

I threw Lora off balance, rolled her over, and then scurried to my feet. She dived forwards again as I wiped the blood from my lip on my snow-soaked sleeve. We spun across the white ground, painting it red.

"I don't want the pack, Lora!" I tried again. "I know it may look that way." I directed us towards the wall of an old building. "But we were doing what we had to. We were dying."

She kicked me against the wall, my back taking the full brunt of the impact and a few bricks falling free and landing beside me.

I landed on my knees, spitting blood to the ground.

That hurt, but nothing could be so painful as fighting her. She wasn't listening; not giving me the chance to explain. It made me so angry that a gulp formed in my throat, and my neck tingled.

I could make her listen…

No.

I'd never mutate again. Not after the news I'd just received, and especially not after the last time I'd fought Lora and broken her arm…

She reached to grab me, but I used her move against her, sending her to the ground.

So, that's what it feels like to be on the other side.

The anger released itself in a victorious laugh which I couldn't hold back. Lora scrambled up, and I pinned an arm against her shoulders, trapping her against the wall.

"Ares, let me go now, or else—"

"Listen!"

"There's no way I'll ever let you take them. They're mine!" Her body shook and swayed as she tried to wriggle free. I'd never seen her so furious. Her under-eyes had bruised with exhaustion, and I swore I could feel the sadness radiating from her. This was Lora at her lowest, her weakest, her most reckless. This was the time she needed me most.

I felt her arms rising behind me, something heavy in her hand.

"Lora, please. I don't want the pack! I've never wanted them!"

"I'll kill you. Let me go and—"

I kissed her.

My lips asked her to listen in a way my words couldn't.

She fell silent, still, and then she heard what I was trying to tell her.

Her body relaxed against the wall. The brick dropped from her fingers, and the weight seemed to fall from her as she embraced my explanation.

My heart raced against hers as though I could feel it through our chests and the air around us. I shouldn't have been able to feel the Alpha bond with Lora; my new hormones had not been altered to work in that way. Yet here we were, wrapped in a spiritual bubble of raising pulses, hurt hearts, and forgiveness.

I could have stayed there forever without care for the snow or the witnesses behind us. But, through the perfect cloud of fog we'd created in our minds, I was well aware of our situation.

"Please listen, for one moment," I whispered against her lips.

I kept her pinned against the wall, worried that she may turn feral on me again at any second, and she slowly met my eyes. She didn't say anything, but she wasn't fighting back, and I assumed that was an answer.

"Being so far away from you was killing us. Dr. White transferred the Alpha hormones to me to keep us alive until we found you. It was possible because I'm a Gen. 3, not a Gen. 2 like the others. But my Gen. 3 alter ego likes to absorb foreign matter, so the Alpha hormones won't last forever, and it's slowly taking over my human state too. The more I mutate, the more I chip away at my soul. It's a big old mess, and I feel like my life has fallen apart since you left. You can stop me from talking any time you want because I'm just rambling now—"

Her lips met mine once more.

This kiss was light and sweeter, and I guessed she'd forgiven me. I dropped my arm from her shoulders, looping it around her waist and reeling her in.

"Get a room!" Jayleigh yelled from the far side of the street.

I smiled, pulling away from Lora and giving her time to ask her questions. I had a few of my own.

"What do you mean, your animal state is taking over your human state? How is that possible?" Concern creased her eyebrows, but her voice was steady. Her usual tone returned.

I cleared my throat, taken aback by her kiss. "The animal state is growing stronger… I guess I'll end up permanently in my animal state, unable to mutate back. Or the two alter egos will merge, like evolving, but without the human side of me to control the energy. I don't know. I'm still trying to process it to understand it. I'm only just coming to terms with being a Gen. 3."

"A Gen. 3." Lora placed a hand on my cheek and tried to make sense of it.

"Yeah, we don't know what it means yet, but it explains my differences from the others."

"So, I'm not ill, and my feelings aren't anything to be ashamed of? And the dark—" she stopped herself from finishing the sentence. "They've altered your hormones to make you an Alpha."

"Dr. White used the word Beta to describe my role during your absence. I think it means second, and I'm very much okay with that. It's fading quickly. I can sense pack Beta, but it's nothing compared to the connection I felt yesterday. We'd have died if we couldn't find you by nightfall."

Lora's confusion turned to an expression of guilt, her gaze

falling to the ground. "I had no idea leaving would hurt you—all of you. I thought I was doing best by everyone," she whispered.

I hugged her to my chest. "We know."

I might not have believed it yesterday, but seeing Lora now, feeling her body shudder against mine as she fought back the tears, I knew she was telling the truth. She wasn't running from her feelings, as I'd initially assumed; she was fulfilling her role of Alpha in hopes of keeping everybody alive.

But she'd failed.

Zee and Indigo were nowhere in sight, and we still needed to reach Hail. I wondered how many pins I'd see if I glanced at the tablet now, but I would only move from this spot once Lora was ready.

I rested my cheek against her head, inhaled, held it, exhaled, and appreciated having her by my side once again. She was safe. Rattled and grieving, but she was here, in my arms.

I'd never take it for granted again.

She pulled back, and I wiped her tears with my thumbs, cupping her cheeks in my hands.

"We'll work it out. It's okay," I tried to sound convincing, but I had no idea how we could rescue Hail.

Dr. White's commands to return to The Farm were gone with the icy breeze wrapped around our ankles. I knew from my little time as a stand-in Alpha that leaving Hail was not an option, and this was our only chance to get him back. We were halfway there. It didn't make sense to turn around now.

Lora nodded, and I kissed her quickly before backing away and nodding toward the others. "Let me introduce you to my pack," I joked.

"Too soon, Ares." Her jaw clenched, but a small smile escaped her as she rolled her eyes and walked away. I lingered for a moment.

She's here. She's back.

I worried I'd blink and she'd disappear, her silhouette dispersing and becoming one with the falling snow. My heart fluttered, and I pushed away from the wall, following close behind so I might collect any broken pieces of her that tried to escape.

The pack turned as we approached and welcomed her in the traditional Titanium way whilst Marshall and Kate lingered a little further down the street, an abandoned car, a pile of rubble, and two curbs between them.

Marshall stepped forwards as Tye expressed how relieved he was to have Lora back and snitched about my lousy job as Beta, so I was glad when my brother intervened. "So, when will we address the elephant in the room?"

I take it back, I thought.

"What the hell are you doing here?" Lora sighed.

"Supervising," he shared her unamused tone. "Where are the other two?"

Lora's gaze dropped to the ground again.

Marshall knew that one of them had died. He'd seen the map and probably knew which color pin represented each pack member, so he must have been trying to hurt Lora by asking the question.

"Indigo is back there." She pointed towards the alley. "And Zee… Zee sacrificed herself to save us."

We had expected something along those lines, yet it didn't make it any more bearable to hear.

My head fell forwards.

Everyone remained silent as we took a moment to come to terms with the news, and I looked back to Lora. She wouldn't meet my eyes, hers seeming glassy and bloodshot.

"What happened?" Marshall asked.

We all glared. Now really wasn't the time.

Lora's throat tightened.

I needed to intervene.

"Night Walkers," Indigo's voice emerged from the alleyway, small. I doubted Marshall and Katie would have heard her.

She looked frail as she rounded the corner to meet us, and I imagined how it might feel to stand in her shoes. The thought crumbled me from the inside.

I looked back to Lora as everyone sympathised with Indigo, greeting her with hugs and appreciation. A small tear ran down the Alpha's cheek, and I placed my hand on her shoulder.

"I don't want to talk about it," she whispered, so I grabbed her hand and led her away from the group, squeezing her fingers like a small hug.

"I'm sure you did everything you could," I said as we reached the truck, and I pulled the door open, shards of glass falling into the snow.

"I said I don't want to talk about it." Lora's tone surprised me, and I dropped her hand to hold mine up in surrender.

She was blaming herself again.

No matter her distance from The Farm, Lora always took responsibility for everyone else. I'd had a taste of that duty, and I was glad to be rid of it. One day was plenty enough for me.

"The keys are still here." Lora rattled them in her fingers. "What happened last night?"

I wiped the remaining glass from the seats as I filled her in on our evening with the Night Walkers and what we'd heard on this street just hours ago. The snow was doing a great job of hiding the bodies, or the Night Walkers had taken them after the attack. I didn't want to imagine what they'd do to the dead.

"We should take the truck," I suggested, "to get Hail."

"We?" Was it shock or worry on Lora's face as she spun the keys around her index finger? "You're not rescuing Hail with us, Ares. If what you said is true, that you can't mutate without losing a piece of your humanity, you'll be digging your own grave by walking into a group of Night Walkers."

My stomach twisted at her words. I wanted to scream. I'd just got her back, and now she wanted to leave me behind?

But it made sense that she wouldn't want me anywhere near the vampires. I'd be susceptible to their mind control, unable to fight back. She was looking out for me.

That didn't make the pill any easier to swallow.

"But I can't be away from you, Lora. You can't send me back to The Farm. I'll die."

"Who said anything about going back to The Farm?" She cocked an eyebrow. "You're not the only one who can't mutate, Ares. You're coming with us, but you'll keep a safe distance... with those two."

I followed her line of sight and groaned.

"You'll be babysitting the farmer and Mad Marshall."

What could possibly go wrong?

CHAPTER EIGHTEEN

ARES

We squeezed into the truck. Lora sat up front with Marshall and Katie, whilst Indigo sat in the back with the rest of us.

She wrapped her arms around herself and stared into what seemed to be a vast emptiness and not—in fact—my crotch. I didn't feel it was an appropriate time to make a joke, so I tilted my body away from her eyesight and towards the front of the vehicle.

"If Daniel asks, you're to tell him that you left me no choice but to allow you to continue your mission," Marshall announced. He charged my tablet via the cable and directed Katie through the streets that would lead us out of this nightmarish town. "Tell him that you planned on killing me if I refused."

Tye muttered under his breath, at a volume only the hybrids could hear, "That can still be arranged."

Lora turned to look at Tye through the wire that separated us but said nothing to him. "I assume you're all aware of Ares' situation?" she asked instead.

The others nodded, except for Indigo, who stared at my thigh. "What do you know about Gen. 3's Marshall?" Lora asked.

He shook his head. "There's no such thing. They didn't exist before Ares. And Mother did a good job of hiding her special little experiment." I winced at his choice of words. "It's not on record, and all of the farmers believed he was a Gen. 2, apart from Daniel and his elite group of scientists. I don't understand it."

That made two of us.

How had Dr. White managed to keep my secret for so long? I'd seen how Marshall acted in the Observatorium, how he'd eyed the monitors and flicked through various folders on his computer. He had access to everything and eyes on everything, so how did I manage to go under the radar?

Dr. White said that Mother used to take me to the Biome to get me away from the confinement of the bunker, which meant I'd walked the corridors of level -3 throughout my childhood. I'd been to the corridor of windows and peered in on the Night Walker inside—the woman with the answers.

"What do you know about a Night Walker trapped in a room near the Safe House?" I asked Marshall. I'd been there and seen her, so I was sure it wasn't just a dream.

Marshall shook his head. "We've never used those rooms, Ares. They're interrogation rooms, built in the military days, before the apocalypse."

Jayleigh gulped at Marshall's words. It was the first time the pack had heard a farmer refer to the current world situation as anything other than a war.

A war was winnable.

An apocalypse was a state of no return.

"There is a camera within each interrogation room, so I think I'd know if one was in use. Besides, how are you suggesting we'd manage to confine a Night Walker in there anyways?"

I shrugged. "I don't know… I just had a dream. Well, it felt more like a memory. I thought you might have known something about it, but I guess it really was a dream after all."

"I've spent my whole life watching those cameras. I'd remember if I'd seen a Night Walker in there."

"Yeah, of course." My voice didn't give away my doubt.

I knew that Night Walker had been in that room. I knew because it was the same Night Walker that I'd seen in the footage of Camera 72. It was the same Night Walker that killed our parents.

There was no possible way that I'd dreamt about her, having never seen her face before. It *had* to be real.

Of course, I believed Marshall when he said he'd never seen anything, but that wasn't to say that the cameras had been telling the truth. What if there had been a cover-up? A loop? What if the Night Walker had been hidden from Marshall, just as I had?

Or perhaps I was overthinking again…

The snow was beginning to drift, collecting against the hedges and making it difficult to see where the road ended and the grass started. The tires sunk now and then. Thankfully, Marshall assured us that the vehicle was fit for off-road use and extreme weather conditions—a little less so now that the windowpanes were missing. Lora had given Katie her jacket. Marshall wrapped himself in our sleeping bag.

"So, tell me about these fancy weapons that Dr. White supplied," said Lora, trying to make conversation.

I pulled my dagger from my pocket and held it out for her to view. "Solid titanium." I spun it through my fingers, watching the light reflect in harsh bursts. "The only thing which can kill a Night Walker."

"Do you all have one?" she questioned.

One by one, the pack revealed their weapons, holding them towards her.

"Good." She smiled. "We're going to need them when we get to Hail."

I only wished that we'd been allowed to take extra.

Marshall reached into the rucksack he'd left in the truck overnight, pulling out a small gun, parts disassembled, and he started fitting them together like pieces of a puzzle.

"I don't think a gun will help against a Night Walker, Marshall." I frowned at the sight before me. Shouldn't he know that already? Or did he bring the gun for another reason?

"They're special titanium bullets, Princess. Do you really think I'm daft enough to come out here unprepared?"

I shrugged. "You were dumb enough to leave your bag in the truck last night."

He rolled his eyes. There was more he wanted to say, but he held it back, finally learning his place amongst us.

Lora's eyes lingered on me whilst the conversation died, and everyone zoned out.

I offered a smile which she returned, but her dimples never appeared, she didn't show her teeth, and her eyes didn't sparkle the way they used to.

It was just the stress of losing Zee and the knowledge that the Night Walkers still had Hail.

Of course, she was allowed to act differently. Of course, it would have been strange if she'd acted unaffected by it all.

But my mind still fought to convince me that I was the problem.

"What's up?" I asked.

She raised her eyebrows and shook her head twice as though she had no idea what I was talking about. "Nothing," she whispered. And then, after a short while, "I'm glad you followed us."

"Yeah. Me too. I didn't fancy dying." I chuckled, but the joke didn't sit right. My eyes flickered to Indigo as the truck dipped again, and we hit a verge, and then the whole vehicle shuttered forwards and stopped.

"Rachel," Marshall's voice was stern, "please don't tell me that we burst a tire."

Katie stayed silent for a while, and then, "We didn't burst a tire... We burst two."

"Shit!" Marshall hit his palm against the glass of the window.

"Is there a spare?" Lora questioned.

Katie rested her head against the steering wheel. "Yes. But only one."

"I'm not sure if it's ever occurred to you that tires are more valuable than gold these days," Marshall spat at Lora. "Either we hunt for one that will fit, which could take days in itself, or we have to walk the rest of the way."

"Can we find another vehicle?" I asked. "I've seen so many left on the roadside and driveways. Can't we take one of those?"

Marshall's tongue clicked against the roof of his mouth. "They're pre-war vehicles and mostly run on gas. This truck is fully dependent on solar power." He pointed upwards. "The roof is made of panels, and the truck's wheels connect to a generator, turning the energy into electricity as they spin. It's self-sufficient, unlike the abandoned cars you've seen on the roadside. Whatever petrol those cars had left would likely have been looted years ago."

I sighed. "Walking it is, then." Lora cocked an eyebrow at my response, and I quickly backtracked. "Unless you have a better idea?"

The words left my mouth, although the decision was no longer mine to make. I'd become more comfortable with leading than I'd cared to realize, but I didn't want the responsibility, so why did I still act as though I were in charge?

The Alpha bond.

I could still feel it tying me to the other three hybrids of pack Beta, although it was dwindling, fading. It made me feel powerful. It boosted my confidence, and part of me would miss it when it vanished altogether.

Lora opened her mouth to suggest another option, but she fell short. "No, it looks like walking is our only choice."

She reached over Marshall's body to open the door and then waded through the snow to meet me at the back of the truck.

"I'm sorry," I said as soon as the others spaced out. "I guess I got used to calling the shots yesterday. I promise it won't happen again." I held my hands up.

"It better not, or I'll have to put you in your place… Show you who's really boss around here." Her smile quirking slightly to one side was the only indication that she was flirting. Her tone was deadly serious.

Confused but intrigued, my eyebrows raised. "And how exactly might that go, Alpha?"

She leaned in and whispered into my ear. "You'll have to wait and see."

Lora left me grinning. My gaze followed her as she retraced her tracks towards Katie, and once she was out of sight, I turned to find Jayleigh leaning against the backdoor of the truck. She was closer than I'd anticipated and watched me with beady eyes. "Wind your tongue in, Ares. It'll freeze at this temperature."

"Crap. You really have a habit of creeping up on me." I

jumped.

"Yeah, and you two really have a habit of grossing me the hell out. I'm glad to see you've made up and everything, but there's a time and place."

"Hey, you're the one who lingers around whenever I'm alone with Lora. I have a few valid arguments to suggest that *you're* the gross one."

"Damn, you've got me," her voice was laced with sarcasm. "I love to watch your public displays of affection. It's like popping a spot; disgusting to watch, but you just can't help yourself."

"I knew it." I smiled and cringed at the same time.

Jayleigh rolled her eyes, and as they stopped, they landed on something to my left.

"I think you're just jealous of us." I followed her gaze towards Diego. "Why don't you go and talk to him?"

"Jealous? Ew. No thanks. You and Lora are cutesy-smootsy enough for us all."

"What's holding you back? Worried that he doesn't feel the same?"

Jayleigh laughed. "Oh, no. He feels the same all right. It's written all over his face."

"It is?"

Diego had all but three expressions, and I couldn't describe any of them as longing. Or maybe I was missing something.

Marshall's voice echoed around us as he yelled from the front of the truck. We circled to see what the commotion was about, and as I looked down, I witnessed a set of traffic spikes half-buried in the snow.

"Shit!" Marshall called out again, holding his hands to his head as he walked in circles.

"Would the Night Walkers have laid them out?" I asked.

Katie shook her head as she turned to view the trees around us. "No, that's not exactly Night Walker style."

I could barely hear her over my brother's breakdown.

"Marshall, shut it!" I commanded. His strop was only going to attract unwanted attention. If Night Walkers hadn't planted this trap, then something else had, and chances were that they could move in sunlight and were probably watching us right now. "You're here to help us, not get us killed."

Katie continued sifting through the snow, revealing the tire's damage. "There's no way of fixing that, and we only have a replacement for one. It does indeed look like we're walking." Katie sighed.

"Shh!" Tye hushed us suddenly, holding his hand in the air and cocking his head. "Do you guys hear that?"

My heart beated faster. I sensed the pack Beta hybrids react the same way as we paused to listen. Three seconds later, I recognized the sound of feet kicking up snow and bodies rustling through the trees.

Marshall looked clueless. "What is it?" His eyes darted around, trying to hear what the hybrids could.

"Run," Lora whispered, her voice high-pitched and panicked.

We quickly grabbed our belongings and hit the road, not looking back. The snow reached my shins. Each hurried step sank. Running in the snow wasn't easy, but whatever followed us seemed to have no problem as they closed the distance.

Crap.

A similar sound appeared from the trees to our right, surrounding us, stalking us. They were fast.

This is it. This is how I die.

We ran for almost two minutes before something jumped out at us. I stopped in my tracks, leaping away from the cluster of brown hair and teeth before me. My mind took a moment to process what I was seeing.

We huddled together in a tight group as more jumped from the trees.

Marshall screamed in the distance, Katie and him unable to keep up with us, and I turned to watch something knock him into the snow.

I'd have laughed if not for the cold fear in my veins.

Wolves.

Several closed in. They had us surrounded.

I spun to count fifteen in total, each slowly creeping forward and forcing us to squeeze closer and closer together.

How ironic, I thought, *that I'd die by a wolf's teeth and not a Night Walker's.*

Despite the snow, I was sweating, my palms clammy. I reached for Lora's hand, squeezing it tightly.

The wolves herded us, walking Marshall and Katie towards our group. "What do we do?" Marshall asked as he approached, the snow soaking his hair.

Lora was still. "Wait until they get close enough and fight them off?" she suggested.

I didn't dare take my eyes from the wolf before me, now barely ten feet away. Its amber eyes pierced through mine, seeming to stare into my soul. I was transfixed as it snarled to reveal a complete set of teeth and stalked forwards slowly.

I felt myself crouching before I realized what I was doing, dropping my hand from Lora's, and reaching to the wolf instead.

"Ares, are you mad?" Lora's voice was pitched higher than I'd ever heard it before.

Probably, I thought, but I didn't respond as I reached eye-level with the wolf. "Everybody, get down," I instructed as I followed my intuition.

My heart never steadied, and I never took my eyes from the wolf.

"Why? To give the wolves an easy target?" Tye argued.

"Just trust me!" I snapped in a demanding whisper.

I heard him sigh before replying, "I swear to God, Ares! Man. I'm gonna kill you if this wolf bites my face off."

The noise around me faded, including Tye's complaining. I focused only on the wolf.

Five feet away.

This could've ended badly for us all. I knew it as I projected my hand forwards towards the teeth of the beast before me.

Three feet.

It lingered a little longer. The snarling stopped.

We're not going to hurt you, I repeated in my mind, hoping it was readable through my eyes. I couldn't consider the alternative. I *had* to trust my instinct.

And my instinct was telling me that the wolf was just as scared of us as we were of it.

The wolf stopped before me, its nose pointing to the ground so it could glare at me from under its brows. Its eyes were wild as fire, burning scars into my soul.

"Shh," I hushed. "We're friends."

It took the wolf a long time to consider my words. My hand was visibly shaking; my arm wobbled through the air. And much to my relief, eventually, the wolf seemed to relax. Slowly, it rested its forehead against my hand.

I was only vaguely aware of the voices behind me as I felt the thick coat of hair beneath my fingertips.

"What am I witnessing right now?" *Jayleigh.*

"He's a fucking wolf whisperer." *Marshall.*

"It's possessed him. Somebody kill it." *Tye.*

I slowly moved my hand, making no sudden movements, and scratched the wolf's head between the ears. It reacted as I imagined a cat would, closing its eyes and tilting towards my hand.

I smiled, still shaking in fear but oh-so giddy. "Hey there. I'm Ares. We're not going to hurt you."

The wolf didn't move as I withdrew my hand.

Once I was sure it was safe, I stood. The other wolves had moved from their place in the circle to stand behind my new friend. They greeted me with sceptical eyes.

So did my own pack.

I turned slowly.

Lora was close, speechless. "What… How?"

"I don't know." I frowned as I asked myself the same question. "Maybe it's my Gen 3 genetics?"

"You're arctic wolf, Ares. Not timber wolf." Marshall was quick to correct me.

"Oh, yeah… Well, either way, you're welcome."

Blank-faced and open-mouthed, they stared as the wolf sat beside me and started to nuzzle into my leg.

"Very impressive!" A voice boomed throughout the forest. My body froze over. "I've never seen that before."

The pack tensed, some taking on fighting positions, ready to fend off the intruder. It couldn't be a Night Walker as the sun was still high in the sky, although hidden by thick clouds.

It must be the person who set the traffic spikes.

They were there to kill us, to sacrifice us to the Night Walkers in replacement of their loved ones, or to feed us to the wolves.

"I'm here to help." The voice sounded again, and I saw movement behind a large fern to my right. A man walked forwards with one hand in the air and a long, thin whistle in the other. He blew a couple of notes of varying lengths into the whistle gently, and the wolves ran off behind him, save for the one still sitting at my feet.

"Interesting." The man stepped over a snow drift and onto the road before us. He was pretty old, yet he looked healthy, not at all like a man living in the brunt of the apocalypse. He dressed in an oversized fur coat, and his face seemed round, well fed, with wrinkles dragging at his olive skin. "Solace, come," he beckoned, but the wolf remained by my side.

I instantly felt on edge. Something about this man didn't sit right with me. Why would he intentionally sabotage our mission? Why had he planned to scare us with his wolves? Why did he claim that he wanted to help us? Why? When all he'd done so far was waste our time and energy.

He stood defenceless, with only his wolves to protect him, yet he didn't seem worried about standing amongst a group of silver-eyed hybrids armed with daggers. He seemed perfectly at ease.

"Forgive me for misunderstanding, but I wouldn't expect an ally to set his wolves on us," Lora spoke for the pack. "Or slash our tires, for that matter."

"I understand how it may come across, but I would never have let the wolves hurt you. They were only there to give me the upper hand in this conversation. I couldn't risk an attack from a hybrid like yourself."

We paused. The air felt thick.

"You know who we are?"

The man nodded. "I've met a few of your kind before and helped them out on occasion."

"Who are you?" Marshall stepped forwards. "The Farm does not know of this."

The man shrugged. "We asked them not to tell you... Marshall, I presume?"

A frown crossed my brother's face. "Tell me who you are or—"

"You can call me Chipper, and I'd like to invite you to join us. I feel that you may need to hear what I have to tell you about the stolen hybrid."

I could feel the doubt amongst the pack—the shock. Chipper knew about Hail, and he knew about us, The Farm, and Marshall. But how?

My eyes drifted towards my brother. His nostrils flared; a hand placed firmly over the gun strapped in its natural habitat across his chest.

"I made acquaintances with Benji's pack maybe four years ago now. Is he still about?" Chipper directed the question at Marshall.

"No." Marshall's jaw clenched. "The pack never returned from their last mission." He gripped the gun so hard that his knuckles began camouflaging with the winter scenery.

"Ah, I see." Chipper looked to the ground. "I'm sorry to hear that."

Marshall turned to Lora. "I don't have a good feeling about this. He claims to know pack D, yet I do not know this man or the part he played in their mission."

"I try to keep my identity a secret for security reasons. You can never be too careful in this world. I do hope you understand." Chipper's smile was warm, as though he were sharing a joke.

"What do you propose, Chipper?" Lora asked, despite Marshall's worry.

"I'd like to invite you to join me. I have food, a place for you to take refuge. It's well hidden and has been a haven for many over the past twenty years. I want to share my information with you."

"And you're offering this out of goodwill?"

Chipper shrugged. "I offer this in return for intel. I want to know what's going on inside The Farm's gates."

"We're on a tight schedule. As you already know, one of our own was taken, and we think the Night Walkers want to turn him."

"It is information about your mission that I'd like to share with you. Without it, I'm afraid you won't survive inside the Night Walkers' nest."

Lora sighed and met my eyes as though asking for my opinion.

I didn't like it one bit.

Not Chipper and his toothy smile. Nor how he already knew about our situation. I especially didn't like how the wolf at my feet seemed to act as a barrier between us, telling me that I should not get close to this man nor trust him.

But we needed to know about the Night Walkers' nest. If we wanted to see Hail again, we'd need as much information as possible. As things were, we were running blind, but maybe we'd have a slight advantage with Chipper's help.

I hated myself for nodding at Lora, but Hail was worth the risk.

"We would be grateful to accept your offer."

Chipper pulled back his arm, pointing through the trees and blew his whistle in two short notes. "It's just a short walk this way," he said and began to follow the wolves as they descended into the forest.

Marshall began to mutter swears as Lora stepped in Chipper's direction.

We'd just agreed to give away valuable information—confidential information. We were about to share The Farm's secrets in hopes of saving a hybrid that Marshall already considered dead.

I followed close behind Lora as we moved into the forest, my new wolf friend, Solace, hot on my heels. She hadn't listened to the whistle like the other wolves, and I was glad, doubting that I'd ever had a pet before. I patted her head as we walked.

"Are you sure about this?" I whispered to Lora.

"No," she replied.

"Me either. But we need to hear what Chipper has to say."

"Right," she agreed, her eyes darting through the woods as though she were looking for something. "We'll trade information, eat the food Chipper had offered, and then we'll get the hell out of this forest."

"And what happens if it's a trap?"

Lora looked at me as though she hadn't considered this, her eyes wide and lips pursing closed. "Then we'll pull an Ares."

I blinked back my confusion. "What does that mean?"

"We'll wing it and hope for the best."

My elbow bumped her arm in response.

Marshall was still complaining behind us, and Lora clicked her tongue as he called my name. "Have fun," she said as I fell back to walk next to my brother. Solace slowed too.

"Ares, tell your girlfriend that she's just made the most stupid decision of her life. We don't know this man. What if it was him who killed Benji and his pack?"

I let out a small laugh. "You need to learn to trust others a little more. Not everyone is out to hurt you, Marshall."

"I beg to differ—"

"Your nose is bleeding," I paused as I noticed it.

Marshall flinched. Then he reached to touch it, wanting to

see the proof with his own eyes. "I'm not surprised. I get them all the time when I panic. Why the fuck am I the only one stressing out about this? Titaniums are supposed to be intelligent creatures, and I've just realized I've been raising a group of morons for the past three years."

"The only thing you've been raising in the past three years is your blood pressure. I bet you're just cranky because of the caffeine withdrawals."

Marshall snorted a laugh through the hand covering his nose.

"Wow… A laugh from Marshall. This really is the damn apocalypse."

I saw him turn to glare through the corner of my eyes as I manoeuvred over a fallen branch. "You are the most annoying person on this entire planet. How am I related to you?"

"You've obviously never looked in the mirror, Marshall. It must run in the family."

He was silent for a short while, much to the group's relief, and there was no way of reading his thoughts. His face was expressionless, but at least the nosebleed had stopped.

"So, I see you made a friend," he sounded uncomfortable, as though making small talk was difficult for him.

Solace looked up at Marshall like she knew he was talking about her. She curled her lip to reveal a pointy set of white teeth. The image reminded me of Dickward and how he'd snarled at me when he mutated in Phase 2.

Marshall tried to appear unfazed but put a little more distance between us as we walked, using me as a shield. "Yeah, she seems lovely… Very nice."

"Have you ever had a pet?" I asked, my mind remaining on Dickward. Marshall had admitted that he'd taken a particular liking to that 'animal'.

Marshall's eyebrows bent in on themselves. "Do you think Father would have allowed a cat to run through the corridors of level -3? Shit everywhere, hair malting all over the chairs… No. And I never wanted one, anyways. You may have already guessed that I'm not fond of animals."

"You don't say?"

We broke from the trees. The snow was slowing now, flakes appearing larger but fewer. The sky seemed brighter than my eyes could focus on as the clouds thinned.

"Not far now," Chipper called back to us. "I have scouts in the trees ahead. Please don't be alarmed."

"Do they have guns?" Marshall asked.

"Well, yes." Chipper laughed. "They'd be useless without guns, but they won't use them on you. We're not savages."

Marshall seemed to tense beside me.

I tried to play off my nerves, but the further we walked, the more I questioned Chipper's intentions.

Solace seemed to sense my worry and nuzzled into my leg. I smiled down at her and wondered how I'd managed to acquire the wolf.

A rustling from above caused me to look up, following Solace's gaze. Upon a small platform within the trees, a man perched with a gun in one hand and a flask in another. One of Chipper's scouts.

"Reckon he has coffee in there?" Marshall asked me.

I pursed my lips. "I doubt it. It's highly unlikely that these people have a tropical biome like we do on The Farm."

Marshall's eyes scowled. "Remember what I said to you in the Observatorium yesterday?"

My brain fought to recall everything which had happened in the past twenty-four hours as it mashed together in a blur of confusion and anger.

"That you don't lie? Or that you're not sorry for stabbing me because I deserved it?"

Marshall's brows pinched for just a second. "No, not that… I told you you're next in line to take over The Farm. So, whatever you decide to share with these strangers, whatever secrets you give away, will affect you in the long run just as much as it'll affect me when we return home. Information is power. Keep that in mind before running your mouth like you usually do."

We passed several more scouts as we approached a cliff, a set of steps leading us down to lower land.

"Is... that what I think it is?" I asked.

"Moon-powered water." Marshall's voice was bland, but I watched his eyes light up as we stopped atop the cliff, looking down to the sea below, waves crashing against the snowy shore.

"It's beautiful." I was mesmerized, hypnotized by the call of the tide.

Marshall looked disgusted by my reaction and began the climb down to the beach, leaving me behind.

Lora also remained on the cliff, and I slipped my hand into hers. We both closed our eyes for just a moment.

"I understand why you want to find a cottage by the sea now. The sound is magical," I whispered.

My eyes remained closed, but her gaze was on me. I was sure of it.

After a few more seconds, she squeezed my hand a little tighter and then let go. "Come on," she beaconed.

I savoured the moment, then opened my eyes and followed her down the rickety wooden steps. We met the pack at the entrance to a cave further down the beach. The walls were damp and smelt thick of salt. Torches were chiselled into the rock, lighting the way to a small gap towards the back of the cavern where the wolves waited for us.

For the faintest of seconds, the smell of smoke surrounded me. *It's just the torches,* I figured.

Single file, we followed Chipper through the gap and side-stepped our way into an enormous cavern via the narrow tunnel. The smokey aroma grew stronger with each step, and I questioned if Chipper was leading us to the gates of hell, deep within the Earth's core.

Instead, we found quite the contrary—a shanty town. My jaw fell as the walls around us revealed the hidden community.

Industrial-style steps led us down to a lower level filled with tables and chairs, stalls, fire-pits, food, tents, wolves, and *people.*

"What... What is this?" Marshall questioned.

Chipper smiled as he revealed his most prized possession. "Hybrids, Marshall, young lady-"

"Katie," she corrected. "My name is Katie."

Chipper nodded and held his hand out before him. "It's my greatest pleasure to introduce you to The Sanctuary."

CHAPTER NINETEEN

ARES

The Sanctuary was built in fire, sweat, and saltwater. The cavern's walls flickered red as the flames danced, smoke rising high and escaping through small gaps in the rock above.

Here, I had never felt so far from home.

I'd become used to the open air, the clean white walls of the bunker, and the organization of The Farm. The Sanctuary was a rude welcome into civilian life.

Gone were the high-tech devices, clean clothes, and privacy. I'd never considered The Farm as luxurious, but it felt expensive to me now. This was poverty. This was realism. This was life outside of the fence.

"The what, now?" Marshall interrupted. "Are you telling me that this army has been living here this *entire time*?"

"Humans have sought refuge here since the early fifties, yes," Chipper replied. "But I wouldn't call them an army, as such."

Marshall backed against the cave wall; his forehead was damp with sweat, and he seemed not to hear me as I called his name.

"This isn't happening..." he reached for the rusty metal railing beside him, wobbling.

"Marshall, are you okay?" I studied him. He looked more out of sorts than usual.

"Get me to the toilet."

Chipper pointed. "We don't have toilets, but you'll find the dunnies down there to the right."

I rushed Marshall in said direction, carrying him through a tunnel and sliding the curtain closed around him as he began spewing into the borehole.

I waited outside the curtain, focusing on the sound of running water beneath the varying tones of busyness that The Sanctuary emitted. *So far from home,* I thought again.

The Farm was never this loud. Even the hundreds of farmers working in the bunker remained quiet so long as the sirens weren't blaring. There was a sense of tranquillity about the place that I'd never stopped to admire until being thrust into this strange underground world. I wondered how Jayleigh was holding up with the contrast.

The wall was warm against my back as I waited. It covered me in soot, but I didn't care much for my appearance.

What would Marshall do once he recovered? That dangerous spark of craziness I knew only too well had loomed in his eyes.

But he wouldn't do anything stupid, would he? To sacrifice our mission now would have been a waste, and I wouldn't risk losing Hail for my brother's temper. I was responsible for keeping Marshall under control if there was ever such a thing.

Solace stalked towards me, her head low. For a moment, I worried that she was stalking me, ready to attack, but her ears dropped as she drew closer and leaned against my leg. Her amber eyes reflected the flames of the torches which lit the walls, and she panted through the noise of bustling human life.

"Are you okay in there?" I called to Marshall, realizing he'd gone quiet.

He didn't reply.

Crap.

"Marshall?"

Knowing my luck, he'd probably escaped through the back of the curtain, and I'd find him setting The Sanctuary alight just a moment too late.

Or he simply needed a little privacy.

But there still needed to be an answer.

I considered peering around the curtain to ensure he hadn't fallen through the hole, given that this man had experienced the luxury of *actual* toilets for most of his life, but I feared I might interrupt him.

One more minute passed.

And then another.

"Marshall?"

Still no reply.

I pushed passed the fear of what I might be walking into and pulled back the curtain.

"Crap," I left Solace outside and rushed in, leaning over Marshall's unconscious body and checking his pulse. He sprawled across the floor with vomit running down his cheek, still breathing, but his temperature was abnormally high.

I picked a clean rag from the basket, dampened it in the stream that ran through this part of the cave, and then placed it on Marshall's clammy forehead.

"Marshall?" I patted his face. "Come on, Marshall, it's not sleep time yet, Pal."

"Hmm?" He slowly opened one eye. "Where am I?"

"A bathroom—cave… thing. How are you feeling? What happened?" I pushed passed the niggling feeling that something about the situation felt off.

He struggled to sit, touching his brows. "What the fuck is on my head, Ares? Get it off." I barely understood his grumbling but removed the damp towel, tossed it into the used rag bin, and helped him find balance in a sitting position. Neither of us said anything for a while. I tried to avoid staring at the dribble from my brother's mouth as we sat there. The shock had really done a number on him.

"They've been hiding down here," his voice sounded empty when he finally spoke.

I frowned. "That's a good thing, right? We're not as alone as we originally thought."

Marshall laughed. It started small, then grew to the point that it sounded almost painful.

"I'm missing something," I whispered.

The laughter slowly died, and a void of silence filled the air between us once more.

He knew that I was onto him. I couldn't shift the conversation I'd overheard between him and Dr. White from my mind whenever I looked at him. I'd tried to distract myself from it because I had more worries than whatever Marshall was hiding. But he'd left The Farm for a reason, and I was now sure it was not the same reason he'd initially given us.

"My entire life, we thought that we were saving the human race," he said. "Do you know how much weight I've had on my shoulders since Father died? We thought that there were only a few of us left. But in there? I just saw several hundred walking, talking humans." Tears stung his eyes, bloodshot and angry. "They've been living down here, knowing about The Farm, and *laughing* at our efforts."

"I don't think they've been laughing—"

"They're living peacefully down here, away from the Night Walkers. Of course, they're laughing. I would be if I were them."

"Marshall, what you and our parents built on The Farm *is* saving the human race. We're able to fight back because of you, so don't for one second think it's all for nothing." I shocked myself with how much I seemed to care for The Farm's efforts, despite how much I hated their methods. Life outside the fence proved how crucial my family's work was. This planet was a mess. "These people down here? Sure, they're living real nice for now, but they wouldn't stand a chance if a Night Walker found them."

Marshall nodded once, sharp, and reached his hand to the stream, which ran alongside the wall, to scoop water and wash his face. "It would have been nice to know they existed. We could have offered them a place on The Farm. We could have built a stronger army, united against the Night Walkers." His hand hung over his face, despite being done cleaning his dribble.

"Yeah," I agreed. "But now we've found them, and it's never too late to rebuild."

Marshall blew air through his nose and dropped his hand, gaze landing on me in what seemed to be a look of pain, eyes squinting, mouth pulled tight. "You're irritatingly optimistic."

"I'm sorry." I copied his sarcastic tone. "Would you rather I sat here whining, like you?

"I'm not—" He stood abruptly. "This conversation's over."

I was relieved to hear it. "Praise the Lord."

Marshall stumbled and swayed as I drew the curtain back, pausing to ensure his shock had worn off as he began the journey back to the hustle and bustle of The Sanctuary.

"Come on, Ares. What the fuck are you waiting for?"

I'm making sure you're okay, I replied, but only in my head because I didn't want Marshall to know I cared about his wellbeing.

Not yet.

I was still trying to work out why I worried about him. But maybe that's what it meant to have family. I felt for Marshall the same way I felt for Tye—although perhaps a little less extreme, with Tye's actions being more excusable than Marshall's—in that I didn't like either of them. We'd fought on multiple occasions, but some part of me still cared.

It was human instinct.

Marshall screamed and leapt aside as Solace sprung out from behind a rock. He stumbled, tumbling into a large pile of dirty fabric that the community had discarded in the tunnel, and I watched in amusement as Solace bared her teeth at him and trotted to my side.

He took a moment to process that he wasn't in real danger, his face a picture of confusion and fear. His chest rose with each panicked breath, and his eyes darted around as he tried to make sense of the situation before landing on me in disapproval.

I couldn't hold back the laughter.

I didn't recognize half the swears that left his mouth as he rose from the sheets and towels, brushing himself off and fixing his rucksack on his shoulders.

"Not a word of this to anyone!" He pointed at me in a warning. "Learn to control your dog if you want to take her back to The Farm."

As my laughter faded, I spied the slightest of smiles crawl across Marshall's face.

"You should know better than anyone that animals can't be controlled, Marshall. Solace does what she wants."

"Not a word," he repeated and continued towards the pack.

I looked down at Solace, scratching the thick mane of fur at her neck and asking, "Aren't you a good girl for knocking Uncle Marshall down a peg or two? Do you want to come back to The Farm? Shall we ask Chipper if that's okay?"

Solace's tail didn't wag because she wasn't a dog, as Marshall had suggested, but her ears perked forward, and she ran off into the crowd. I assumed it was to find Chipper, but upon more thought, I realized that Solace was a wolf and hadn't understood a word of what I'd just said. I searched the crowd for Chipper as I returned to the pack.

They had claimed a table and ate as though they hadn't seen food in days. Most of them didn't turn as I approached, but Lora pushed away her bowl of untouched stew and stood to greet me.

"Is he okay?" Her arms crossed at her chest, eyes lingering on something behind me. Lora seemed just as uncomfortable with our current situation as I was.

I tipped my head from side to side. "He's Marshall. He's never okay."

My brother filled the empty seat next to Jayleigh, posture stiff, giving her a side glance as she turned to talk to Diego.

Was he scared of her?

The idea was laughable. Marshall wasn't the kind to fear anything... except wolves. He'd been careless even when the

Night Walkers breached The Farm's gates, although he'd been on multiple painkillers at that moment, and I assumed that he wasn't now.

Thinking about it, I'd not seen him take any form of medication since leaving The Farm.

"Lora!" Chipper's voice bounced from the cave walls, and I jumped. The people of The Sanctuary swarmed around our host as though his voice was a welcome signal to gawk at us. I'd never felt more exposed. "It's time to talk."

Lora reached for my hand and squeezed my thumb.

"Do you mind if I tag along?" I asked. I didn't actually want to, I wanted to grab a bowl full of stew and take a nap, but if Lora was going, I'd go.

Breathe.

They're only human. They just want to talk. But something still felt off.

Lora's holding my hand.

Everybody is watching us.

She's squeezing my thumb instead of her own.

What does it mean?

What does it mean?

Think about that later. Concentrate on Chipper's words.

But what does it mean?

"Oh, we only need the Alpha. Feel free to stay with your

friends and enjoy the refreshments." Chipper denied me, then his gaze dropped to my hand, fingers intertwined with Lora's.

"Where I go, he goes," Lora laid down her terms, and I couldn't help but smile, despite the anxiety swelling up inside.

"We're kind of a package deal," I added. There was no way I was letting Lora go with a group of strangers, human or not.

Not because she couldn't handle herself, I'd have bet Jayleigh my next two meals that Lora could have taken out the whole of The Sanctuary alone if she'd wanted to.

She had that kind of power, and although I was yet to witness the full extent of what Lora was capable of, I knew it was there. I could sense it.

No.

The last time I'd been separated from Lora, she'd left The Farm, and we'd both almost died. That was something I didn't want to risk again.

Not the dying part, I knew I'd die one day—probably soon with the way my luck was running out—and that was fine because I couldn't allow my alter ego to take away my humanity. If I came face to face with a Night Walker, then I'd be left with no choice but to mutate, and Lora had to be there with me when the time came. I needed to be able to say goodbye.

So, I followed close behind, so close that when we entered a room which branched off from the main cave, our bodies pressed together, and it was nothing short of magic.

I needed her there when I died to tell her that she was the reason I lived, for the small, stolen moments like these where I felt most alive.

The world fizzled away, and it was just the two of us. She set my body alight with just a smile, and I squeezed her hand and nodded in reassurance as we pushed through the growing crowd, wishing more than anything that we were leaving the room of people rather than entering it.

Benches filled with men and women of different ages, and heads turned as we made our way towards the platform at the front.

We took a seat as Chipper addressed the twenty-something people before us. "I'm sure you'll all join me in welcoming our new hybrids to The Sanctuary."

A small round of applause echoed throughout the cave. The flames on the walls flickered to the stuttered beat. A sweat broke over my skin.

This doesn't feel right.

"Would you like to introduce yourselves?" Chipper seemed not to notice my discomfort.

Lora dropped my hand and slowly stood before the crowd, gripping her hands into fists behind her back. "I am Lora, Alpha of the Titanium pack." Her voice was confident. Calm.

She was radiating positivity. "And this is Ares, my…" she paused as she looked back at me, unsure of how to finish the sentence.

I stood to rescue her from having to put a label on our relationship. "I'm the Beta of the Titanium pack." I rested a hand on her shoulder and gave a light squeeze.

A slight murmur rose from the group. Apparently, The Sanctuary knew more about us hybrids than I'd first realized. Chipper controlled the crowd as he continued. "Interesting. This is the first time we've heard of a Beta. "Lora... and Ares," he added my name in an afterthought, "there's a reason I've called the two of you to this meeting, not Marshall. He could share more information about The Farm than you, but we've heard a lot about The Farm and how they treat you there, we have seen what the farmers put you through, and that's the reason why we haven't made ourselves known to Marshall or his people."

"What do you mean, you have seen it?" I stopped him. There was no way they'd be able to get into The Farm without being spotted on camera or alerting the gatekeepers. Even the Night Walkers had sounded the alarms.

Danger flashed in Chipper's eyes, and I felt threatened. Not physically, I knew I could take on the older man if I had to.

But the sense of wrongdoing came from my growing

dedication to The Farm.

I didn't support how Marshall and my father had run it.

I didn't support Mother's experiments.

But I *did* believe in the cause. I knew that it stood for a peaceful, sustainable future. And I knew that these people were about to threaten it.

These people had been spying on our home.

"We have the equipment to hack into old technology, such as the systems used on The Farm. It's how we can hack into the Night Walker's nest and give you the information you need to save your friend."

My stomach flipped, and I was glad I'd not had time to eat anything before the meeting. I wasn't sure if I could stomach what I was about to hear.

"The real reason I wanted to call you here is to give you an ultimatum… an escape from The Farm. We have plans regarding taking down the Night Walkers, but we need equipment used on The Farm. So why not kill two birds with one stone? We wondered if you might consider joining us to stop The Farm's brutal ways."

CHAPTER TWENTY

LORA

Putting a stop to The Farm.

The Sanctuary had been monitoring The Farm to attack it, and Chipper invited us to join his rebellion. Instead of teaming up, as we should, he wanted to risk more human lives. For what?

Did Chipper have information about Hail at all? Or was bringing us here a ruse to get us to join his efforts?

The Sanctuary's plans angered me, but I had no real connection to The Farm, as Ares did. To me, The Farm was a temporary home. But Ares had roots there, and Chipper had just marched in with a chainsaw, hoping to cut the tree down.

Through my shock, I sensed the darkness surrounding Ares begin to grow, reaching out and taking no prisoners.

How had this storm cloud been hiding in Ares? How did somebody with so much love to give have such a wicked alter ego? It was like his aura was alive, a shadow crawling from the human vessel and spewing out into the air around him.

His head bowed forwards just an inch.

Jaw clenching, he was losing control.

I scrambled to find his hand and squeezed, forcing his eyes away from Chipper to look at me. If only I were in my evolved state and able to speak directly to his mind, I'd have been able to reassure him. My heart melted as our gazes locked. It was rare to see a severe expression on Ares' face, brows drawn, and nose flaring. Fury looked good on him, but I knew it shouldn't be encouraged.

Heat radiated from his hand to mine. The smokey aura around him closed in, and, for a moment, I felt it snake up my arm, down my shoulder blades, and circle my torso, where it settled for a while and then dispersed.

My body reacted in a short volt of energy, kickstarting my heart which had surely stopped for a moment in surprise.

What the hell was that? I asked myself. *What just happened?*

Ares's eyes were still setting me alight. *"I don't know."* He seemed to reply.

But that wasn't possible. We weren't in our evolved state, and mind jumping wasn't something a hybrid could do in their human state. But Ares wasn't like the others. I had no idea what a Gen. 3 was capable of, and with the mutant side slowly taking over his humanity, did this change how he could control the energy that the hormones within us unlocked?

I had felt the exchange of energy; my light extinguished his darkness.

Had it sparked a reaction? Had it allowed us to connect in a sixth sense for just a moment?

We stared. My body was alight from his gaze, the energy that had just charged me, or both.

The leader of The Sanctuary didn't seem to see whatever was going on between the two of us, so he continued to talk, despite the fact that neither of us were listening. "The conditions that The Farm forces upon you are less than acceptable, and the Sanctuary would like to offer you safety and protection without any of these life-threatening trials…"

"Ares?" I called out to him, wanting nothing more than to hear his voice in my mind again, but the dark cloud around him had faded, and I took this as a sign that he'd regained control.

We continued to stare, but he didn't seem to hear me, his eyes searching mine as though trying to pull words from my mind.

Whatever allowed us to mind jump in our human forms had now passed.

"Lora?" Chipper was waiting for a response, having finished his speech at some point. "Ares?"

It was safe to assume that neither of us had heard a word. We both turned back to face the crowd, and I wondered if they'd seen anything or if they were just as blind to our energy as Chipper.

The crowd met us with blank faces.

"I… Um." Eyes. Too many peering eyes. I was flustered and confused. "I need some air," I admitted. "Can we have a moment to talk in private?"

Chipper rolled his head on his shoulders in impatience. I predicted this was different from how he'd expected the meeting to go. "We are offering you a chance at a normal life," he persisted. "A chance to—"

"We cannot agree to anything until we've had time to talk about it," I said with finality, but his words were not the reason I needed air.

My feet removed me from the make-shift stage, fingers locked with Ares' so that I dragged him along too, although I sensed he was glad for thc interruption.

Everybody's attention was on us as we fled.

We picked up speed as we retreated through the tunnel, shoes hitting the floor with urgency, and the rock echoed our racing rhythm as we shared the growing need to escape. The walls were closing in on me. The air was heavy and burnt; the smoke stung my lungs.

My eyes located my pack as we lined the outer wall of The Sanctuary. They seemed settled, laughing at Marshall, who had fallen asleep with his head resting on the table as Jayleigh balanced chunks of bread atop his cheek.

They'd be fine for a bit longer. Tye was still absent after running off with a human girl in a bid to make me jealous. It surprised me that he thought I'd care, there were many more unsettling matters at hand, but Tye had always been on the immature side.

Surprisingly, it was Marshall I found myself worrying for. Who knew what Jayleigh would do to him if he didn't wake up soon? He deserved anything she had in store, I decided.

As I pulled Ares towards the exit, our feet rattled up the metal staircase, shaking as the two of us made our escape. One more narrow tunnel and we'd be free. The cave tried to keep us. The walls swallowed us whole. I fought to reach the sea before the claustrophobia unlocked the chains of my inner animal.

I gasped for air.

My knees hit the rock as I scrambled.

And then the cold winter morning air welcomed me, the cave spitting me out. The urgency propelled me forwards, and I tumbled from the tunnel, pulling Ares over in the process. We rolled across the sand of the open cave, the tide attempting to catch us but narrowly missing our feet. My breath formed clouds on Ares' face as he hovered above me.

And the overload of emotion and confusion bubbled in my stomach, spilling out of me in an uncontrollable laugh. It bounced from the walls, echoing around us in a chorus of chirps like baby birds in the late spring.

Infectious, it seemed.

Ares' laughter joined the choir, and his smile made it challenging to see the cloud of darkness which followed him; it made it difficult to see anything other than how utterly perfect he was. The gentle breeze was blowing at the waves of his hair. The torches illuminated the freckles on his nose, which scrunched as he laughed.

My breath caught.

He must have sensed it, if not *seen*, as the cloud of my breath vanished and our laughter fizzled away. The echoes continued as he leaned closer.

We had more important things to be doing with our time. We had people to save and rebellions to vanquish, but I *needed* this. Ares was, and somehow always had been, the person I ran to when emotions got too high, and stress became unbearable. He found a way of lifting the weight from my shoulders—often without realizing it—and right now, I was crushed.

Not by Ares, although he was lying on top of me, elbows propped on either side of my head. I suddenly became very aware of our proximity as our lips met.

It was like magic.

Instant.

Gone were the worries of Night Walkers, stolen hybrids, and human armies wanting to take down The Farm.

I should have felt guilty for abandoning my duties, and I knew that I would later, but right now?

My only worry was that Ares wasn't close enough.

I wrapped my arm around his shoulders, reeling him in so that his chest was flat against mine, parting my lips to deepen the kiss.

It was blissful.

A moment I'd forever cherish, as it was the first kiss we'd ever had *alone*. No prying eyes or interruptions.

I reached a hand to his face and pulled away slightly, ending the kiss on our terms and nobody else's. Any longer, and Chipper, or Tye, or Jayleigh, or Marshall, or whoever else felt the need to pry would have come looking for us.

This was *our* moment, and I wanted it to stay that way.

"That was…" Ares started but didn't finish.

I smiled and agreed, "It was."

Ares toppled to the side, arm flying over his chest as he lay next to me, looking up at the rock ceiling. The sea approached our feet in a giant wave as though trying to hurry us back inside.

But we *did* have to talk.

I just had to catch my breath first.

"What happened in there?" I finally asked when I was sure my heart rate had returned to a reasonable level. "How were you able to mind jump?"

Ares propped himself onto his side, running his hands through the sand. "I was hoping you'd know the answer to that question, Alpha."

I tried to hide the smile, but I failed. It was no secret that I loved to hate his nickname for me. In fact, I didn't hate it at all.

I enjoyed the way the word played on his tongue.

"A have a theory," I suggested.

"Your theories have never convinced me before." He smirked. "But let's hear it."

"I think that your energy is slightly different to a Gen. 1 or a Gen. 2. It could explain why your eyes glow blue when you mutate and why you've struggled to evolve in the past. And maybe, with your animal state merging into your human state, your body releases hormones at different rates too."

"So it was like I evolved for a short while, but my energy is weaker than a Gen. 1 or 2? So, I didn't get the glowing white eyes or that electric feeling Hail describes?"

"Maybe. Although I wouldn't say that your energy is weaker."

"My mutant state kicked your butt, so I have evidence to support *that* theory."

I rolled my eyes. If only he knew I'd been holding back on him.

"If my energy isn't weaker, how could it be different? It's the Titanium frog which allows us to harness this energy, and the last thing I checked, I was a Titanium hybrid."

"As I said, it's a theory. I'm no scientist, Ares. We'll leave that to The Farm."

At the mention of it, Ares' smile dimmed. *Shit.*

I was going to have to watch my words from now on. I'd have to filter whatever might encourage the mutant to surface.

"Oh, look," Ares distracted himself with whatever he'd found in the sand. He held a frosty stone to the sky, and we watched the light illuminate the rock.

"It's pretty," I admitted, "Although I never thought I'd say such a thing about a pebble."

"Sea glass," Ares confirmed, "battered and beaten by the ocean to create a perfectly smooth stone."

He held my palm out and dropped the stone into it, wrapping my fingers around the sea glass as though it were a sacred item.

And to me, it was.

My first gift.

I clung to it as Ares said, "A pretty pebble for the gorgeous girl."

My smile was larger than the sun.

It didn't matter that the stone was a vibrant blue, the same color as Ares' eyes when he mutated—the blue I feared would replace the slate grey of his usual eyes—because if I ever lost Ares to the animal inside of him, now I had *this* to remind me of the person he really was inside.

"Thank you," I whispered and kissed his cheek, then I placed the stone in my pocket and zipped it closed. My heart was butter.

"Psst."

A noise rippled through the waves.

Both of us stumbled to our feet and scrambled into a fighting position on the sand, facing the figures at the mouth of the cave.

"Keep your voice down." One silhouette held a finger to his mouth and crouched slightly. Another three lingered behind. "You're all in danger. I need you to come with us."

Ares scoffed beside me. "We've heard that once today already. Look where it's gotten us."

The figure crept forward. "That's your own fault for trusting the humans."

Fear struck me like lightning.

The humans.

If this being wasn't human, then what the hell was it?

Then I felt it…

Not the call of a Night Walker; I had experienced that before sunrise, and I knew this was different.

Different, but familiar. Oh, so familiar.

"Don't come any closer!" I held my hands out, ready to evolve and blast them from the cave… if I remembered how to project the energy.

I had also sensed *this* feeling this morning when I first saw Ares with his Alpha hormones.

"Whoa, easy there." The figure crept into the torch's light on the wall, his silver hair and eyes reflecting my own. The rest of his pack followed.

"No… you're supposed to be dead." I recognized the man as the Titanium Alpha from pack D. Tim had played a video of this Alpha yesterday. This was the Alpha who *knew* how to project his energy. I did the maths and figured that this was the Alpha that Chipper and Marshall had been talking about. "You're supposed to be dead, Benji."

This was the pack that died four years ago.

The pack Chipper claimed to have met just before they went missing.

And now they turned up on The Sanctuary's doorstep, just after we the humans invited to join their rebellion against The Farm…

Had the older Titaniums been here this whole time?

"You know who I am? That's a good sign." He didn't come any closer, but his pack moved to join him in the cave, one by one. "Please. We are all the same. We are family. I need you to trust us."

I glared at Benji. Every impulse was begging me to attack for there was only room for one Titanium Alpha.

It was the Gen. 1 curse.

It's why I'd killed so many in the Alpha Arena and struggled to trust anyone other than myself.

Yet here we stood, neither of us attacking.

"Mind filling me in?" Ares stepped forwards, resting his hand on my arm as he sensed my discomfort. It worked both ways, and I instantly felt grounded with him by my side.

Benji's eyes fell upon Ares, and he took a step backwards, holding his body in front of his three hybrids as though to protect them.

"Whoa. What are you? And what the heck is going on with your aura?"

CHAPTER TWENTY-ONE

HAIL

I breathed the murky air from the mask over my mouth and nose.

Donnah was gone.

I hadn't seen her in hours since the woman with the red eyes placed me against the wall and left me. The room lit in an orange haze, and others sat around me. Their heads slumped forwards. Were they asleep or dead?

My eyes landed on the boy next to me. "Bro," I mouthed the word, but there was no sound.

I tried to move, but my body didn't respond.

Through the haze of my mind, I recalled the red-eyed woman ordering me to stay put, and it seemed that I had no choice.

My throat grumbled to life over the next few minutes, yet my words were still mush.

I tried to call for help, wake one of the sleeping bodies around me, or get Donnah back. I didn't care that it was just a vision of her. A dream was better than *this* sad sight.

I grumbled again.

The sleeping bodies were hooked to tubes, too, like me, pumping blood up the walls where the liquid vanished into a machine.

They were draining us, sucking the life from us.

My small whimpers welcomed footsteps from the room next door, and I swallowed back the regret. I shouldn't have made a noise. Why would I want those *things* anywhere near me?

A man walked through the door.

Not a man.

That familiar stink followed him, and his eyes were red too. He was one of them, heading in my direction, sweeping across the wooden floor with speed and grace.

He crouched beside me, and I squeezed my eyes shut, trying to turn my head away.

"Hail," he willed me to look at him.

Not the eyes.

Not the eyes.

They were able to control me when I looked them in the eyes.

He released a puff of breath as though he were laughing, but I didn't believe these beings had a sense of humor. They were dead, after all, surely, they were emotionless.

"Have it your way," the dead man said as he rose to fiddle with something above me.

A hiss vibrated the mask over my mouth, and a drowsiness claimed me before I knew it.

I barely felt the dead man biting into my neck—probably because of the dirty air I was breathing and not because I'd become immune to the pain from experience—but my eyes still flew open upon contact. I remembered two other red-eyed people had bitten me over the past few days. I'd realized at some point that this was the key to the visions. They could only plant dreams in my mind once they'd sunk their teeth into my neck. And now the red-eyed man was going to fill my mind with red and blue. And hopefully, Donnah.

She was the only good thing to come from the visions.

Was she singing again?

For a moment, I could smell her through the deadness of the man next to me. But then he began to glide away. One step, two step.

The wooden boards slipped and slid beneath me, the gaps

between them growing and growing, threatening to drag me down into a bottomless pit of blue fog below.

It wasn't like anything I'd experienced before. I could feel things that weren't there. My foot dangled over the edge of the ledge, and I fought to keep my balance.

It's not real, I reminded myself, but it looked so real, and it *felt* so real.

The floor shook, and I clung to the tubes that drained my blood, hoping they'd keep me from falling.

This man's visions were unlike those of the two women. These were nightmares brought to life. There was no sign of Donnah. No trees. No pie.

The blue fog within the gaps of the floorboards cleared to reveal thousands of pointy stakes, all red, all facing up.

Red from the vision, or red from the blood of previous victims?

I was crying now. Falling to my death wasn't how I wanted to leave this world.

The man *was* laughing, calling my name as he witnessed my hopelessness. "Hail…"

He wanted me to fall.

And then the floorboards stopped shaking. They moved back to their original places, and I was on solid ground once more.

But it wasn't over…

The room was now thick with the blue smoke. It wrapped around my ankles; scorched my skin. I screamed. The pain felt so real despite it all being a trick of the mind.

Magic.

Thick, black, magic.

The sea of fog became dense, clouding the room.

The man stood in the doorway with his eyes on me, and then two more shadows entered, carrying something between them. They placed it down next to me. I couldn't see clearly through the mist of my mind, but it looked like Tye.

Then the ceiling peeled away. Red rain poured down on me, bubbling away at my skin where it made contact. Blistering. Scarring.

I screamed.

The red-eyed man laughed again, and I figured that he must be the devil, and I must be in hell.

CHAPTER TWENTY-TWO

ARES

"My aura?" I looked between Lora and the stranger she knew as Benji.

How did she know him? And why was he looking at me like I'd insulted him? This man had just interrupted *our* moment, yet he made me feel like the interruption.

"What the hell is an aura?" I continued, attempting to hide the annoyance in my voice.

Lora's eyes widened, and she turned back to Benji in a panic.

"Lora?" My heart rate picked up, and I concentrated on the feel of her fingers interlocking with mine, her skin dry from the cold weather.

And the sound of the ocean.

And the feel of the breeze through my hair.

And the smell of lilies, only just noticeable over the salt of the rocks and water surrounding us.

And anything else I could think of to calm myself. To stay in *control.*

"What aren't you telling me?" I asked through gritted teeth.

Lora had no reason to hide anything from me. I thought we'd overcome that barrier between us, the one where she kept secrets to protect me. Because lying, whether for my sake or not, always had a way of coming back to haunt us later—or my animal alter ego did.

And it was stirring now, begging to be set free.

The scariest part was that I *wanted* to give over my control, just as I'd wanted to let the mutant take over and destroy The Sanctuary and everything it stood for.

I knew that I shouldn't.

The boy I'd been when I first awoke on The Farm wouldn't believe I was happy to consider challenging the mystery Alpha before me, and it was only then that I stopped myself and withdrew from that line of thinking.

Because if I was so happy to fight Benji, a fellow Titanium hybrid offering help, then I was no better than the people of The Sanctuary wanting to infiltrate The Farm. I was no better than Beckle challenging Hail for the sake of Donnah's love. And I was no better than my inner animal as it tried desperately to claim my body as its own.

Lora's eyes studied my face, but I sensed her focus was again on something behind me. Or *around* me.

"An aura is how an Alpha sees its pack's energy. And I was telling you that your energy may be different as you're a Gen. 3…"

"I remember feeling it, although it wasn't something I could visibly see," I recalled the moment in the truck when I'd been able to focus on the spiritual connection between myself and pack Beta. That feeling was now long gone. "Each hybrid was emitting a warmth that only I could feel."

"A warmth. Yes." Lora's words didn't sit right. If her tone were anything to go by, she wouldn't even describe my aura as tepid.

"And mine is… cold?"

"It used to be just like the others," Lora said, "but it's been a cloud of darkness since I found you this morning."

"Your aura is out of control, my friend," Benji said.

Oh? I'll show you out of control.

"I'm not your friend!" I snapped. "Who do you think you are, sneaking up on us? Insulting me? Why the hell should we trust a word—"

"Ares!" I fought against Lora as she tried to hold me back, and I only stopped when she stood between us, grabbing me by the forearms and squeezing gently, her eyes pleading. "Ares, stop."

Was it… Was she scared?

Of me?

My heart liquified, spilling from me and sinking into the sand. The last thing I ever wanted was for Lora to fear me. I'd made jokes about my strength, my mutant being stronger than hers, but I'd never once meant it.

I would never hurt her, and she knew that, right?

Only I *had.*

I'd broken her arm and cast her aside.

I'd fought her.

Even this morning, she'd held a brick to my head, ready to make contact if I took it too far.

Because I'd given her too many reasons to doubt me. Despite my differences in my first few weeks, she had claimed to trust me. But that had changed along the line. Most likely around the time I started mutating, believing it was okay.

I was too unpredictable.

Too out of control, just as my aura claimed.

"I'm sorry," I whispered. And then I began to cry. The kind of tears that pooled from my eyes in an endless stream, despite how many times I tried to wipe them away.

Lora wrapped her arms tightly around me, and I was so thankful to have her there because I may have caved without her. Fallen. Lost all will to stand.

I didn't deserve her, this embrace, or a minute of her time.

She was everything right about the world and deserved peace, not chaos. She deserved her cottage overlooking the sea, not the cave underneath it. She deserved so much better than anything I could offer.

And that was the moment it clicked.

I didn't have much luck in this world because I'd already lucked out on her, and if risking my humanity was the price I had to pay for her love, then I'd pay in titanium and gold. And if I had the choice to change it? I wouldn't. Not in a million years.

Control yourself, I fought, for her sake. *Be what she deserves.*

She squeezed a little tighter as though she could hear my internal battle.

"I love you, Lora." The words slipped out in a moment of high emotion. It certainly wasn't how I'd planned to confess my feelings, but it needed to be said.

Lora broke the embrace to look at me, her mouth hanging open just slightly and her eyes gleaming as though they'd stolen starlight.

"I know it's not the most appropriate time, but—"

She kissed me as if our lives depended on it. And maybe, in a way, they did.

If Benji and his pack were still lingering in the cave entrance, then I didn't notice. I wouldn't have noticed if a Night Walker crept up behind me and tried to claim my mind because my mind was only in one place, the here and now, the moment I decided that all the pain, confusion, and chaos was worth it.

If I died tonight, I would die a happy man for having experienced the way Lora accepted me, even at my worst. *Especially* at my worst.

She didn't need to return the words, the kiss spoke for itself, but my body temperature rocketed as she replied, "I love you too, Ares."

I savoured every sound as it rolled from her tongue.

Be what she deserves, I repeated as my heart rate began to settle.

"Interesting." Benji's voice caused me to flinch back. "Do you know that your auras intertwine when you kiss?" This talk of auras was already getting to me, but the idea spiked my curiosity enough to lift my eyes from Lora's. "Your light and your darkness," he pointed, having not been introduced to our names, "fuse, and it drains the chaos from the dark aura. Do you feel any different?"

"I feel exposed, knowing that you were watching," I replied. "But I guess I feel... more myself."

It was true that the fury had simmered to a controllable panic.

What did it mean? Could Lora hold back my mutant? Could she prolong the inevitable madness?

Benji motioned to his pack with his hand, and they retreated from the cave whilst he said, "Great. So now you've regained control and shared a nice loving moment. We need to leave," he ushered. "I wasn't kidding earlier when I said you're in danger."

Lora's body tensed against mine.

"It's midday, so we don't have much time to get your friend out of the nest. Gather your pack, and let's go. I'll explain on the way." He clicked his fingers twice as though it would snap us back into the reality of the situation, and it did.

"What do you mean we're in danger? It's daylight—"

"Get your pack. Now." His voice was no longer friendly, reminding me that Alphas must earn their title. This man had killed Titaniums to be here today, and I was sure he'd add a couple more to his list if we made him wait any longer.

CHAPTER TWENTY-THREE

MARSHALL

I awoke feeling like shit. I spluttered into my arm and wiped my mouth on my coat sleeve.

My body ached from the events of the last couple of days, and I regretted my muscle mass. Keeping up with the hybrids was difficult enough without the extra weight. Endurance had never been my strong suit. I was built to protect myself from animals.

My joints clicked as I sat upright.

Where was I?

The room was alive, loud, and freakin' cold.

I crossed my arms over my chest and searched for the Titaniums. They'd been here earlier, at this table, but where were they now? Had they left without me?

"Shit!"

How could I have been so stupid? *Of course,* they'd leave without me.

I checked my tablet for their location, only to find that it was no longer attached to my arm, stolen in my sleep.

"Those rats!" I cursed under my breath and fought the urge to kick something. I was on my feet and throwing my bag over my shoulder when I spotted Ares' dog at a nearby table, and I slowed my rushing to consider why he'd leave his pet behind.

"Oi," I called to it, hoping it wouldn't eat me like it had tried to earlier. "Hey!"

What was its name?

Shit.

I gave up on the dog and searched for Rachel instead. As the only other human in the party, I assumed they'd have left her behind, too, for her own safety.

I weaved between trading stalls roofed in washed-out fabrics, each table housing weapons, fruit, or bedding. The occupants glared, knowing that I didn't belong to The Sanctuary, my gray uniform giving me away.

I lingered too long at one stall, glancing over the small tubs and what they contained. I regretted it instantly.

"See anything you like?" A woman's voice appeared from behind a curtain.

My words faltered for a moment. "Oh... I'm not buying. I'm searching for someone," I replied as a curvy brunette came into view. I tried not to stare, but my eyes deceived me. Her beauty was dangerous, and she smiled like she knew the effect a woman like her could have on a guy like me. "I'm on a tight schedule, so…"

I began to walk away.

"You can take it," the woman reeled me back, offering out the red container I'd had my eye on. "On the house."

"Oh, no. I don't—"

"Take it." She waltzed around the table to place it in my hand, and I had no idea what to do with her generosity.

"Um." I struggled to think of a way to repay her. "Do you like coffee?"

"Coffee? Can't say I've ever tried it." She laughed at me as if I were offering her the moon.

Placing the container into my rucksack, I retrieved some of the beans I had saved and scooped them onto the table.

"What… How?" Her mouth hung open as she reached for them, smelling them, studying them against the candlelight.

"I grew them myself." I offered a tight smile, and she placed a small kiss on my cheek.

"Thank you." her cheeks tainted red.

I'd never made anyone blush before. My reputation made

everybody the wrong kind of nervous in my presence, but stories of my madness hadn't escaped The Farm. I could be anyone I wanted on this side of the fence.

"You're welcome." My eyes studied the area, and I decided the easiest way to find somebody in a crowded room would be with the help of others. Maybe she'd accompany my search. I moved back to a more comfortable distance before asking, "Have you seen anybody dressed like me? She goes by the name of Rachel or Katie."

It was the wrong thing to say.

The woman's eyes turned from honey to ice, and she quickly retreated towards the curtain, refusing to look at me again.

"Is everything okay? I didn't mean to offend you—"

"You need to leave..." Her voice was low, a warning clear in her tone. "You need to leave The Sanctuary," she clarified.

My body was already too cold, but it dropped another few degrees as her eyes swiftly darted towards other stalls, and then she vanished behind her curtain.

I considered following her but figured that no good would come of it. She was scared of something. And she was, apparently, afraid of Rachel's name.

Odd, I thought, turning to look at whatever the woman had been searching for in the crowd, but I found nothing that struck me as unusual.

Moving through the bodies, I continued my search for Rachel, my panic rising after such a strange encounter.

"Marshall!"

I didn't want to face the person that voice belonged to, but I turned, against my better judgement. "Chipper," I responded as we came face to face.

What had the hybrids told him about The Farm? How much did he know about my work, and how much did he know about me?

"Where are the Titaniums? And I was searching for—"

"They're all fine! No need to worry," he interrupted and placed an arm around my shoulders to lead me away.

"Well, where are they?"

Chipper sucked air through his widely gapped teeth. "They're currently preoccupied, but you'll see them soon enough."

Lies.

"Take me to them. Now."

Chipper laughed, "Look at you, barking orders as though you own the place." He patted my arm in a less-than-friendly gesture. "You need to stay here, where we can keep an eye on you and ensure that you're not causing any trouble, *Mad Marshall.* Help yourself to the food available. Just tell the stall manager you're a special friend of Chipper's."

He was playing with me, toying with my mind, and if he thought I'd fall for his bullshit, then at least the hybrids hadn't shared too much about me. "Quit the games, Chipper. I see straight through them."

"Oh, but my friend," he handed me a slip of canvas paper, folded several times into a small square, "The games have only just begun."

He slipped into the crowd as I unfolded the paper, my heart racing as the severity of the situation sank in.

And then the world slowed.

Stopped.

I had to lean on somebody in the crowd to keep my balance.

Written on the paper were my words, *Father's* words, "Keep to the rules, and you'll get along just fine."

CHAPTER TWENTY-FOUR

ARES

Benji's eagerness left me feeling unsettled.

I side-stepped my way through the narrow tunnel, with a growing sense of doom in the smokey air around us.

Ten steps… twenty steps…

The closer we got; the slower Lora walked.

"Everything okay?" I asked as she came to a complete halt.

"No." She tilted her head to the side. "Something isn't right."

My stomach churned, and the lack of food only contributed to my nausea. "Not right how?"

Lora's concern rocketed as she spoke, "We're getting closer to the pack, yet I don't feel like we're closing any distance. They're moving further away if anything."

My eyes moved to the tablet on my arm, and I squeezed it across my body for a better view of the map, failing to believe what the screen revealed.

"Um, Lora?" I beckoned her backwards, manoeuvring between the rock walls to show her the tablet.

Love really is a distraction, I thought as I watched the pins move across the map.

One hybrid had joined Hail in the Night Walker's nest whilst the others were halfway to joining them.

Jayleigh…

I leaned against the wall and glanced up into the darkness. I felt dizzy and light-headed. The Night Walkers had my two closest friends, and I'd been so distracted with Lora that neither of us had noticed until it was too late.

My Alpha bond with pack Beta was now completely severed, I realized. I couldn't sense them, and I had no idea how much danger they were in.

"Shit." Lora tugged at my arm to get a closer look. "Shit!" Her eyes glossed over, and she pulled her hands through her hair. "How is that possible? We've been at the entrance this entire time."

Her chest rose and fell in rapid, panicked breaths.

"Maybe this isn't the only entrance?" I thought about the underground town and how easy it would be to hide an exit.

We'd been naive to leave the pack alone with these strangers, thinking they were harmless because they were human, to believe that The Sanctuary was safe. I mentally kicked myself. *It's underground.* Night Walkers could travel during the day so long as they didn't walk in sunlight, so an underground system of tunnels would be the perfect way for them to get about.

Had Benji known this?

Was he aware that Night Walkers could infiltrate The Sanctuary, and was this why he'd been so eager to get us out of there?

My heart stuttered as I questioned what we'd find at the end of the tunnel. Were the Night Walkers awaiting our return? Was there anything left of The Sanctuary at all? Or would we find the community in pieces, with bite marks on their necks and bloody acid foaming from their eyes, nose, and mouths?

I shuddered.

"Should we follow them? Or should we find another way to the nest?" My voice was barely audible, fearing the Night Walkers could hear us.

"We need to make sure everyone is okay." Lora nodded, trying to convince herself that this was the right path. "To make sure The Sanctuary is still standing."

"We could be walking into a trap." My mind feared the idea

that the Night Walkers had turned every human within the cave.

"What alternative do we have?" she said. Time was ticking away as we considered our best option, and each passing second had deadly consequences.

My reply left a bitter taste, "We go back to Benji and ask for help."

"So, you trust him?" she sounded defeated.

"I don't trust anybody!" My whispers were becoming loud and fast. "Not Benji, and certainly not Chipper. I trust you and the pack, and that's it."

We both paused to watch the pins move across the map. "Okay, Benji seems the better option." Lora finally released her hair from her grasp. "Let's hear what he has to say."

I held my breath, hoping to steady my heart rate as we shuffled around and headed back towards the sea.

Benji waited for us at the mouth of the cave, a trying expression on his face. "Where are the others? What's going on?" he asked, slowly retreating from us.

"Is there another entrance to The Sanctuary? The pack is gone, and they're traveling towards the Night Walker's nest," Lora panted.

"Whoa, take a breath," Benji instructed. "Let me see the map."

He motioned for my tablet, and I reached my arm up to

show him. There was no way I'd willingly hand it over.

"Yep, that's the Night Walkers' nest, alright," he agreed. "Don't panic. We have two paddle boats, and they'll get us to the nest far faster than running."

"So, you'll help us?" Lora said, guarded and unsure.

"That's all I've been trying to do since we caught track of your scent. Titaniums unite, whether Gen. 1, 2, or Gen. 3." He glanced at me.

His acceptance of my differences almost made me regret how I'd treated him earlier. I was fast to judge and form opinions of him, and then I'd been angry that he'd done the same to me.

"How did you know that we were in danger?" I asked as we hurried after him towards the sea.

"Chipper controls The Sanctuary, and Night Walkers control Chipper. Did you really think that this collective group of humans could go undiscovered by Night Walkers for so many years? That a few guards in trees would be enough to hold off the Night Walkers?" he said as we crossed the snow-covered sand, feet sinking into it. The flurry had cleared now. The sky remained thick with clouds but bright. "The Night Walkers use The Sanctuary as a food bank, allowing them to reproduce and live a confined life until the Night Walkers need new blood. Most of The Sanctuary don't realize they're under mind control and live happily in ignorance."

Ironic, I thought. A nervous laugh escaped me, and Lora and Benji met me with worried eyes.

"Oh no, I'm not laughing at the situation. It's just… it's a farm. The Sanctuary is a human farm for Night Walkers."

Lora was hesitant as she held onto one of the boats, eyebrows creasing as she glanced back towards the cave. "If The Sanctuary is a farm, then what does that make the nest?"

My eyes followed hers, knowing that the pack would be in real danger once they reached the end of the tunnel. "A slaughterhouse," I whispered, chilled to the bones.

I thought of Hail and Jayleigh again, wondering what they were going through and whether they'd managed to evolve, praying they were okay. Jayleigh wouldn't go down without a fight, and Hail had already survived this long, so he must have been doing something right.

Just a little longer.

It kicked us into motion, running the boats over the waves and jumping in once we were deep enough. We had to move fast.

But with each row closer to the nest, my heart raced faster, my anxiety grew stronger, and I found myself losing more and more control…

CHAPTER TWENTY-FIVE

MARSHALL

"What rules?" I demanded, but nobody seemed to hear. "Is this a joke?"

I reread the words on the paper, the letters slowly mixing as I stared, and small splatters dropped onto the ink and painted the page red. I wiped the blood from my nose with my sleeve and swore under my breath. "This *must* be a joke."

My mind struggled to find an explanation; it was more than I could process. How could Chipper know these words?

I scrunched the paper into a ball and lobbed it as far as possible into the crowd of bodies.

The hybrids were gone, Ares was gone, Katie was nowhere to be found. I knew no good would come of trusting these people because they'd been hiding from The Farm for decades, and there had to be a reason for it.

It all seemed cagey to me.

I searched the crowd again, my body threatening to pull me to the ground. My knees were unstable, and I needed a moment to sit and process what was happening. I found a table and slumped into the chair, scanning the cave for familiar faces.

Anyone.

I needed help finding the hybrids as I was sure now that they hadn't left me behind, as I'd initially thought, but had been sucked into Chipper's game.

The leader of The Sanctuary had vanished now, but I felt his gaze tattooed on my skin. "Chipper!" I called out, met with sideways glances from strangers passing by. They could call me crazy, but I didn't care.

This is how Ares felt on The Farm, I realized, knowing that I was watching and planning his future.

I wiped my nose again.

I swore again.

I scanned the crowd again.

So, this was how it felt to be kept in the dark… I didn't like it. I almost felt sorry for Ares, knowing his curious nature, how much I'd hidden from him, and how much I was still hiding.

I needed to find him. He deserved to know the truth.

"Chipper? Come out, come out, wherever you are!" I raised

my voice so that the whole of The Sanctuary could hear. Mad Marshall had stuck, and it was time to meet expectations. If this were a game, I'd at least have some fun.

It was like one of those games that the kids in the Infirmary used to play, the kind I'd watch from a distance as I drew my maps and researched various animals.

Where would I be hiding if I were Chipper?

Somewhere with a good view was essential. He'd want to be able to see me throughout The Sanctuary, so it would have to be somewhere without blind spots.

He'd give himself height.

My gaze rose to the cave's roof, scanning for balconies, platforms, anything that could give him a visual over his kingdom.

And that's when I spotted a camera.

"You've got to be shitting me," I murmured and slowly turned my head, looking for more lenses. The rough refuge image was just for show. This place had *electricity*.

What else were they hiding?

My animals.

I stood abruptly, deciding to turn this place inside out before I rested, starting with the tunnel that led me to the dunnies. I wondered if there were branches I'd missed earlier that would lead me elsewhere.

But it didn't.

I followed the wall until I reached a tent built against the rock, canvas tied high. It seemed strategically placed. My eyes scanned the area to ensure nobody was watching, and I let myself in, closing the zipper behind me.

Surely enough, I found a dimly lit tunnel on the other side.

I laughed in satisfaction and followed the path to what I assumed would be a viewing room. The tunnel stretched further than I'd expected, and doubts started to creep in as I walked.

Was this leading anywhere? Or would it be a dead end?

Part of me wanted to turn back.

The temperature dropped, and I thought the main cave had been cold enough. I could see my breath form in the pale light before me.

And then there was an opening…

I slowed my pace. They'd have seen me step inside the tent and anticipated my approach if this were a room full of screens. So why hadn't they tried to stop me?

A semi-transparent plastic covered the gap in the tunnel. *Plastic.*

That was enough to spike my adrenaline.

Somebody had outsourced the material and placed it here for a specific reason. But why?

I could see nothing but blurs through the plastic,

illuminated by blue light.

My hands shook as I reached to pull back the sheet. I was not supposed to see this.

I was not supposed to be here.

It was against the rules.

My fingers clung to the rare material and regretfully pulled it back.

I pulled my arm to my face to relieve my nose from the stench of the room, slowly stepping inside.

My eyes took a moment to adjust to the new light, but I didn't need perfect vision to know what the blurs were.

Bodies.

Rows upon rows of dead humans, each one was foaming at the eyes and mouth; Night Walker victims.

It was a morgue.

My body shut down on itself, my mind racing back to the night of the attack on The Farm eight years ago, watching my parents die on the screen and resurfacing hours later to find hundreds of bodies similarly scattered across The Farm to these.

My eyes glanced downward.

I drew a sharp gasp, then blinked twice to ensure I saw correctly, to confirm that my eyes weren't playing tricks on me.

I wanted it to be a part of the game.

The body was the woman I'd traded coffee with on the stall; there was no doubt about it.

But that had been less than thirty minutes ago. How had she ended up here? How was this possible? Why?

I reached down to touch her skin. It should still have been warm, shouldn't it?

Her eyes were bloodshot, glaring up at me in tears of red as though to say, 'You did this to me. It's your fault I'm dead.'

I recalled how she'd looked over her shoulder in fear and told me to get away from The Sanctuary before retreating behind her curtain. She'd been so scared because she knew there were Night Walkers in these caves, and they were watching, waiting.

They'd killed her for helping me.

I was sure of it, although I couldn't understand why.

My eyes closed. I tried to inhale a deep breath, but the stench was too much. It was only a reminder of my situation. I'd caused many deaths in my time, but somehow this one hit the hardest.

Until I opened my eyes.

My breath caught.

Ringing appeared in my ears; no matter how much I tried to cover them and shake my head, the squealing wouldn't stop.

Rachel.

Katie.

Whatever she wanted to call herself.

Katie. I should have called her Katie.

She was as pale as the day I met her, as she'd first loaded onto The Farm; too old for metamorphosis, too young to search for refugees—as it was in those days. My family had saved her, and I'd signed her death warrant by forcing her to leave The Farm.

Her eyes didn't bleed, but it didn't make the sight any less gruesome.

She'd deserved better.

So much better.

I'd told her not to trust the animals on her first day. But after it all, it should have been *me* she kept an eye on.

My stomach kicked up everything inside me, and I backed away, tripping over arms and legs, stumbling through the plastic sheet in the door and tearing it down. I screamed, that hollow sound the warmest thing in the tunnel, frantically trying to unwrap myself and run.

But then something was tackling me.

It pinned me against the ground and stopped me from escaping. So, this was it. *This* was how I'd fucking go; before I got to share my story with Ares.

The rocks pressed into my back as I fought, rough edges

scraping wounds into the flesh of my hands and neck as I thrashed about relentlessly. I couldn't reach my knife through the plastic sheet which entrapped my arms.

I screamed out again, and the scream twisted into a laugh.

Maybe it was my intended punishment to leave this world without the one thing I needed most. It would be fair. I didn't deserve a happy ending after all the lives I'd taken, intentional or not.

I'd die a piece of somebody else's game, and I found humor in that. I found *peace* in that. I'd played God for too long, and as death faced me in every direction, I felt relieved that my rein was over. I'd done my part.

I witnessed the teeth through the snarls.

My body stopped fighting back.

And then my attacker backed away.

I lay there for a moment, wondering what was happening and why I wasn't dead yet, and once I built up the courage, I moved my eyes toward the silhouette. A wolf's profile…

"Dog?" I called out to Ares' pet, not knowing if it was her or another wolf. They'd all look the same in this light. "Where's Ares, Dog?"

I slowly unravelled myself from the plastic, feeling somewhat embarrassed. I was sure I was about to die. The animal had only been trying to get my attention before I started fighting it.

It retreated down the tunnel, stopping after a few steps and looking back at me whilst I wiped my wounds on my clothes. There were Night Walkers here, and I was bleeding...

"You want me to follow you?" I asked. I was indeed as mad as the rumors said, talking to an animal like it would understand.

I stood, wiped my eyes, coughed the dust into my sleeve, and then headed towards the wolf. Ares' pet hadn't left his side for long since we'd been here, so I felt inclined to follow it. It would take me to Ares.

Or it wouldn't.

Either way, it would lead me away from The Sanctuary, and that was all I could ask for.

I spat into the rock.

"Come on then, Dog. What the fuck are you waiting for?"

CHAPTER TWENTY-SIX

ARES

We followed the shore in the direction of the Night Walkers' nest. Listening to the sound of the waves was doing frighteningly little to ease the anxiety within. I felt the animal scratching to get out, clawing his way to the surface with each nervous row of my paddle.

"Okay there, Gen. 3?" Benji asked from the front of our boat. He'd shared one with Lora and me whilst his pack grouped into the second boat.

There was no use in lying in response. Both he and Lora could feel the hybrid within me growing stronger.

"Trying my best." I cast my eyes on the horizon, broken wind turbines idly watching as we weaved between them, the fractured blades dangled into the sea and algae turning them green. We'd been on the ocean for almost an hour. The hybrids had reached the nest, so my tablet told me, and I knew that Benji was about to lay down a plan. We'd shared information, caught up on where his pack had been hiding out all this time, and I'd listened to the Gen. 1s discuss how to draw the energy from their hands, knowing that I'd most likely never get the chance to try.

Evolving was never going to be an option for me. I was like the Venos, unable to harness that area of gray between human and animal states.

I tried not to feel bitter about it.

The near-freezing water splashing against my face didn't make me feel any better about the situation.

"We need to split into two groups when we reach the nest," Benji began. "Ares, you'll have to stay out of trouble with Myrheen. Lora should join me in locating her pack."

"We're splitting up?" I questioned, hairs on my neck raising to the wind, "No. I don't like that at all."

"It would be the safest solution for everybody. From what you've told me, all hell will break loose if you mutate in there. And not to mention that you may never return to your human state, and we can't risk that."

I looked to Lora for backup, waiting for her to hate the idea just as much as I did, to throw in an alternative and claim her terms. But instead, she gave me an apologetic look and shook her head.

"Sorry, Ares. I'm with Benji on this one." She focused on pulling the ore through the water as though it were a novelty task, and she hadn't been repeating that same action for the past hour. My temperature raised a few degrees. Was she siding with Benji over me? "Not because I want to, but it's the safest option."

Lora looked back at me when I didn't reply, and I shifted my attention across the sea, watching the birds glide over the water.

"Fine. It's not like we might die there and never see each other again. Yeah. Splitting up seems like the perfect idea."

"We're not going to die," Lora and Benji said simultaneously with such fire. I almost believed them.

Gen. 1s were good at that. Was it a common trait? Had they been modified to encourage their pack and lead us into battle without doubt of our success?

Or were they delusional?

Because from where I was standing, the Night Walkers certainly appeared to have the upper hand.

"I appreciate your positivity, guys." I smiled. "But you need to consider what will happen if things go wrong. If you two die in there, your pack will die too. You understand that, right? My

Alpha hormones are gone. The pack won't return to The Farm in time to find a new Alpha, and we are humanity's last hope. Lora, if you die, Jayleigh, Hail, Tye, Diego, Indigo and I will die with you. You need to be careful."

Our eyes met. Lora looked as beautiful as ever, her fury framed by snow-covered lands, turquoise seas, and skies as pink as her cheeks. She belonged to this world; she was the world.

"Don't push me, Ares," she warned. "Do you think I haven't already considered that? I know what will happen if I die, and I know that you cannot be with me when we enter the Night Walkers nest, not only because of your alter ego, but because I know in the heat of the moment, I would gladly sacrifice myself to save you." Her eyes glazed over as the wind picked up, and I had to fight not to rock the boat and scoop her into my arms.

"That... That would be a foolish thing to do." I paused my rowing to appreciate what she'd just confessed. The feeling radiated from my skin and bones, and I swore it was enough to thaw the entire country. "And I'd never expect you to do such a thing. If I ever get myself into a dangerous position, it will be my fault, and I should face the consequences."

A small smile appeared on Lora's lips. "It would be a stupid thing to do," she agreed, "but it would be as easy as breathing."

Benji looked uncomfortable. "We're getting close, and we

could do with a plan that avoids either of you dying."

I nodded. "Fine. I'll stay out of the nest. But you must promise you'll return to me, okay?"

"I give you my word," Lora agreed, "We're all getting out of this alive."

And I believed her.

We sailed ashore, pulling the boats onto the beach, hiding them in the dunes, and burying them in the snow. I followed Benji over the hills and stopped beside him as he pointed. "There it is."

I heard it before I saw it.

An abandoned theme park was built on the seafront and sprawled across a wooden pier with lights flashing, music playing, and not a soul in sight.

The whole place screamed 'trap' to me.

I searched the shadows. The Night Walkers would be waiting for us because this had been their plan all along. They'd taken Hail as bait and been toying with us since our first night outside the fence. Why?

What were they gaining from this?

Why hadn't they attacked us in the town?

Why hadn't they killed or turned us into one of their own?

We descended from the hill towards the eery music, and I was suddenly thankful that I wouldn't be entering the nest.

"Everybody ready?" Lora asked as she fastened my tablet tighter against her arm. Benji's pack had weapons they'd taken on their last mission from The Farm. Only half of their pack now remained, so they offered Lora a dagger of her own, and she gripped her fingers around it, still squeezing her thumb.

The group replied to Lora with yeses.

I remained silent.

My heart was racing faster than the music, which slowly picked up tempo as we walked closer.

"That's the town." Benji pointed towards the cluster of buildings where I would hide until they returned.

I nodded, slowing my step and searching the group for the hybrid named Myrheen, a stocky woman with a big smile and wide eyes.

Lora lingered next to me. This is where we'd part ways, and it was every bit as painful as I imagined. I pulled her aside from the group, out of earshot of the others, needing a moment alone with her before she ran into the most dangerous challenge we'd ever faced.

"Tell me that this is a good idea?" I said.

"I don't think hearing me say it will convince either of us on this occasion," she kept her voice low, a sad smile on her face. "Whatever you do, stay out of trouble. Okay?"

"Eye-eye, Alpha. I'd ask you to do the same, but we both know that would be a waste of valuable time I could have spent kissing you. Just promise you'll be the one creating the trouble?"

"Eye-eye, Beta." Her laugh was nervous, it scared me, so I kissed her like it was our last day on Earth or Earth's last day. I was sure the sky vanished, and the ground melted beneath me as I held her in my arms, never wanting to let her go. "Hey," I said as she turned to leave. I snatched hold of her wrist and reeled her back towards me, catching her in my arms. "I love you."

Lora didn't respond straight away, her face just as unreadable as always, but her eyes softened. "I love you too, Ares."

She smiled and squeezed my hand whilst the group split in two, them heading towards the amusement park's entrance and me and Myrheen towards the walls of the overgrown town.

"I'll see you soon," she whispered and walked away.

"Soon," I repeated her words as though I were praying, looking to the sky. If there ever was a God, we needed him now.

She turned back once as we departed, and I gave a small wave in her direction, then created a new path in the snow towards the crumbling buildings.

We had a view over the theme park and watched in dread as the pack reached the gates. The abandoned park buzzed to life, the music growing louder, the carousel beginning to spin and send the snow flying from the roof, the Ferris wheel churning, and the roller coaster leaving the station in a whir.

Myrheen shared my worried expression.

"Crap," is all I could muster through my panic. My heart beat so fast I feared I'd die of natural causes instead of Night Walker-inflicted injuries.

My jaw tightened, and I took several deep breaths.

The gates opened.

The pack evolved simultaneously, a bright white exploding from them, and they entered at full speed.

I swallowed my hope of the Titaniums' control over the situation.

How could I sit and wait for their return?

How could I watch from afar?

How could I put myself before my family? The Titaniums needed me; they were in more danger than my mind could comprehend.

My body moved into line with Myrheen, following her into the town and trying to keep my mind focused on something. Anything.

We turned corners, delving deeper into the town and

further from the theme park, but as the music faded with distance, I feared something about the image before me didn't seem right.

The town was older than the one we'd camped in the night previous, the buildings made of wood and stone, with thatched roofs. Cars sat perfectly untouched. There were no broken windows, and doors still hung on their hinges. Except for the evergreens taking over the town, it looked pristine. Perfect and cared for.

Sure, the snow could have hidden a lot of mess, but—

That's when I noticed it.

In the snow.

I held my hand out to grab Myrheen's attention, willing her not to take another step as I pointed.

Fresh footprints.

Had the hybrids been here? Above ground? Or were these human footprints?

Was this town under Night Walker's control, like The Sanctuary?

If so, where were the humans now?

I remained still, looking in every direction but seeing nobody. And then I felt the tiniest prick of a needle against my neck, and I collapsed into the pillow of white.

The sky was grey and then blue and red. A solid chunk of

marble.

I couldn't make sense of it.

The only thing I knew for sure was that this was *not* part of the plan.

CHAPTER TWENTY-SEVEN

LORA

We weaved through the abandoned stalls, rollercoaster framework, and attractions, heading for the building at the end where the pins on the tablet revealed the hybrids were located.

The plan was simple: kill any Night Walker to stand in our way.

Benji would search for the leader, which he referred to as the Queen of the Night Walkers and alert us if he found her. Killing her would wipe out the rest of her bloodline, meaning that every Night Walker she had ever turned would die, and then we'd be free to rescue the hybrids.

Benji and his pack had been monitoring the nest for years. They'd faked their deaths to free themselves from The Farm, which could they'd done by removing the clothes that The

Farm supplied and trading them in for whatever they could find within nearby towns, and they'd lived in a hidden cave only accessible by boat.

Each night they tracked the Night Walkers, following where they went from a safe distance and recording patterns and abnormalities.

They'd lost half their pack in the last four years, each member able to evolve.

It didn't fill me with hope for our mission, but I had to remain positive, or else I'd convince myself into a dangerous frame of mind.

I slowed as I spotted the building we'd been searching for, a large sign above it reading 'House of Nightmares'. I'd known that the Night Walkers were intelligent creatures, but I hadn't expected them to have a sense of humor.

It shocked me, and I paused, looking up at the rickety house painted black. We still had an hour of sunlight left, but that wouldn't make any difference under this roof. Once we entered, we'd be in shark-infested waters.

I pointed, unable to mind jump to Benji's pack. It meant I'd have to be extremely cautious as I couldn't hear their instructions.

Benji gave a brief nod and approached the door.

The hybrids around me began to draw the energy from

their hands, creating orbs of sparking light and power. I tried to copy, but as I'd found this morning, I could not produce even a flicker.

I held my dagger ready instead. The others could paralyze the Night Walkers, and I'd go for the kill.

Benji opened the door and stepped inside. I followed at the back of the line.

We were in darkness, as I'd expected, but neon signs lit the walls in luminous pinks and greens. Arrows pointed us deeper into the building, switching on as they came into view, the walls seeming to close in as we crept forwards.

They knew that we were here.

It was all a part of their game.

My heart stammered, my whole body seeming to twitch in fear. There were two things I hated more than Night Walkers: heights and enclosed spaces. Yet, I was delving further into the narrow-walled nest of the vampires.

I didn't have a choice.

My skin pricked with static energy, the sensation seeming exaggerated by the cold. It left my body coated in a nervous, clammy sweat that stuck to my clothes' fabric. It made me irritable.

But that was only because I was on high alert.

I focused so intently on the sounds around us that I could

hear the buzz of electricity through the dimmed neon lights, the breath of the other Titaniums, and the wind howling against the outside walls of the building.

Something crashed behind me.

I spun on my heels, dagger ready to plunge into the heart of the imposing Night Walker, but there was nothing there… only a neon arrow on the wall which buzzed and flickered out.

I kept my eyes on the darkness as I backed away. I couldn't hear anything and didn't smell death, as Hail had described, but I imagined them hiding there, stalking us.

It was just a part of their game.

They were trying to scare us.

I focused on putting one step in front of the other to distract myself from my imagination.

I thought of the missing hybrids.

They were near. I could sense them, but much like it had been with Hail, I found it difficult to pinpoint their exact location once they were under a Night Walker's control.

The tablet suggested that we were getting close.

I followed Benji's pack around the corner and into a large room staged to look like a modern amphitheatre. The middle of the room sunk into the ground, ringed by steps and angled towards a drain at the center.

Worrying, I thought, imagining why they'd need a drain in

an arena, *to collect blood, convenient for Night Walkers.*

I kept to the wall, staring at the tablet and freezing over. This is where the hybrids should have been, where the pins located them.

And then I noticed the map shift into motion, and Ares' pin was moving away from the town and towards the theme park.

No…

No.

No.

This wasn't right. He wasn't supposed to move, and the hybrids should have been here.

Everything was spiralling out of control in a haze of neon light. "Um, Benji?" I started to tell him there was a problem, but then another crash came from behind me, and a sliding door slammed closed, locking us in.

My heart leapt.

I'd never felt a fear like this in my evolved state, but I didn't think I'd ever been *this* scared.

I turned back to Benji's pack for guidance, but they'd grouped further across the room, their stance unwelcoming and defensive as they smiled at me.

It wasn't part of the plan at all.

It was a set-up.

These Titaniums had been feeding us lies since we'd met them, and I threw my arms in defence as I realized that I should have listened to Ares when he'd said to trust nobody but ourselves.

These Titaniums were with the Night Walkers.

We'd walked straight into their trap.

Internally, I cried as I reminded myself of the first rule I'd learned in the Alpha Arena.

Never trust another Gen. 1.

CHAPTER TWENTY-EIGHT

ARES

"Psst."

Red and blue danced in my vision. Had I gone blind?

My body shivered, a feeling I wasn't used to.

Haziness.

I barely registered the sounds of somebody shuffling beside me until they whispered in my ear.

"Psst. Ares…"

My brain couldn't connect the dots. Where was I?

"Lora?"

I recognized the laughter instantly. That hiccup was his signature, no matter how faint and weak it sounded. "I will punch you if you try to kiss me, Bro."

"Hail?" My hands scrambled around to find him. "Hail!"

"Dude… Keep your voice down. It's like you're *trying* to wake the dead."

"Are you actually here, or am I imagining you?"

"I'm here." A hand rested against mine, and I could have cried—if I wasn't already, my eyes burned so badly that I couldn't tell.

"Why can't I see you? What's going on?"

"It's the bite. It takes a while to wear off, but yours seems to have faded faster than the others. They're still out cold."

Now I was sure that I was crying. "All of them? Is Lora here?"

"Not all of them; Lora and Zee are missing."

I squinted my eyes closed, "We have so much to catch up on." I rubbed the lids with my fingers. "Oh, that's not a good idea…" the dizziness claimed me again.

"Just give it a minute. It clears eventually."

I listened to him, and the clouds evaporated after a couple of minutes. I held my hands in front of me, counting each finger, and then I turned.

"You're here." I couldn't believe my eyes, and part of me didn't *want* to. He looked terrible, with blue circles under his eyes and veins piercing through his skin. He sat against the wall beside me, tubes hanging from his wrists. I'd never seen him so pale.

I held my hand up, and frail fingers met mine, slapping them back and forward in our handshake.

"I've missed you." My voice quivered.

"I've missed you too, Bro. But you shouldn't have come. They were planning—"

"They knew we were coming." I nodded, and my eyes landed on the other bodies in the room. "What is this place? What are they doing to you?"

Hail wasn't the only one with tubes attached to him. The room was large, lit only by the red and orange lights surrounding the sign, which announced that we were in the Funhouse. It cast hues over the bodies, each just as pale as Hail. The pack were to my left, not yet connected to machines.

I needed to get them out—all of them.

I stumbled to my feet, staggering to find my balance. "What is this stuff?" I began to fiddle with the tubes in Hail's wrist, following them up to the machine on the wall. "Why's it so dark?"

The container at the top was half-full. I poked at it, and the liquid sloshed around, thick. Warm.

I jumped back.

Blood.

Of course it was.

The Night Walkers weren't injecting the humans; they were

draining them. "Crap. Hail, we need to get these out of your wrists right now."

I hurried to remove the needles, covering the open wounds with the dressing I found in a bin near the door.

The room was a hospital of sorts. I hadn't expected the Night Walkers to care for hygiene or to drain the humans in this manner.

I left the oxygen tank in Hail's nose to aid his breathing and started to free the other humans in the room. They were barely conscious. One or two muttered thanks as I disconnected them and placed their masks on, too, wondering how long they'd been stuck here like this.

"Wait." Only as I reached the last body and then checked over the pack did I realize we were missing more than Lora. The fact that we were alive and somewhat well reassured me that she was okay, wherever she was. "Where's Marshall and Katie?"

"Marshall? Hopefully dead," Hail muttered, seeming sleepy. His eyes began to roll. "I've not seen him, or whoever Katie is…."

My heart sank.

I'd assumed they'd escorted Marshall and Katie alongside the pack. I checked over the sleeping bodies once more, but they were all strangers.

Crap.

Had we left them at The Sanctuary?

If I'd eaten anything since breakfast, I was sure I'd have thrown it up now.

I'd left my brother alone in a Night Walker-controlled human farm.

But at least a farm is better than a slaughterhouse, I reminded myself. And that's if The Sanctuary still stood.

We'd turned back before finding if the humans had survived the Night Walker infiltration. Had they taken the pack and left everyone else alive? I prayed that was the case. Maybe the Night Walkers had been there all along.

The guilt twisted into anger, but I didn't have anything here to bring me back if I mutated. Lora was gone, and the Funhouse was a windowless box.

But I *did* have Hail and Jayleigh.

"We're going to get out of here," I told Hail, but he was unconscious now, just like everybody else in the room.

I was utterly alone.

My mind flipped through a hundred worries and questions without any answer. The energy was rising with my panic, and I needed an outlet, or at least a distraction.

An escape.

The main door was sealed closed with no obvious way of

opening it from this side, so I searched the room for fire exits, hidden entrances, moving tiles in the floor or panels in the walls, but I found nothing. I started to move objects, knowing that there must be a way.

But that's where I fell short.

Because this wasn't The Farm, and this wasn't a challenge. There was no loophole. Sometimes there were just dead ends and false hope.

Pull yourself together, Ares. I wouldn't sit around and wait for Lora to rescue us or for the Night Walkers to return. I may have lost the Alpha hormones, but I was still the Beta of this pack as far as I was concerned, and I could find a way.

I walked towards the door and used the dagger from my pocket to try and open it, sliding it around the frame.

"Come on… Come on!" I yelled in frustration.

"Ares? Is that you?"

My blood ran cold.

"Marshall?" I was so confused. All I could do was stare at the closed door and wonder what he was doing on the other side. So, they *had* brought him along? Was he hooked up to a machine too? It didn't matter. He was here, alive, and I wasn't alone. "Are you okay?" I asked.

"Define okay..." he replied. "Look, Ares, there's something I need to tell you before shit hits the fan—"

"Yeah, you're still hiding stuff from us, I know. And I want to hear it," I *really* did, "but first, we need to get out of here. The sooner we're out of the nest, the better."

"Right, yeah. Let's get this door open."

"I think it's electronic." I searched the wall again. "Is there a button on your end?"

"Um… No, but there's a load of bodies and tubes. It looks like something from Mother's lab."

"They're extracting blood," I explained. "What about a control panel? A lever, anything?"

"I'm looking." Marshall went quiet as he searched.

"Any luck?" I asked after thirty seconds or so, but there was no answer. "Marshall? Are you there?" Panic rose throughout my body. There were no other sounds from that side of the door, so I assumed he was safe from the Night Walkers for now. "Marshall?"

"I'm here." Marshall's voice was barely a whisper. It sounded close, as though he hadn't moved, standing to the door's left. "I'm here, Ares."

"Marshall, what's going on? You're scaring me."

Silence hung in the air.

When Marshall finally spoke, I could hear the gulp in his throat and the sniffle of his nose.

"It's Mother, Ares. She's here."

CHAPTER TWENTY-NINE

LORA

"Benji… what have you done?" My voice shook.

The door behind the Titaniums slid open, and Night Walkers seeped in through the darkness, seeming to glide across the room as though they floated, their red eyes fixated on me.

My back pressed against the wall as I backed away, my dagger pointing towards them.

You silly, silly girl. How could I have let this happen? *Ten… fifteen… twenty…* I counted the vampires as they passed through the door, knowing full well that it took only two Night Walkers to kill fifty farmers. I tried to act strong and unbreakable, but my mind was already wavering. *Don't let them in.*

The room paused, and I sensed even the Night Walkers held their breath as a woman strolled into the room. The

Queen. So at least there was some truth to Benji's stories, but I questioned if killing her would end her entire bloodline, as Benji had suggested. There was only one way to find out, but I knew it would be impossible to lay a scratch on the Queen's doll-like skin or pluck a delicately styled strand of black hair from her head, never mind impaling her with the dagger in my hand. The vampire was stunning. Not in the same way Indigo or Shyla had been; the Titaniums had a rugged, natural beauty, but the Night Walker Queen was flawless, from her perfect complexion and subtly sharp features to her plump, wicked smile. Immortality could do that to you, apparently.

I felt like cowering, but I stood firm and imagined my shoes stuck into the ground.

The Queen could not know that I feared her.

She stopped next to the Titaniums, whispering something that only they could hear, and they relaxed, the ball of energy in their palms extinguishing.

They couldn't have been under the Night Walker's control as they were in their evolved state, which meant they were following her orders voluntarily. That was far worse.

"Join us, Allora," the Queen called out, her voice wrapping itself around me and coating my skin in ice. "Allora... Allora..." The hairs on my neck stood on end, ready to fight the sound away. "We can show you a new way of life,"

I swallowed hard. My breath halted, and my mouth ran dry.

"What do you know about life?" I asked. "Other than taking it?"

The Queen smiled at my attempted confidence, but I knew she saw straight through it. She was already in my mind for her to know my name, so she knew I was bluffing.

"We are not what you think we are, Allora." She held her hand out and one of her Night Walker minions rushed forwards, placing something in her hands. I could barely make it out in the dim light. Then she struck the wood along the ground and produced a flame, proceeding to light the torches at the top of the steps as she spoke. It was ritualistic—a ceremony. "We're not trying to take over the planet or kill off the human race. We *need* humans to survive…"

Her voice sounded like single strands of magic, and it entranced me.

"I don't care for anything you have to say," I fought back.

"Oh, but you should…" she moved towards the next torch as though she had all the time in the world, and maybe she did? Perhaps she was stalling. "And you will."

I gripped the dagger so tight that my knuckles began to stiffen. I didn't like the warning in her words as they dispersed around me.

"Why am I here? What do you want from me?" I asked as I eyed the Night Walkers along the far wall. They stood motionless, turning into shadows and appearing as dead as they smelt. Each one was just as beautiful as the Queen, yet their skin appeared faded, red eyes not quite the scarlet orbs of their leader.

The Queen trailed the outer side of the pit, continuing to set fire to the torches. I swore that she was feeding on the drama and suspense. She'd chosen The House of Nightmares as her backdrop and dressed up in her fancy red armor, which glistened and glinted under the flames. The Night Walkers loved their mind games, seeming to enjoy scaring poor, defenceless humans. It took the term 'playing with your food' to a new level.

"You and your pack have been on trial for the past twenty-four hours." She held the burning stake in her right hand, facing me from across the pit with a hint of a smile. "We've been testing your loyalty, finding those worthy of joining us."

She descended the steps into the arena and stomped on the stake the extinguish the flame, sliding it into the drain with her shiny boot.

"You passed your trial, Allora, as did Ares, Jayleigh and Diego. Unfortunately, Tye and Indigo did not pass their trial, and we will not offer them a place amongst us."

My mind stuttered.

I couldn't begin to comprehend her words or what they would mean for my pack. I couldn't think. I couldn't speak. I couldn't hear anything over the ringing in my ears.

My skin began to radiate with energy, and the room appeared brighter.

She was threatening us.

They're going to kill Tye and Indigo.

And she'd probably kill the rest of us if we refused to join her.

"Don't you dare touch them." I glared at her through glowing eyes. The inner animal was channeling my hatred into power, and I was visibly shaking. My hand on the dagger gripped so tightly that the electrical currents which began to pass through my fingers zapped across the titanium, coating the weapon in white and blue lightning.

"Oh wow, nice trick, Allora," the Queen snarked, revealing a pointed and pristine set of teeth, "It's a shame that plans are already in motion, and you're too late to stop them."

"You're a monster!" I yelled, fearing for my pack and whatever they were about to face. "I will never join you. We will never follow your orders."

The energy circulated my body at a speed I wasn't comfortable with, so I swallowed and contained the building current inside.

The Queen let out an audible sigh. "I thought you might say that." She motioned for Benji and his pack to push me forwards.

I pointed the dagger in their direction, knowing there was no possible way of fighting everybody in this room.

Except…

My body knew exactly how to escape this situation; only I couldn't allow it. I wouldn't let history repeat itself. My fingers twitched around the dagger as I realized it was too late. History had already repeated itself. I'd been betrayed by a Gen. 1 in the Alpha Arena, and here I was again, reliving past mistakes.

Panic spread like wildfire through my veins.

Dread in its purest form.

"Don't walk any closer, Benji!" My hand wobbled as I moved the dagger in his direction. I'd use it if I had to.

The Queen laughed from below, her voice carrying through the room and bouncing from walls. The other Night Walkers were creeping forwards, enclosing the space behind me.

I saw light.

I felt hopeless.

I needed Ares. The world was getting too loud, and the pressure was becoming too much. I had to hear him tell me that it would be okay, that we'd work it out together.

But I had yet to learn where he truly was.

None of the hybrids were where the map suggested they'd be, and Ares was certainly not where we'd planned for him to stay.

He was not safe.

None of us were.

And if I didn't descend the steps to meet the Night Walker Queen, my entire pack would die alongside me.

The bodies around me pushed in, closer. I stepped forwards. I needed more time. I had to think. *Think.*

Join the Night Walkers or indirectly kill my pack?

Or…

No. You can't.

Turn into a monster and fight on the wrong side of the war, or die fighting for the right side?

The creatures around me were too close.

My mind spun.

The energy raged through my veins, eyes, hair, and skin, and the static began to warp into the air around me. I could see it shimmering, distorting everybody to the point where they were just fuzzy shapes in my vision.

No. You promised that you wouldn't.

But I was no good at keeping promises.

I slowly raised the dagger in the Queen's direction.

It's too late. Already too late.

I was light. I was vengeance. I was death.

"Let my pack walk free, and I'll let you live," I laid down my conditions, knowing that there was no other possible way out of this where my pack survived.

For the greater good, I thought as my mind jumped to my Beta and wondered if he'd ever find himself to love me again after what I was about to do. *"I'm sorry, Ares. I hope you'll forgive me,"*

The Queen charged towards me, not realizing the strength of the storm brewing inside until it was too late. Her face twisted in horror as the light erupted from within, release so sharp and satisfying that it left me feeling revolted. It felt good to let go of everything. I wiped my soul clean, but the consequences would haunt me for an eternity.

The static energy was audible, lightning wrapping my body in a protective bubble, building… growing…

The Queen turned to run away as I dropped the dagger to the ground and screamed. The energy escaped me in white and blue light. The building exploded around me, and I turned everybody inside into ash.

CHAPTER THIRTY

ARES

"I don't understand, Marshall," my voice cracked, "Mom is dead. You showed me— We watched her die on Camera 72. Are you sure you're not hallucinating? The Night Walkers can plant visions in your mind. Maybe—"

"I know what I'm seeing, Ares. God, *damn* it." He was sobbing. "She's been here all this time."

I tried to think clearly, but all I could focus on was the adrenaline racing through my veins. "Marshall, it's okay." I barely heard my voice through the high-pitched ringing.

"It's not fucking okay!" He hit something against the door. I guessed it was his fist. "They've been feeding on her for eight years!"

My heart shattered. I had no solid memory of this woman,

only the stories I'd been told, yet my body felt numb at the thought of having her back.

She's alive.

Mother is alive.

We could take her back to The Farm, and she could tell me all about our life together before the metamorphosis, teach me everything she knew, and answer my questions. I had *so* many questions.

And Dr White would have his sister back.

We could be a family again.

We *would* be a family again.

"We've got her now, Marshall. That's all we need to focus on. We just need to get her and the pack out of here..." I was panting through the shock.

Marshall didn't reply.

My hands shook as I held them over my heart, beating so unbelievably fast. I called out to him, pressing my ear to the door, trying to make sense of the mumbled voices I could hear on the other side.

He'd woken her.

Her voice was weak, but it was *her.*

I was sure of it.

I recalled it from some part of my brain to which I no longer had access, and I recognized it from my dreams.

"Mom?" I asked quietly. I wasn't sure she'd even be able to hear me. There was a pause, Marshall's voice, and then I heard them walk towards the door. "Mom, are you there?" I held my palm to the metal separating us, wishing I could mould myself into it and sink through it.

"I'm here, Ares," her voice was soft, weak, a ghost of a memory.

Tears fell as though I'd never cried before. A barrier had been opened, and it swept me away, my heart aching with rekindled love. "Are you okay?"

"I'm fine, Mom. I— I can't believe you're here."

Marshall was yelling swears in the distance.

"You sound older than I remember." Mom coughed through her whisper. "How long have I been here?"

"Too long," Marshall's voice sounded guarded, blaming himself even though he had no reason to feel responsible. There was no way he could have known that Mother survived. *How* had she survived? "I'm going to find a way to open the door, and then we can get the fuck out of here."

"Are you okay, Mom?" My eyelids squeezed in worry, and I breathed through the immense emotions building within me. I couldn't bear to think of everything she'd been through. I wanted her to promise that they hadn't hurt her, to reassure me that she hadn't been in pain for the last eight years.

"I don't feel much at all right now… just numb," she replied.

Numb was okay; numb wasn't pain.

"I have so much to ask you. So much to talk about." I pulled the photo of her from my pocket, the one Dr. White had given to me just before sending me to the Safe House, and I wiped my thumb over the image, putting a face to the voice on the other side of the door.

"I'm sure you do," she said and coughed again.

"Save your energy, Mom. We're a long way from The Farm and getting back isn't going to be easy." I wiped my face with my sleeve and tried to collect myself. I needed to preserve my own energy to get everyone out of there alive.

"Tell me a story, Ares." My skin tingled, and I frowned, recalling the words but not knowing why. Was this a game we used to play? It seemed to hold sentimental value, but I couldn't remember why.

"Um. Sure."

She might want to hear about my training and that I was doing well despite my lack of control over my alter ego. But that would be too heavy. She wouldn't care about the training. I changed my mind, sure that hearing how many times I'd nearly died in the past few weeks wasn't the story she was requesting.

She'd want a lighter and happier story, reassurance that her life's work was paying off. She'd like a story of friendship and love, so I planned to tell her about Lora, but when I opened my mouth, my words took a different course.

"Marshall's been doing a great job since you left." I wiped my face once more, only now noticing a hole in my sleeve as though somebody had been at it with scissors, and they'd stolen my tablet in the process. A rush of panic shot through me, and I grabbed at my calf for my dagger, only to find that it was gone, too.

I tried not to overthink. I couldn't imagine the worst, but I'd be completely defenceless if the Night Walkers returned. I placed the photo of Mom on my bent knee as I sat and fiddled with a loose thread to distract myself. "He's successfully raised two Titanium packs, both of which are still alive, and a Veno pack, too. The Farm is making a difference in the world, and our future is looking much brighter because of it. I'm sure you'll be really proud of what he's achieved since you… since you've been gone. Sure, his methods have been questionable. Sometimes they were completely unethical and psychotic, but we are alive today because of him. He stood up to the challenge, even when Dr. Wh—Uncle Daniel," I corrected myself. "Even when Uncle Daniel couldn't… Yeah, it's not been easy for Marshall, and we don't always see eye to eye, but I'm starting to think that maybe he's—"

The Funhouse came to life as the power in the building turned on, introduced by strange music and moving objects on the walls. The door clanged. I climbed to my feet and backed away as it moved, holding Mom's photo between my fingers and tidying myself in hopes of making a good impression. Not that it would matter. Mom was probably too weak to see clearly, never mind judging me for my unkempt appearance.

This is it. I'm about to meet Mom. I was *so* ready to meet a woman who raised me, took me to the Biome to help me escape the underground bunker, and taught me to read and write.

I wiped the palm of my free hand on my jeans. Despite how cold the room was, I was sweating.

What should I say?

Should I hug her?

What will she think of my eyes?

I wouldn't look like the same boy she remembered.

My vision swept over her as the door screeched to a stop, and my breath caught in my throat, tears giving way in confusion as I stared at what I found on the other side.

"Ares, run!" Marshall's words cut through the air.

For the first time in history, I wanted to obey Marshall's orders and accept that he sometimes talked sense and wasn't mad. I tried to move as fast and far as possible, to follow my brother's commands, like the human in me was so used to doing; well-practiced in abandoning those I cared about to save myself. I should have called on those skills now. I should have put my humanity first, run for the door on the far side of the room, and escaped the Night Walker.

But I didn't.

I was frozen senseless. Not even my inner animal fought to move me as I stood in the open doorway, staring. My mind ticked over.

It didn't make sense.

Marshall was standing exactly where I'd expected him to be if he hadn't gone to switch the power on and open the door. His eyes screamed at me, urging me to get out before it was too late.

And there was Mom.

Not at all like the woman I'd seen in the photo. She was pale and drawn but not from the lack of blood in her body like Hail and the others in the room around me. If anything, she had too much blood as she stood strong beside Marshall, an arm around his chest and a hand tilting his neck aside. She was no longer my mother at all.

"That's a lovely story, Dear." Her smile revealed pointed teeth stained red with blood.

Marshall's blood.

I choked.

My body still fought against me as my mind forced me to move.

This can't be happening. It's a vision. It's not real.

It had to be a hallucination; planted into my mind to cause extreme pain, and it was a living nightmare.

I let go of mother's photo and stared in horror as she twisted Marshall's neck until it cracked, then dropped his lifeless body to the ground like nothing more than a bag of dirt.

The sound echoed throughout my ears.

It can't be real.

It can't be real.

It can't be real.

CHAPTER THIRTY-ONE

ARES

The vibration of Marshall's head hitting the wooden floorboard I stood on released me from my trance.

I crumbled, feeling the dread pour through my body like molten lava, burning me from the inside out. It scalded, and I wanted nothing more than to melt between the planks of the Funhouse floor and disappear forever.

My body moved whilst my mind stayed behind.

I couldn't think straight.

All the Funhouse's noises had fizzled away into one single note, which rang through my ears like a warning siren.

I crawled towards Marshall's body, unable to process anything other than the need to sit with him.

My vision blurred through tears or shock, and I was

halfway towards my brother's body when two bare feet interrupted my path.

"Rise, Ares," my mother commanded, and I had no choice but to stand. I was already under her compulsion, and my body turned to follow as she began to walk back towards the pack.

It wasn't like mutating, where I could still influence my alter ego if I trained my thoughts and focused on different emotions. Being under Night Walker control made me feel like a machine. I was a robot. Mother's mind was the remote, and she twisted and turned me, boasting her power, and stopped me in front of Jayleigh. I looked down at my friend in a panic, wanting to scream. She needed to wake up. Run as fast as she could. She was in danger.

We all were.

My throat closed itself as I tried to yell and choked. The more I fought, the more I struggled. I attempted to turn back to Marshall to confirm that my eyes hadn't deceived me. He was still dead. It was real. But my head didn't move, and I could only make out the outline of his body through the corner of my eye.

My heart shattered.

It *was* real.

"You have many questions," the Night Walker beside me stated. I couldn't call her Mom because my mother truly had died on The Farm eight years ago, and this monster had claimed her body as its own. I refused to believe that this Night Walker was my mother. I couldn't accept it. "I will answer them, Ares, but first, we have a small matter that we need to address."

I didn't have a choice but to stand by her side, barely even hearing Lora's words as the Alpha mind jumped an apology, asking for forgiveness.

Forgiveness for what?

I couldn't understand what she meant, and the ability to think it over was a luxury I didn't have. Thankfully, a distraction came just as my mother walked towards the pack.

The floor rumbled beneath our feet, a violent explosion rippling through the building, shaking the walls and knocking me off balance.

I stumbled. Mom quickly corrected my clumsiness as her red eyes settled on me.

The back of my neck tingled.

"It's time," she said.

Time for what?

I didn't want to know.

I wanted to find Lora and make sure she was okay, ask why she needed my forgiveness, and then get the pack the hell away from the Night Walker's nest.

But Mom was moving. She approached Indigo, who sat at the far end of the line, and closed her eyes. I watched in horror as Indigo began to scream Zee's name, reaching out to her as though she was standing in Mom's place.

Mom laughed, an entirely evil sound. Through the haze of my mind, I could remember the sweet sound of her giggle as she wiped dirt from my face in the Biome. She hadn't appeared to age since the image in my mind, yet she looked like a different person.

The crazy lights of the Funhouse flickered in her armor, and her eyes screamed danger.

"We've been testing you, Ares." Mom tilted her head in one sharp motion, and Indigo's screams stopped, her arms falling limp and her eyes slowly opening, panic evident on her face.

Go back to sleep. I doubted whatever nightmare Mom had planted in her mind could be any worse than what was about to happen.

"Some of you passed the test. Others, such as young Indigo here, failed miserably." The smile on her face was foreign. I fought against my body again, straining and struggling to help Indigo from the monster before me, but I was frozen in place, stuck with no option but to watch.

Just like Marshall had been as he watched our parents die on the screens of the Observatorium.

How did Mom survive? I'd seen the video for myself…

I also saw the Night Walker carry my mother's body away after my father had drowned her.

"We believe that only the loyal, the brave, and the selfless deserve a place beside us. Only those worthy of immortality shall live to see the world we create."

I wanted to tell her that she'd lost her mind. She was a monster, and she was about to *kill* my friends.

Mom lifted Indigo's body from the ground by the neck with a strength that would match any hybrid's. Indigo's eyes bulged. Her feet kicked out desperately beneath her.

"This one," Mom glared Indigo directly in the eyes as she spoke, "failed the loyalty test miserably. She was ready to hand Lora over without a second thought. Of course, we fed her a few lies, as we'd lied to you and Lora about The Sanctuary's plans to ambush The Farm."

Heat rose from my feet to my chest.

The Night Walkers *had* been in control all along. They'd been playing us, and we'd fallen straight into their trap.

Mum turned back to look at me as Indigo scrambled to break free from her grasp. "It's a shame really, because she showed so much promise."

My heart raced for Indigo, witnessing the fear in her eyes turn to hopelessness. And then she looked to the ceiling and embraced the fact that she wasn't getting out of this alive. Her kicking stopped. A single tear rolled down her cheek, and Mom's teeth were in her neck before the tear reached the floor.

Time slowed.

My skin crawled with hatred.

I had never wanted to mutate as much as I did now, the anger sweeping over me and the fury driving me forward.

I screamed, although my body didn't allow the noise to leave my mouth.

Trapped. A prisoner in my own skin.

How dare she.

She spoke of loyalty, yet she was one of the sole creators of The Farm. She had been crucial in aiding the war and fighting back against the Night Walkers.

Yet, there she stood, judging *us* for our decisions and how we coped under pressure.

Since leaving The Farm, Indigo barely had time to process everything she'd experienced. She was angry, mourning, and broken. I could understand why she blamed Lora, but she didn't deserve to die for it. Her way of coping with the grief was to hold somebody responsible. Her loyalty test shouldn't have been focused on an area of such pain and sorrow.

Who was I kidding?

There shouldn't have been a loyalty test *at all.*

Mom dropped Indigo's body similarly to Marshall's, however, as Indigo's life faded away, her body began to convulse, jolting on the ground. Blood poured from her eyes, foam forming in her mouth and burning away at the skin on her face.

I watched it in horror.

My stomach couldn't hold it.

I couldn't do this.

I couldn't watch Mom kill my friends.

As she moved one step aside, her gaze landed on Tye, and I fought harder than I'd ever fought before.

I was not a coward.

I would not stand by and let the Night Walkers win.

I would sacrifice everything I was to save the ones I loved.

"Don't... you... dare." I forced the words from my lips, straining.

Tye was awake, watching me with pleading eyes.

I had to save him. Not because he was Lora's friend, and not because I liked him—because that would never be a possibility after everything he'd done—but because he was family.

Tye was more family to me than this Night Walker would ever be.

"Hmm, able to break through the mind control, are we?"

Mom looked at me, her eyes drawing me in like Hail to food. A cruel smile crossed her lips, eyebrows tilting down instead of rising. She let go of Tye like a toy she was no longer interested in playing with, a shiny new object now holding her attention; me.

"Your mind is a mess," she stated as she walked closer to me, stepping over Indigo's shuddering body. "The animal and human states are merging, not quite one or the other. I predicted this might happen."

"Why?" I punched the word out, focusing on the animal which raged inside. It allowed me to overcome the mind control just enough, so long as I didn't let it too much reign.

"Daniel hasn't told you? Well, he always did stay true to his word. How is my brother, by the way? Does he still obsess over me? He was certainly the protective type and always thought he knew best." She snarled the words out. "And how is he coming along with that cure?"

So Dr. White *did* know why I was losing control of my animal state? He knew this could have been possible, even when he'd pushed me to mutatc, promising it would help me evolve.

I glared at the monster before me. How would my uncle cope with the news that Mom was standing before me, a Night Walker, hiding away in the nest for the past eight years despite the footage on Camera 72. "How?"

"Oh, Dear, please stop with the questions. You'll pop a blood vessel if you try to fight the mind control for too long," she drawled and walked away. Tye was sprawled across the floor, unconscious again, and Mom's focus returned to Marshall's body, so I presumed that Tye was safe for the time being.

I just had to find a way to distract her until Lora and Benji found a way to kill the Night Walker Queen, taking out the entire bloodline, including my mother.

She dragged Marshall's body from the adjoining room and placed it before me. I couldn't look, no longer wanting to hold my brother in fear that I might vomit.

"How?" I asked again. "You… died." Short sentences were just about manageable.

"Yes," she agreed. "After receiving a bite from Gretta."

My skin coated itself in a deeper sweat.

Gretta. I knew that name.

A blonde-haired woman with a large nose and skin so pale she looked ill; the Night Walker that Mom had been keeping in the room with windows. The one I'd dreamt about. The red-eyed woman with the answers. The Night Walker that had ripped Father's head clean off his shoulders.

Gretta.

Gretta.

Finally, I had a name—a confirmation that this memory was real and not a fragment of my imagination. I knew I hadn't dreamt it as Marshall suggested.

It shouldn't have been good news to me. I shouldn't have been so relieved to hear that they'd hidden a Night Walker underneath The Farm.

I recalled the window I'd passed on my way to the safe house, the chair tipped onto its side, and I connected the dots. Gretta had been trapped in the bunker and somehow managed to escape whilst I'd been in hibernation eight years ago.

It explained how so many farmers had died that day. The Night Walkers hadn't broken into The Farm as I'd presumed; Gretta had broken out, and she'd taken out the people who'd kept her prisoner in her escape.

"That's how it works, you see," Mom continued. "Mind control through the eyes. Visions from a bite. Death through venom…"

Marshall's body moved before me, his neck snapping back into form and his limbs flying out to the sides as though a piece of string pulled at his chest.

"And drinking the blood of a human before killing them will continue your bloodline."

I couldn't breathe; I couldn't process that Marshall was about to become the one thing he'd fought his entire life to overcome. He'd been mad enough as a human. "You're turning him."

I wondered if Mom could sense the blood racing through my veins faster and faster. Could she smell my fear?

"Yes, I'm turning him," she confirmed. "And once I kill Tye, I'll turn you, too. And Hail, Jayleigh, and Diego. And when we have the entire pack together, we'll take on that firecracker girlfriend of yours, and turn her too. She'll feel so heartbroken that she'll give in. And then we can start on a new world. A better world." Her eyes lit up like blood in the light of a flame. "One big, happy family, just like you've always wanted. Isn't that right, Ares?"

CHAPTER THIRTY-TWO

LORA

I watched the clouds slowly pass over, wondering if they were looking down on me with as much disappointment as my ancestors must be feeling.

My body was working on building back enough energy to lift the beam, which had me trapped, but honestly, I wished it wouldn't. I didn't deserve freedom. I'd accepted life trapped on The Farm just as soon as I'd killed everyone in the Alpha Arena, believing that it was a fair payment, following orders, training hybrids, and risking my life for the war. As the Titanium Alpha, I could help save the lives of Gen. 2s to redeem the Gen. 1 lives I'd taken.

Sure, I'd have never made it out of the Alpha Arena without killing every one of them and earning my title, but I hadn't played fair. I wasn't the smartest, most skilled, fastest, or strongest. But I was the most careless.

I used a power that nobody else could conjure, so at least I could claim to be the most powerful, but that in no way justified the fact that I'd cheated my way to the top.

I'd killed every last one of the challenging Alphas in a single betrayal-inflicted outburst, a few by-standing farmers caught in the crossfire.

From that day forwards, I'd promised to keep control of my emotions. I vowed to act selflessly, keep to the rules, to gain control of the energy inside. To never let myself *feel* too much.

To never kill another Titanium.

Yet, I'd just killed Benji and his pack… save for the woman marking Ares. She'd be dead soon enough, though, unable to last without her Alpha, and her blood was on my hands.

I'd done it again.

This time it was for selfless reasons, but that didn't make it any easier. I'd saved my pack by using my secret weapon—my curse—and possibly several hundred humans by taking out the Night Walker Queen.

I hadn't impaled her with titanium as recommended, but everybody around me had turned to ash in the explosion, and I doubted any Night Walker could come back from that. Even Benji's pack, who had been able to control and contain the energy, couldn't withstand the power I released.

I sobbed.

My body shook against the beam that pinned me down, and I welcomed the pain, staying in my human state to fully feel its weight. I'd earned it.

What would Ares say when he found out what I'd done? How could I ever begin to tell him?

Would he ever look me in the eye again?

I didn't deserve his forgiveness. Maybe he could accept what I'd done today, but I had never told him about what happened in the Alpha Arena, continually fearing he'd look at me differently and run, but I'd have to tell him one day. I couldn't go on pretending to be the person he believed I was. And I knew it would change our dynamic once he learned the truth.

I was a natural killer.

I was no better than the Night Walkers.

And that's why I had to do my damn best to win this war. I had a debt to pay, lives to avenge, and tremendous guilt to overcome.

I swallowed my self-pity and tried to focus on the fact that I'd at least managed to tick one of those boxes by taking out the Night Walker Queen. *Benji and his pack chose the wrong side,* I tried to convince myself, *they were just as much of an enemy as the vampires.*

Gripping my thumbs to the point they threatened to break, I decided it was time to face the music, but the song was a staccato scale creeping slowly upwards in pitch and never resolving. It made me uncomfortable, and my spine tingled.

I was just able to evolve, regaining enough strength to shift the beam from my chest and throw it aside; the wisps of hair crossed my vision flickering only a faint light.

How long had I been lying there?

Where were the pack now?

I zoned in on them through the Alpha bond but couldn't pinpoint their location, as though they were still under Night Walker compulsion.

But I killed the Queen.

I rose to my feet, wiping dust and debris from my clothes which were now torn from the building which had collapsed around me. My dagger was buried within the rubble, and for a few minutes, I rummaged to find it before turning to witness the state of the theme park and noticing the sun begin to shrink beyond the sea.

I needed to hurry, stop dwelling on my actions, and find my pack.

They were close, and I could at least rule out the two stalls on either side of The House of Nightmares' remnants because they too had been wiped out, so I started in the next building. This one was full of arcade games, shooting ranges, bowling alleys, and Night Walker bodies. Unlike hybrids, the vampires must drop like flies when their leader dies, the magic in their blood no longer active.

That was a kinder way to go, instantly, unlike the Gen. 2s or Ares if I had ever died before them.

Something rattled outside the building.

I ducked out of surprise more than anything else. Had they seen me? Did they know I was here?

I held up my dagger in defence and considered if there could be more than one bloodline of Night Walker living within the nest, then crept around the dust-riddled machine I'd been hiding behind. If there were more of them, I would be in big trouble.

We didn't have many minutes of sunlight left; I guessed thirty at a push.

I made for a smaller machine near the door, leaping over a Night Walker body as I ran, ducking behind a round game with glass on the upper half and insides strewn with spiderwebs and coins.

Through the glass, I could just about peer through the door.

I kept my breathing steady, rhythmic, calm, and ready for

whatever I might find on the path outside the building.

But it was clear.

Maybe I'd imagined it?

It could have been a building shedding any weight I'd loosened during my explosion.

My eyes landed on The Funhouse, and suddenly I was sure of where I needed to go. Ares. I could sense the shadow of his aura snaking through the Alpha bond, growing, reaching out to me for help, and it was coming from the building lit with red and orange lights, calling out to me like a beacon.

A crash echoed in my ears.

This time, it was coming from behind me. *Inside* the building. My body reacted, fleeing whatever stalked me from the darkness, and I sprinted onto the pier and towards The Funhouse.

It wasn't far. An abandoned Hook-a-Duck stall was the only thing to intercept my path, and as I dodged the faded sign, I found myself pulled back, my clothes cutting into my neck as somebody caught hold of my top.

My arm yanked it free, and I spun to find a pair of gleaming red eyes staring back at me.

Katie. She was here, a Night Walker, standing before me in broad *daylight.*

"Surprise, Allora," she whispered.

My heart raced, and I wanted to run, to find my pack and escape, but confusion had me frozen.

I stared.

How is she standing in the light of the sun?

Why wasn't her skin frying?

"How…" My eyes must have portrayed just how horrified I felt because she laughed, "How did you— How are you able—" I couldn't finish any string of thought, my mind glitching over the new information.

"Thanks for abandoning me at The Sanctuary. I guess Marshall was right when he told me not to trust animals."

I *had* abandoned her. We knew that Night Walkers had taken the pack and that The Sanctuary had therefore been infiltrated, yet we didn't check to see if she'd been taken too. Nor Marshall, for that matter.

"Katie, I'm so sorry—"

"Save it." She cut me off and let go of my clothes.

More Night Walkers crawled out from the shadows of the not-so-abandoned theme park and began to circle me.

"How are you able to withstand the sunlight?" I asked, eyeing the Night Walkers as they inched closer like spiders stalking their prey… me. Some showed their teeth, and others laughed as though I'd said something amusing.

I gripped my hand around the dagger.

My energy was dwindling.

I needed to form a plan and quickly.

"We're not Night Walkers, Dumbass." I looked again at their red eyes and razor-sharp teeth, words failing me. "We're so much worse."

My heart dropped so far, I believed it vanished below the pier and into the depths of the icy ocean below. Just as the panic finally took over, a rippling pain I knew only too well took over my body, damn near killing me in the process.

Indigo.

She was dying.

Most likely already dead. The connection was unstable as she was under a Night Walker's control, like how I'd felt the day Teri died in Phase Two. She was in trouble either way, and there was nothing I could do to help. It was too late.

My raspy breath halted altogether.

As though Katie could smell my helplessness, she added, "We're Day Walkers, Lora. And soon enough, you'll be one too."

CHAPTER THIRTY-THREE

ARES

"No." I watched Marshall's body judder on the ground before me. My mouth ran dry, and I gasped for air. "I'd rather die than turn. I'd rather lose my humanity to my inner animal than you."

"That's not what your mind is telling me, Ares. You're only lying to yourself."

She was still playing games, putting words in my mouth and ideas in my head, trying to convince me that this would be the right choice for everybody.

Of course, there was *some* truth to her words. I wanted a happy family, to feel accepted and part of something larger than myself. My Gen. 3 differences would always segregate me from the Gen. 2s, and I'd never feel a part of the pack because of it.

But that didn't mean I wanted us all to join the enemy and fight on the wrong side of the war. I didn't want to kill my friends, and I didn't want to murder innocent humans or drink their blood to survive.

I just wanted peace.

I wanted to live in a world where everybody felt safe.

I wanted unity.

Ironic, considering I couldn't even unite my human and mutant states.

The scales were tipping, wobbling, tipping back again, forever unbalanced; it gave me enough power to overcome the mind control as Mom took a step towards Tye to hold true to her word.

"Put him down." The words were less of a struggle now, but my rage was stirring wild and free. I'd mutate if I had to. I'd already lost Indigo and my brother; I couldn't allow Mom to kill anybody else.

My body lurched into action as she reached forwards, and I knocked her to the side, over Indigo's limp body and into the wall. I didn't have a plan. There were no loopholes on this side of The Farm's fence. I was acting on instinct, fear, adrenaline, and exhaustion, and I reached for my dagger, only to remember that they'd stolen my weapon.

Crap.

Crap.

Triple crap.

I rolled away from Mom as she leapt towards me, wondering how far she was willing to take this. How far *I* was ready to take this.

Could I kill my own mother? Did I hate her enough to plunge titanium through her heart?

Yes.

She planned on taking everything from me and had already taken so much. I didn't realize how much I'd come to enjoy Marshall's company. Not that he was good company in any form, but seeing him do and be better was satisfying, and he *had* been trying.

If only he'd had more time.

His body was still again now, but his eyes were open, staring up at the ceiling and unblinking.

How long before he was one of them? A Night Walker? Roaming the shadows for an eternity.

How long before we all joined them?

Unless…

There could be a way that the pack could still make it out alive. My odds weren't good, but they hadn't been for a while, and I'd prepared myself for an abrupt ending. At least this way, I could do right by my family. Who would have guessed that I might die a hero after it all?

I just wished I'd said goodbye to Lora and told her everything I needed her to know when I had the chance. *Splitting up is always a bad idea,* I thought as I slowly backed through the sliding door and scanned the room.

There.

I hovered at the far end, watching as Mom followed with determination.

"You can turn me, Mom," I said, my heart racing so fast I thought I might die before she got the chance. "Just let my friends live. Me, you, and Marshall, we can be a family again. I want that for us, but I also want my friends to live. They at least deserve that."

"You might think otherwise once you're a Day Walker," she smiled, barely giving me time to process what she'd called herself as she charged towards me. I fell backwards into the lever on the door as I'd planned, opening it and sprawling out into the evening sun.

Day Walker?

I planned to trick her, get her outside, and let her sizzle away in the sunlight.

But a *Day* Walker?

I rolled across the pier, Mom laughing as she tumbled with me, menacing and evil. She'd been one step ahead and seen straight through my plans, purposely keeping the truth about her ability to walk in the sun to herself.

I knew Lora was behind me as I rose from the ground as though I could sense her just as easily as she could sense me. What happened to us at The Sanctuary earlier still impacted our spiritual connection.

"Lora!" I called out to her, Mom pinning my arms by my side and turning me to face my Alpha. Lora stood in a circle of vampires—Day Walkers—and looked like she'd been through hell.

"Ares!" She sounded defeated.

My eyes flickered sideways for a moment, catching sight of a face behind her. "Katie?" I was too exhausted to do anything but stare. Fighting Mom's compulsion was taking its toll.

The red-eyed girl no longer looked kind. "Ares." she bit, quirking an eyebrow.

"Ares, are you okay? Are you hurt?" Lora stole a glance at me beyond her circle.

"I'm fine, don't worry about me. Just focus on getting yourself out of there."

Mom squeezed my arms, my shoulder popping. "Well, Ares, aren't you going to introduce me to your girlfriend?" Her teeth were uncomfortably close to my neck. I feared what she might do if I refused her, what she might still do if I obliged.

"Lora, this… this *was* my mother, Samantha. That is not exactly how I imagined this would go in an ideal world. But, as you can see, she's now a Day Walker and wants to turn us all."

"Over my dead body!" Lora yelled back, barely paying attention to the first half of my introduction.

"She'd a feisty one. I'll give her that," Mom sounded amused, "You've got my approval."

"Samantha…" Lora's eyes darted towards Katie, then to the Day Walkers surrounding her, and then back to us. "She's the Queen, Ares."

I could hear Mom's lips move over her teeth in a smile. "Intelligent, too. A worthy Titanium Alpha indeed. Thank you, Lora, for tying up my loose ends with your outburst in The House of Nightmares. Those Night Walkers were more trouble than they were worth. But they got your pack here, and that's all that matters."

"Loose ends? What is she talking about?" I asked Lora what she'd done to help my mother's mission.

"Go ahead, tell Ares what you did to those poor Titaniums." Mom's arm tightened around me, and Lora's eyes widened in fear. Then she looked at me, and the expression on her face was one I'd only ever seen once before, as Tye had spilt Lora's plans to keep me alive by leading me on. It was the same look of guilt. My stomach churned at all the possibilities in my mind.

"They were working with the Night Walkers, Ares," she began. "I don't know why, but they led me into a trap, and the Night Walker Queen tried to turn me."

"So…" Mom enticed the story from her.

Lora gave the Day Walker behind me a hateful glare. If only looks could kill. "So, I killed them all."

"Wonderful." Mom laughed into my ear. "I couldn't have planned it better if I'd tried."

I remained silent. Even as Lora's eyes pleaded, I couldn't bring myself to say what I felt inside. I should have been mad and yelled at her. It was against my moral code, yet I struggled to process that I was pleased. I was *thankful.*

"You knew I'd kill them?" Lora asked my mother. "You set them up. Why?"

"I've been working with the Night Walkers for a while now, striking a deal with their Queen to join forces and ambush The Farm. She wanted the Titaniums, although she wouldn't tell me what she had planned, and I wanted my son, so I agreed to her terms. I agreed to follow her orders, but it didn't matter because I knew how to play both sides to get what I wanted."

It was her. Mom had been playing us all, Titaniums and Night Walkers, like puppets.

"It is wonderful to see inside your Titanium minds. It's

surprising how well you can get to know somebody by spending a little time in their thoughts, right, Allora?"

"Get out of my head." Lora's voice was low, warning.

"You don't think you're worthy of Ares' love, do you? You've killed more people than you'd ever admit to him. You'd gladly lie and hide who you are, *what* you are, to keep his respect."

I sensed Lora's defeat through the look in her eyes.

Mom was tearing down her walls, praying on her guilt. I'd already destroyed Mom's plans by drawing her outside before she could kill Tye and turn the rest of us. She'd confessed that the heartbreak would destroy Lora, and then she'd be able to turn her too, so Mom was improvising. She was still trying to turn Lora.

And she was using *me* to do it. The anger reached a new limit, tilting me further out of control.

"I don't blame you, Lora," desperation laced my voice. "Don't listen to her. I know you." I couldn't hold it back any longer, the rage growing as Mom fought harder to silence me. It was okay that Lora had killed the Titaniums, and I finally admitted to myself that I'd have done the same in her position, welcoming the mutant thoughts. "I know you wouldn't kill unless there were no other options. And I know that you'll forgive me for *this*."

Lora looked between Mom and me, her face twisting as she understood the situation and what I had to do to get us out of there alive.

I had prepared a speech in the boat, thinking of the perfect way to tell Lora just how much she meant to me, should it have ever come to this moment. But, as I had the time to say goodbye, I realized my words were nothing but a fragment of the mind, an over-rehearsed rambling of why I loved her and what she meant to me, and it wasn't good enough. It was not my mind that I wanted to share with her in my final moments of humanity, but my heart.

So, I stayed silent for what may have been the first time in my life. Our eyes shared everything we needed to say, and I knew she understood what I was trying to tell her.

I see you.

I love you.

I always have, and I always will.

The darkness burned through my veins like sea water infiltrating the lungs, and I let it drown me.

CHAPTER THIRTY-FOUR

LORA

Part of me wanted to uncage my own inner animal and tear the theme park to shreds.

Most of me wanted to kill Samantha for everything she'd already done and was yet to do.

All of me wanted to stop Ares from mutating, fearing he'd never fully regain his humanity.

But none of it was possible with the Day Walkers surrounding me in a cage-like ring. I didn't have enough energy to break free after exerting it all on the Night Walkers. Fighting was my only way out, but I was greatly outnumbered.

I should have been paying attention to my battles instead of staring hopelessly at Ares as the shadows within him swarmed out and stretched. A commotion broke out around me, figures moving as though in slow motion, running, fighting, screaming.

I focused on slate gray, capturing every speck of silver and granite, chiselling it into my mind like stone. *Ares' eyes may never return to this color*, but I wanted to preserve this moment to fall back on if the vibrant blue ever became too much, and I struggled to remember the innocent boy who stood before me now. If the mutant blurred the lines of who Ares was and what he stood for, I'd remember how he sacrificed his humanity to save us.

The brawl sent me flying to the side, bringing me back to the present, unable to see Ares or Samantha through the feet and paws around me.

Wolves.

My head darted around, witnessing the wolf pack tear into the vampires who had me surrounded. How? Why? I didn't care. It only mattered that they were here and willing to help.

I jumped to my feet, dagger in my hand.

Solace was distracting Samantha, although the wolves wouldn't be able to put up much of a fight. The vampires were faster and stronger, but the Day Walkers' compulsion couldn't control Solace and her pack, giving them a slight advantage. The vampires had always influenced their enemies, but they'd have to work to win this battle.

Ares was on the ground, a Day Walker hovering over him and pinning him to the wooden pier.

A sour taste filled my mouth as I ran towards them, taking down anything in my way.

I drowned out the sound of screaming and wolves whining, hearing only the sound of my feet echoing against the wood and a voice so familiar. My focus remained on the Day Walker as he leaned closer to Ares neck. I could barely breathe.

And then the words, "I don't have long. Trust me. Close your eyes and stay down," from the Day Walker's lips into Ares' ear.

As he turned to face me, I registered the copper hair, the jacket and the heavy boots, and the scar above his red eyes.

I stilled.

"Marshall."

We'd left him at The Sanctuary with Katie, and they'd got to him, too.

He gave me a wink, then glanced down to the blood-covered dagger clenched in my hand. And he was charging towards me, his arm flying out around my torso, slamming into my shoulder and dropping the weapon from my fingers. I focused only on retrieving the dagger as Marshall whispered into my ear.

"I have a dagger in my boot. It's burning into my skin, and

I need you to grab it when I floor you. Then we're both going to kill my mother. She's unable to read my mind now, so I'll pin her down. You need to use that dagger to kill her."

I didn't understand what was happening, but I nodded quickly and faked an attack, glad to be away from Marshall's new teeth. As promised, he dropped me to the ground, and I whipped the dagger from his pocket with haste, holding it between the two of us. I grabbed the second dagger from the floor with my spare hand.

"Is she looking?" Marshall asked, referring to his mother.

"She's squeezing Solace's chest."

"Good, she's distracted. Now."

We ran toward Samantha, Marshall reaching her before I could, and I struggled to comprehend what was happening as he ripped her arms back. Solace cowered away to Ares' side, who followed Marshall's orders to stay out of trouble. He hadn't mutated.

Marshall had interrupted just in time.

I watched as Marshall and Samantha fought. Red eyes and teeth. Samantha was faster, but Marshall was stronger. He overpowered her, and I waited for my chance to pounce.

And then somebody yanked my hair and twisted, my head jolting backwards. I scrambled to face my attacker. As I slashed the dagger across her arm, Katie screamed out, the skin turning gray and oozing blood. I focused only on surviving, not thinking about who I was fighting and how this was sure to end. I twisted, buckled her knee, and planted the dagger firmly through her heart.

"Lora, now!" Marshall called.

I spun on my knees, grunting through the effort, and threw the second dagger at Samantha, thankful for my years of target practice. It embedded itself into her chest, and I wiped Katie's blood from my face as I waited for the Day Walker Queen to turn gray.

Only she didn't.

She laughed, mocking my efforts.

"It's not Titanium, you fool. I take back what I said earlier. Ares could do better than you."

The energy ignited at the idea of Ares with anyone other than myself, and the rage burned in my fingertips. I let the lightning seep through my skin. This time I could barely hold it back, forming a perfect orb of hate-filled light.

Maybe it was panic which allowed me to project the energy?

I launched it towards Samantha, and her body stilled upon impact, paralysed.

"I believe *that* was a hundred per cent Titanium," I could hold back the snide comment as I whipped around and yanked

Marshall's dagger from Katie's corpse. I stalked towards her, probably a little too confidently, and withdrew the blade that Benji had supplied from Samantha's motionless body.

Of course, I should have considered that the traitor would have handed me a useless weapon.

Then I motioned for Marshall to step aside. He nodded, seeming to brace himself as he complied.

I paused.

Samantha was the Queen, and killing her would kill them all…

I pushed her to the ground and placed the dagger into her shoulder with so much force that it pinned her to the pier. I witnessed the pain in her eyes, yet she couldn't scream.

Marshall frowned. "What are you doing? Kill her! I don't have much time—"

"I'm giving you time," I interrupted him and looked towards Ares, "to say goodbye."

CHAPTER THIRTY-FIVE

ARES

Marshall had come to my rescue, the monster saving me from the beast.

I didn't quite understand at first that he was still transitioning into a Day Walker, he was still himself, despite the appearance, and he asked me to trust him. As crazy as it seemed, I found it easier to trust him now than I had in my entire life. He'd saved me from myself. He'd allowed me more time with Lora, and I owed him.

So, I did as he asked, squeezed my eyes shut, and prayed that whatever he had planned would pay off. My inner animal was still raging under the surface, and I'd easily switch if needed. I listened, waiting for my queue, but it never came.

Solace was by my side when Lora called my name. I opened

my eyes to find Lora coated in blood and leaning over me with a smile so large it burst my heart. Behind her, Mom was pinned to the ground and completely motionless, and Marshall was staring at me over Lora's shoulder.

Red eyes suit him—finally, a visual representation of the madness inside his head.

Lora placed a hand on my cheek, and I cupped it with my own, not caring for the blood that would once have made me feel queasy.

"You're here," she said.

I didn't need her to elaborate, "I'm here." I nodded. "And for the record, this was a *very* bad idea."

"I'm not going to argue with you on that one." She looked back to Marshall and nodded in his direction. "Do you know what's happening?"

"Yeah..." my voice dropped as I processed everything, "Thank you."

I squeezed her hand as I looked back to Marshall. I'd already watched him die once today, and I wasn't sure I could do it again. But this time, I had the chance to say goodbye. That was a luxury that most people didn't have. I wouldn't take it for granted.

"I'll finish off the remaining Day Walkers, and then I'll be with the pack when you're ready." Lora motioned towards the

Funhouse and offered a small smile as she walked towards four Day Walkers staring at their helpless Queen.

I climbed to my feet, following her towards my brother, my bottom lip trembling.

My heart raced.

My stomach churned.

"Marshall, I'm so sorry—"

"Save your precious breath, Princess." Marshall cut me off. "We don't have time for that." He sat on a bench and rested his elbows on his knees, looking across at our mother's body. There was a moment of silence as I pulled myself together. Marshall played over his words. "Do you know how many nights I lost sleep, wishing I could bring Mom back from the dead?" He snorted.

"I can imagine…"

"You know what this all means, right? Me being… this. And Mom being the Queen. Lora thinks that when we kill her, I'm going to die too, and that's okay because I'd much rather be dead than a monster."

"You've always been a monster, Marshall," I joked.

He didn't laugh, "Yeah, well… I've been dying for a long time. I guess death was eating away at me, piece by piece."

I held my breath. "What do you mean? What— you—" *No, he wasn't ill.* Dr. White had been flushing the drugs from his system, fixing him.

I knew he'd been sick, but not *ill*, and I'd mocked him about it and made jokes because he'd assured me he was getting better.

I'd been rubbing his weakness in his face and not once had he tried to stop me.

Marshall pursed his lips and glanced towards the horizon, the sun nothing but a sliver of light on a teal sea. He rested his chin on his knuckles.

"This would look good on a postcard." He took a breath and nodded slowly to himself.

"A post— Marshall, what the hell are you talking about? I asked you if you were well enough to leave The Farm, and you'd promised me that you were okay! I shouldn't have—"

He interrupted me, "It wasn't your decision to make, Ares. I'd have left whether you *allowed* me to or not. I've lived my entire life on that farm. I didn't want to die there, too. I wanted to see a glimpse of the world outside the fence."

I stared, sinking onto the bench next to him, realization kicking in. Now we both stared out to sea.

"You were never planning on going back, were you?"

He cleared his throat. "The day of the attack, Dr White ran some tests, and I realized that my… condition… had worsened significantly. Then I heard that you were leaving The Farm and

— call it a moment of madness, sickness, or whatever the fuck you like—I realized I wanted to go with you." He took a deep breath, and I wondered if he was fighting back tears or the vampirism that would soon take complete control. "I wanted to positively impact your life, to help you, before I died so that you won't look back on your memories of me in the same way I look back on memories of Father."

I was speechless. The sea rippled beneath us, and I thanked it for filling the silence. So, Marshall *had* been telling the truth when he said he wanted to help us.

He'd succeeded, too.

"You saved me today, Marshall." I clenched my jaw to stop my voice from shaking. "I don't know what you think of Dad, but I can honestly say that you're not all that bad, and I'm glad that you blackmailed me into bringing you along."

Marshall laughed. A genuine, honest laugh. Not the kind I heard on The Farm. Not the kind that ended in a cough. I glanced down at his blooded sleeve, wondering how I'd missed the signs, the extensive sweating, the nosebleeds, the coughing, the fainting.

He was ill.

And he wanted to spend his final days with me. Not Dr. White or Wilson. Me.

"It's your turn now, Ares. I know you haven't had the

training I did, but you're intelligent and have a good heart. You need to return to The Farm, ask Wilson for Protocol Six, and do whatever it takes to win this war. Do you hear me?"

"I can't, Marshall." My head was still shaking. "I'm a sheep in wolf's clothing. You said so yourself."

Marshall smirked. "You've never been a sheep in wolf's clothing, Ares. That was a scare tactic. You *can* do it, and you *will* do it. I believe in you."

It lingered in the air.

"That's the nicest thing you've ever said to me." My body seemed to relax as I breathed in his faith and acceptance.

"Well, don't get used to it. I might try to kill you in the next minute or so." He grimaced.

"I'm so sorry, Marshall—"

"Shut up." His red eyes glared into my soul. "I need to ask you something whilst I still have time. Did you mean what you said in the Funhouse? Do you think Mom should be proud of me?"

My heart faltered.

The man before me was a boy, still looking for his parents' approval. Marshall may not have liked our father, but he'd always upheld his legacy, followed his rules, and always tried to make him proud, even in death.

"Yeah, Marshall." For some reason, I reached a hand out to

pat his leg. It should have felt like the weirdest thing in the world, but it didn't.

Marshall sobbed.

"They should be proud. You should be proud of yourself. I'm proud of you." I added in my mind, not for killing my friends, but for trying to be better than the person my father created.

I wondered, if not for the first time, what kind of person Marshall might have been if given a normal childhood, caring parents, or even a couple of friends. The world could be lonely, especially for a man who'd worked his life to make people fear him. I'd feared him. I'd hated him more than anything in the world. But now, given the luxury of time, I decided I might have eventually considered Marshall a friend; a twisted and traumatized friend, but I'd have been there for him if he ever needed me.

Marshall sniffled and swallowed. "Good. Then I only have one request left to ask."

The words made me nervous, but I did owe him for everything he'd done today, so I nodded regretfully. "Anything."

He wasted no time in getting to the point. "You have to be the one to kill Mother."

I said nothing, my blood running cold.

I was sure my heart had stopped. Maybe *I* was the one dying after all.

"Come on, Ares," he said.

'Ares.' The name echoed around me. 'Ares.'

He was losing himself, the Day Walker magic growing stronger. The longer I debated it, the more danger I was putting myself in because Marshall, full Day Walker, *would* have been a danger.

"You're going to kill a lot of vampires in the future. You'll have to make tough decisions, and running The Farm is a heavy burden. I need to know that you can do it."

"You're really sick. You know that?" I muttered and ran my hands over my eyes, but I knew there was no other way out for my family. Mom and Marshall were dying today. There was no escaping it.

They're already dead.

I'd watched Mom snap Marshall's neck. I'd watched Dad drown Mom and Gretta behead Dad on the screens in the Observatorium.

And the weight of the words Marshall had shared with me in that room came crashing down around me.

I didn't have a choice.

It was my war now, my family's legacy.

I stared into the distance and felt as numb as the winter.

"Knowing when sacrifices are necessary," I whispered, and Marshall exhaled in relief.

He nodded. "For the greater good."

I filled my lungs with ocean air, closed my eyes, and built the courage. One day I'd have to kill; as with most wars, death was inevitable. Running The Farm would put me right in the middle of it. Should my first kill be on the battlefield? Or here, where it would be somewhat *appreciated*? Welcomed?

"Come on, Ares." Marshall urged.

'Ares.'

'Ares.'

The echo in the wind was enough to make me move, following Marshall towards our mother.

They're already dead, I reminded myself.

Mom could now move but was still pinned to the pier by the dagger through her shoulder. "Oh, look at my boys." Her lips curled into a smile. "Have you come to finish the job your girlfriend started? What happened to her, Ares? Did she get cold feet?"

Marshall covered Mom's mouth with his hand, pinning her down by the shoulders. "Ready?" He asked.

No.

Never.

There's not enough time in the world for me to ever be

ready for this.

"Marshall, I am so sorry," I said again, shoulders slumping and head bowing. It should never have come to this.

He nodded. This time he didn't interrupt or tell me to shut up. "I know. So am I," he replied quietly. He closed his red eyes, and I took one final moment to remember the scar above his eye, his unkempt hair, and that wicked smile I had hated for far too long.

I couldn't look at Mom. I kept my eyes on my older brother as I felt for the dagger, pulled it from the Day Walker's shoulder, and then aimed it over her heart.

I paused.

My brother's eyes opened. "This tension is killing me." His voice was blunt, but I knew he was joking, trying to ease my nerves with dry humor as I always did to others in horrible situations. He'd noticed.

"Sorry." My hands shook so hard it was visible, even in my peripheral vision. Marshall removed his hand from Mom's mouth and rested his fingers over mine.

It's okay, his eyes told me, and I took another deep breath.

"Come on, Princess," he chuckled his iconic, chaotic way. "What the fuck are you waiting for?"

And then I pushed, and the laughter stopped.

CHAPTER THIRTY-SIX

ARES

We buried Marshall and Mom on the hill overlooking the sea and the theme park. It wasn't ideal. I'd have preferred them back at The Farm to reunite Mom with Dad so that I could visit their grave often, but Marshall would have approved of this resting place. He had lived his entire life trapped on The Farm. At least in death, he could be free.

From this spot, I could see the pier and the gray bodies that remained there, the sea before us, and a large forest behind. Marshall had said that he'd wanted to see the world, and there was not much I couldn't see from here. If his spirit rested near his body, he'd have a view of every season in its fullest glory.

We'd scouted the town near the theme park to find equipment and proceeded to dig as night fell.

The pack remained silent.

We dug a grave big enough for four, and as we neared six feet in depth, I climbed out and proceeded to wrap my family's bodies in old blankets whilst Lora prepared Indigo and Katie, watching me to ensure I didn't break.

"I'm okay," I said as I tied a rope around the legs. My voice was steady, almost calm. The shock was wearing off, and I found peace knowing that my mother and brother wouldn't spend eternity as a plague to humankind, and they could rest now.

"That's what's worrying me," Lora whispered gently, the evening breeze drifting whisps of hair across her face.

My hands were still shaking. They hadn't stopped since—

I blocked out the memory.

It wasn't one I wanted to remember.

"Okay, maybe I'm lying to myself, but I'm trying my best to hold it together, for their sakes." I nodded towards Jayleigh, Diego, Hail, and Tye, who were still digging. Their mind control ended as soon as Mom died.

"Hey," I grabbed Lora's hand and placed it over my chest. She was panicking for my humanity, scared I'd pushed it a little too close to my limit and lost a little more in the process. "Don't worry."

"It could have been you." She pulled her hand away and

continued to tie the rope. I followed suit and nodded.

Mom's teeth had hovered too close to my neck, and I'd been seconds away from mutating. Either option would have turned me into a monster, mutant or vampire.

It really could have gone in so many different directions.

"It could have been you, too," I replied. "Do you want to talk about what happened with the Night Walkers and Benji's pack?"

I saw the evidence of Lora's massacre as we left the theme park, but it hadn't been what I expected. A building lay in ruins. The stench of burning filled my nostrils, and I regretfully searched for the bodies but found none. There was no fire.

There was nothing to forgive in my eyes, but she seemed hesitant to talk about it, and I didn't want to push her.

"Not today," she said finally.

Nodding, I whispered, "Okay. I'm here if you ever change your mind, but I understand if you don't."

She smiled. It wasn't a happy expression but a look of relief.

I finished wrapping my mother's gray body. She'd stolen Marshall's tablet, so I claimed it and fixed it to my arm. Something caught my eye just as I covered her face with a cloth and reached for her necklace, the symbol resonating deep within my mind.

I'd decided to keep Marshall's dagger as a reminder of him. Part of me wanted the cap, but I didn't think any number of washes could bring it back to white. It deserved to be buried with him, anyways. So, I kept the dagger instead, safe in my pocket, and removed the necklace from my mother. The chain felt dainty through my fingers, and I wondered how she'd kept it for so long without snapping or losing it.

I placed the necklace in a separate pocket, and then we covered her face and lowered her into the ground. We did the same with Marshall, Katie, and then Indigo.

It felt different seeing them now, like this. Painful. I glanced out to sea instead, watching the winter waves roll in with the wind, gripping at the necklace and dagger as though each item carried the souls of my family. I clung to them.

Solace nuzzled into my leg, comforting me through it.

"Ares?" Lora whispered. I blinked a couple of times, trying to focus on what she was asking. "Do you want to say a few words?"

"Oh." I nodded. A gulp filled my throat, and it made talking almost impossible. "Um. Yeah."

Clearing my throat, and then again, I tried to find my voice as I stepped forward. "Marshall." My hand gripped tighter to the object in my pocket. "You once buried *me* alive. I at least had the decency to kill you before returning the favor."

I knew that he would have laughed; the nice laugh from the pier, not the menacing one he used way too often for anyone's liking. I was glad to hear the chuckle of the Titaniums around me. It made it easier to imagine his voice within the crowd.

"You deserved better than the cards you were dealt in this world." I chewed my bottom lip as the pack fell silent. If they disagreed with my words, then they kept it to themselves. "I don't blame you, and I hope you've found peace."

I wiped my eyes. The bitter wind poisoned my tears.

"Mom… The person I met today was not you. I'm sure of that. I'll try to remember you as Dr. White describes you, loving, thoughtful, and intelligent. A marvel. I'll end this war for you, our family, and humankind…" I didn't know how much to share with the nearby hybrids, so I decided to cut it there. "I love you both."

The idea that The Farm was now mine—the fate of humanity resting solely in my hands—scared me to my core, but I was sure Marshall had been preparing me for it since he discovered that we were family. He'd been testing me, challenging my thinking, and carving me into a leader without my noticing.

I felt I needed more time to be ready. But time, I'd come to realize, was a luxury.

I had a world of support; Lora, Jayleigh, and Hail. I had Dr. White. I had Solace, and I knew that if I ever wavered, they'd be there to set me straight. They would not allow me to follow in Father or Marshall's footsteps.

I helped to fill in the graves after Lora gave a few words for Indigo and Katie, and then we bunkered into a nearby building, covering the windows and doors with whatever we could find, and slept in shifts.

I took the first shift with Lora and Jayleigh, staring into oblivion.

"So, there are Day Walkers?" Jayleigh asked, trying to wrap her head around the idea. "As if Night Walkers weren't bad enough, now they're evolving too."

I let Jayleigh and Lora consider possibilities amongst themselves whilst my mind roamed back to my mother. She had turned Marshall, Katie, and all the Day Walkers who'd had Lora surrounded, making her a Queen. But Gretta had turned Mom, and who knew how many others, and she was still out there.

My head spun as I considered everything I knew about Gretta.

She'd been trapped on The Farm, with no footage of her on the cameras except the one on Camera 72.

The farmers didn't know she was there. Marshall hadn't known, and if anyone found out, they'd likely try to kill her.

Had my parents been protecting her?

That wasn't right.

She wouldn't have killed them if they were doing her a favor.

So, they were ashamed of her?

I watched a flap of paper blow in the window's breeze as the questions overloaded my brain. My hand buried itself in the fur of Solace's neck.

It started to click into place.

Ashamed.

They'd hidden her because they were ashamed of what they'd done.

They'd hidden her because she was a monster, a mistake, but then she'd *escaped* The Farm.

She was a product of The Farm, much like us.

She'd been an experiment, just like us.

"Mom did it…" the words left my lips in a horrifying realization, my gaze landing on the two confused, sleep-deprived girls before me.

"What?" Jayleigh and Lora squinted, not following my train of thought.

"Earlier, Mom asked how Dr. White was coming along with a cure," I recalled her words, "I assumed she had somehow found out about my mutant cure, but what if…" I was too emotionally and mentally exhausted to form the words. "What if they were trying to find a cure for Night Walkers? To turn them back. To make them human again. And what if my parents half succeeded, making the Night Walkers able to walk in sunlight and hold onto their humanity for a short while before they turned?"

"You think that your parents *created* Day Walkers?" Lora's eyebrows raised.

"I'm not sure, but it makes sense, doesn't it?"

"You could tell me that horses fly, and I would believe it with this Day Walker venom still lingering in my body," Jayleigh added.

"It does make sense." Lora ignored Jayleigh.

"If Gretta escaped, of course, the first person she'd want vengeance on would be my father for entrapping her. And then she turned my mother into a Day Walker as payback for experimenting on her…"

Lora tried not to look relieved by my story, but I could see she was happy to have somewhere to start.

Jaylcigh didn't care so much. "Nice! So, we kill this Gretta bitch, and we wipe out the entire Day Walker population."

"We kill Gretta." I nodded. For once, this sounded like a solid idea. It's what my family would have wanted. They'd created the Day Walkers, so ending this evolved species seemed like a form of closure.

"Are you sure that's the right move?" Lora asked. I shared a look with Jayleigh, wondering when she had become one to back down from ending the war. "I mean, is that the *first* move?"

"We're not safe morning or night whilst the Day Walkers roam the Earth. Ridding ourselves of the evolved species would allow us safety whilst the sun is in the sky," I suggested. "But first, we need to go home."

We were low on supplies, intel, and energy. We needed a good night's sleep; my body yearned for the springy mattress of my bed in the barn. I longed to wake in my stall, the sun creeping through the gaps in the walls, a light breeze filtering in.

"Home," Lora repeated with a quick nod and a small smile. "That sounds nice."

"Are you homesick, Alpha?" I asked.

"I think I am," Lora agreed.

"I miss our routine," Jayleigh agreed. "Training was hard, but at least we knew what to expect from day to day. I'm even starting to miss Tim's grouchiness. Remind me, does he have black or brown hair?"

"None," I chuckled quietly, glad to have the group back together and a half-plan in place. Come to think of it, I was starting to miss Tim's bald head too.

HAIL

I listened to Ares, Jayleigh, and Lora talk quietly whilst everybody else slept.

I didn't usually have a problem getting to sleep, but my body was still recovering from the dead people's bites. Memories mixed with nightmares every time I closed my eyes, and I could no longer remember which were real and which were illusions.

I was pretty sure that Ares had saved me. He'd pulled the tubes from my arms, but there were red clouds above him, raining blood onto his head, and he'd had blue eyes, so maybe my memory of that moment wasn't at all trustworthy. Perhaps I'd mixed too many memories and visions into one.

That's the problem with nightmares; they find a way to creep into your waking life.

If only Donnah was a nightmare.

She'd been the best thing to come from this whole

experience, and at least I'd been able to see her face again, even if it had only been in my imagination.

It had been worth it.

All the pain.

All the suffering.

I'd do it all again to hear her sweet song just one last time.

I closed my eyes and thought about it, but my mind didn't do her voice justice.

After a while, my mind drifted back to Ares and the handshake he'd done after I'd woken him from the red-eyed peoples' dreams. I'd missed that handshake, and I'd missed my friend.

But something didn't seem right about that memory.

Before I woke Ares, we'd both been sitting in a field of red grass. I'd looked at him but not seen him. I'd listened to him but not heard him.

Something seemed strange about it.

Maybe it was the dreams.

They were still messing with my mind.

And I was really, *really* hungry.

CHAPTER THIRTY-SEVEN

ARES

The following evening, we followed the track that meandered for miles towards The Farm's gates.

I'd found Marshall's backpack in the Funhouse and charged the tablet through his portable stick. I also found a couple of escaped coffee beans and a tub of something red among the usual items. Opening it, I realized it was paint.

"What the crap?" I poked my finger into it and smudged it on the back of my hand. "Paint. Why the hell did he bring this?"

"He was mad, Ares." Jayleigh rolled her eyes. "I've spent a long time analyzing that man, and there's no explaining somc of the things he did."

I let out a sad laugh and returned the paint to his backpack, turning my attention to the charging tablet to alert Dr. White of our arrival. We were nearing the gates of The Farm.

As I watched the metal crank up and reveal the dust track leading us to the silo, I considered running.

For a split second, I experienced that same fear I had felt upon waking on The Farm and needing out. It played with my mind, making me feel trapped even though The Farm's lands stretched on for miles. I understood how Marshall had viewed The Farm; a cage.

They were ready to trap me.

But then I felt Lora's fingers intertwine with mine. Maybe she'd noticed the panic in my eyes or felt the shift of energy, or perhaps she felt that same revelation.

And as we crossed under the gates, I squeezed her thumb with my own, knowing that whatever was about to happen, we'd experience it together. It was scary, but it was nothing we couldn't manage. So long as we actually *stayed* together this time. The world had a habit of splitting us up.

Dr. White didn't greet us at the gates as I'd expected, so we strolled along the track to the silo. Every few seconds, my eyes would land on Lora.

"Stop looking at me." She tried to hide her smile. "Enjoy the scenery."

I laughed softly. The Farm looked brown and mushy, and

remnants of snow made the land seem dull. Once upon a time, I could have found something to marvel over, the branches of leafless trees entwining one another. The cold breeze against my skin. But not today. "Why would I? The most beautiful thing this world has ever created is you."

She didn't try to hide the smile this time, and a pink blush swept over her cheeks. Yes, I may once have looked to nature for comfort and peace, but no sunset or autumn forest could ever compare to the happiness I felt around Lora.

We approached the lift of the silo, and I suggested that everybody meet us on level -1 in ten minutes. The pack entered the lift to the common room, and I held Lora back as she tried to leave with them. I pushed the button to -3, and as soon as the doors closed, my lips were on hers.

Finally, alone.

She voiced her surprise through a small yelp, but it soon died away as we sank. My hands were in her hair, down her back, holding her face, pressing her against the lift's wall, whilst her hands rested steadily on the back of my neck and stroked small circles into my curls. We were bruised lips and breathless sighs.

"I love you, Lora," I whispered, our noses resting against each other as the lift slowed.

She kissed me once more for good measure. "I love you

too, Beta."

Was it too much to ask for the lift to break down for an hour or so? I could have done with time stopping for a while, leaving us suspended in this moment.

We jerked to a stop, and then the doors opened. Dr. White stood before us with a clipboard in one hand and his other adjusting his glasses.

"Oh. Ares, Lora!" If he'd realized we were in the middle of a personal moment, he didn't care about breaking it. "It's so good to have you back!"

My uncle ushered us out of the lift as though he'd expected somebody else to hide in the corner. When he found it empty, his smile faded, and his shoulders sagged. I didn't need to ask to know he was looking for Marshall.

"He… um…" I started, feeling the dread and hurt bubble within me. *Be strong, Ares.* "He didn't make it."

Dr. White was silent but nodded slowly as his eyes fell to the ground.

We'd decided it would be best to tell him in person rather than the call the night previous, with nobody there to comfort him. But Dr. White didn't seek support from either of us. He didn't even ask how Marshall died. Instead, he coughed to clear the gulp in his throat and then proceeded down the corridor which led to the Observatorium.

We rushed after him, taking a right turn at the end, and entered the room full of cameras. "Marshall made arrangements before he left," he said as he began clicking through files on my brother's computer, wiping a tear as though it were a side effect of hay fever. "This was always his plan, Ares. I'm not sure how much he told you of his condition, but he never intended to return to The Farm. He planned on sacrificing himself to save you if his illness didn't kill him first. He was more like your mother than I gave him credit for."

His words lingered.

I'd planned to tell Dr. White that my mother had been the Day Walker to kill Marshall, and up until this moment, I thought it had been the right thing to do. Because telling the truth was always best, wasn't it?

Except, in situations like this?

My uncle still worshiped the ground that my mother walked on. He remembered her as she was in life, and I didn't want to tarnish his memory of her. He still believed that she was dead. To tell him that she had been out there for eight years would destroy him. But to tell Dr. White that Samantha had killed her son? I couldn't do it, and I *wouldn't.*

When I'd been asking for answers about who I was and what my Gen. 3 basis meant for me, Dr. White had once told me that some things were better left buried.

This was one of those things.

"Marshall mentioned something about Protocol Six. He said I should talk to Greenman—Wilson," I corrected myself. "I should ask Wilson about Protocol Six."

Dr. White nodded, scanned the Observatorium for the man dressed in green uniform, and then waved him up. "Don't worry, Ares."

I tried my best not to.

"But, Dr. White—"

He cut me off with a laugh. "Please stop calling me that. Refer to me as Daniel or Danny. That's what Samantha and Flynn used to call me."

"Danny?" I tried it out. "I don't know, it sounds wrong, Daniel. Uncle Danny." My nerves were showing. "Can't I stick with Dr. White?"

"Sir?" Wilson joined the three of us on the higher level of the Observatorium.

"Marshall asked for Protocol Six?" I asked, and Wilson's face tensed as he understood what it meant.

He had been Marshall's only friend growing up, and he lived in another Safe Zone. They'd been reunited for less than a month before Marshall died, and I wondered if Marshall might have changed if Greenman had returned to The Farm with my brother after I was born.

"Right away," Wilson turned.

"Wait!" I called after him, unsure if I wanted to know the answer to my next question, "What does it mean? Protocol Six?"

Wilson gave me a tight-lipped smile. "It's his collection of postcards. He wanted you to have them."

My mouth hung open.

I was baffled by his words, not understanding what Marshall would be doing collecting postcards or how he'd retrieved new ones without leaving The Farm.

"Postcards?" I repeated.

Wilson nodded. "In the early days, when The Farm had enough resources to recruit refugees, your parents would raid old shops for postcards to give Marshall insight into the world beyond the fence. He loved them and kept them in a box. He even started painting some of his own, I believe."

I almost laughed at the idea of Marshall holding a paintbrush. He'd never struck me as the creative type. But then, I'd only just scratched the surface when it came to my brother. At least it explained the red container in his backpack.

"I'm sorry, Wilson. I know that you were friends," I offered.

Wilson smiled sadly. "We were. Not many would believe me when I say this, but Marshall had a good heart, even though it wasn't always in the right place. Now, I'll go and fetch those postcards."

He turned and vanished into the sea of farmers below, not wanting to speak any more about it.

My eyes fell on the screened wall.

Lora said nothing, but she held my hand a little tighter. Dr. White said quietly, "Take all the time you need, Ares, to get used to this view."

CHAPTER THIRTY-EIGHT

LORA

I sat on the sofa in White's medical room while he rummaged through file cabinets. He looked tired, his eyes sunken and the skin underneath seeming a shade of purple. Marshall's had been similar. It seemed that sleep deprivation was a side effect of running The Farm.

"Breathe, White," I said. "It's just a folder."

"Sometimes I wonder why I bother with paper files, Lora. Everybody tells me that computers are easier, but I've always insisted on handwriting my notes. It feels more personal. And it stopped Marshall from snooping. But here I am, at a complete loss for what I've done with yours. My system is usually impeccable. I don't see how I could have misplaced it."

"Well, you've been busy over the last few days. How about

you write your notes on that?" I pointed to a notepad on the desk, and he turned to pick it up. "And you can find my folder later?"

Dr. White nodded briskly and joined me on the sofa, drawing in a deep gulp of air, holding it, and releasing it.

"Marshall's death has hit you harder than you're willing to admit?" I asked.

White raised his eyebrows at my observation and chuckled. "Am I that easy to read?"

I shrugged my shoulders and helped myself to a glass of water from the jug in the corner. "I've known you for years, Old Man, and picking up on changes in behaviour is second nature to me." I placed the jug back onto the table and brought the cup to my lips.

"There's no need to apologise. It's nice to know that I have somebody looking out for me, too."

I returned to him on the sofa and sat at an angle to chat casually, throwing an arm over the cushion. "Do you want to talk about it?"

White shook his head. "No. It's best not to, I think. I see that you and Ares have kissed and made up."

The water splurged up my nose, and I wiped it away with my sleeve. "What do you mean?" Had he seen us kissing in the lift yesterday?

"There was a tension between you before you left but being away from The Farm seems to have brought you closer together. You look happy."

I nodded and picked at the lip of the cup, remembering how Ares' fingers felt laced with mine. "I am happy. Stressed, but that comes with the job. And I'm worried about Ares' Gen. 3 problem..."

White's eye twitched ever so slightly as the words left my mouth, and I knew there was a story to be told.

"What can we do?" I asked. "Is there a cure or an operation? A way to give him more human genes and fewer animal ones? I don't know how this science works, but there has to be something."

"It doesn't quite work like that, but we are trying to find a way—"

"What can I do? Can I help?"

White's brows creased together. "I'm afraid not. This is science and magic, Lora. It's a difficult balance."

It wasn't the news I wanted to hear.

"I can't lose him, White. I can't." I sobbed, and the doctor reached to his desk to grab me a tissue.

How had this boy crept into my life and destroyed my defences? I didn't cry before Ares. I didn't even laugh, but he'd come along and thawed me like spring blossom, shedding morning frost, and I feared I'd turn back to ice again if Ares lost himself. I didn't want to return to that closed-off girl I used to be. Ares had brought me to life, and if I lost him, my humanity might slip away with his because I didn't want to be part of this world without the sunshine he cast over me. I didn't want to live in darkness again.

I dabbed my eyes, the tissue soaking through.

"We're doing everything we can, Lora. I've had a team working on something since you left, but there's no way of being certain it will work, considering how quickly his body absorbed foreign matter."

"How long do we have?" I didn't want to ask the question, but I needed to know. "Will he be okay so long as he never mutates again?"

White pursed his lips. "From the data we've collected, the animal takes over a little more each time he mutates, although there was a spike between the time his monitor disappeared in the nest to the tests we ran this morning. Ares claims that he didn't mutate then, so we don't know how or why he might have spiked."

"I've been with him. He didn't mutate; I would have felt it."

White let out a sigh and pinched his nose beneath his glasses. "Well, that is a massive cause for concern because there is a certain spike. The animal hormones are now consistently in his bloodstream."

"What does that mean?"

My heart stilled.

White placed a hand on my shoulder. "He's just as much of a ticking time bomb as you are."

CHAPTER THIRTY-NINE

ARES

We'd been back on The Farm for two weeks, and I was starting to understand my role as leader and what the world expected of me.

Lora had been by my side, which made things easier. We were a team. We could both run The Farm, as my parents had. It almost made me feel as though everything that had happened to my family had been to bring us here.

Solace also stuck at my heels whilst the Titanium pack planned and schemed our next move. I liked to imagine The Farm was a democracy rather than a dictatorship; our council consisted of hybrids and farmers.

We all agreed to go after the Day Walker Queen, Gretta, and the sooner we could locate her, the better. I needed to end the creature that my mother had created, and as a result, it would take out all of the Day Walkers that the Queen had made. We could wipe out the *entire* Day Walker bloodline in one move.

Wilson had intel from his time in the Northern Safe Zone, and we could contact Chipper through The Sanctuary radio now that he was no longer under vampire control.

We planned to work as a team, united against a mutual enemy. He approved of my plans for The Farm. They deviated from how my father and Marshall had run things, and I just hoped it would get the results we needed.

We didn't have time to continue our training. The war was coming for us and leading The Farm and its people was far more important.

At least it gave Tim and Sally some much-needed time off. However, I suspected that the Venos were keeping them busy enough. Thankfully, Dr. White hadn't executed our old rivals once Marshall disrupted Phase Two. We were supposed to kill Dickward and his pack, but the majority survived, and they'd continued with their training since we'd been gone.

It was a relief. The Venos would make an excellent addition to our growing team so long as they could accept that I was their new leader; Venos were obedient once they learned who to follow.

Things were looking up.

And The Farm was about to become a whole lot busier.

After days of running plans passed Daniel, Tim, Sally, Wilson, and various farmers within the Observatorium, I took a few moments to myself, wandering through the tropical leaves of the Biome with the humid air clinging to my skin and clothes.

It was suffocating.

Being in the bunker was starting to bring back memories of my life before the metamorphosis, especially when I spent time in the leafy oasis buried hundreds of feet below ground.

I'd recently recalled Mom's laughter as we planted trees. Warm and loving, my real mother deeply cared for me and would do whatever it took to ensure I was safe and well, and she always asked if I was okay. Was there anything I needed? Did I want help peeling my orange? Did I want to play a game?

I sat on a rock near the stream and closed my eyes, allowing the sounds to transport me back to an area of my memory that my human alter ego couldn't access. The merging of my two states was manageable, and it currently wasn't as bad as I'd predicted. I was able to pick up early warning signs of my mutant alter ego taking control and calm myself. For the time being, I could enjoy the best of both egos at once.

A memory of the rock I sat on seeped through the cracks

in my mental barrier.

"Tell me a story, Ares," Mom tried to distract me from my tears as she washed my bleeding finger and wrapped it. I'd cut it whilst planting new trees, and now Mom tried to comfort me, my tears still falling and my lip wobbling.

"A boy gave me a map today." My five-year-old voice was so riddled with self-pity that it was a wonder Mom understood what I'd said.

"Wow!" she beamed. "Can I see it?"

I nodded, pulling the paper from my pocket and handing it over. Mom studied the map with a strange expression, her eyes glassing over, and she gave me a small smile.

"He must be very clever to draw a map like this. Look." She tilted the map so I could follow her finger. "We're here, in the Biome. This is where you go to school, in the Infirmary, and this is where Mommy, Uncle Danny, and Uncle Flynn work, in the Lab."

"Where does Daddy work?" I asked, eyeing the drawing.

She pointed to the other side of the map. "Right here."

"Ob-torum." I tried to read the perfect writing.

"Daddy can't see us right now, but he'll watch on his secret screens later. Do you want to give him a wave?"

I nodded eagerly, waving my hand in the direction Mom pointed. I didn't know exactly what I should have been waving at.

"Did the boy tell you his name?" she asked as she folded the map back down to pocket size.

I shrugged my shoulders. "I asked him, but he said I could call him what I wanted. So I called him Floppy!"

Mom laughed, "Why Floppy, Ares?"

"'Cause his hair flops over his face like this." I pulled Mom's hair forward, so it covered her eyes, and she giggled, messing mine up in return.

"Well, maybe I should see about getting Floppy a haircut, huh?" She returned the map and wiped what remained of my tears, my barely injured finger now long forgotten. "How about we go and stick that map on your wall?"

I nodded again, holding Mom's hand and leaving the Biome with Floppy's map tucked safely in my pocket.

I didn't recall what happened once we left the Biome. I doubted I ever stuck the map to my wall, as my childhood room in the Infirmary was as clear as Dr. White's hospital room.

The tablet on my arm rang an alarm, disrupting the blissful silence. It was time…

I turned off the reminder and sighed deeply, enjoying the peace of the rainforest for just a moment longer. Marshall had prepared me for the difficult decisions, the death, and the pressure, but he'd forgotten to mention just how noisy life as leader of The Farm really was.

The vacuum sealed as I exited, and I met Lora in the bustling corridor on the other side.

She'd been a saviour since our return. I kissed her quickly, despite the moving bodies around us.

"Ready?" She asked.

I tried to look convincing, "As I'll ever be. Did Jayleigh organise the—"

"It's all under control. Everything's ready."

I sighed deeply and said, "Thank you, Alpha." Although, those three little words didn't seem nearly enough. I hugged her close and the nervous energy passed between us.

We walked arm in arm towards the Infirmary, a large crowd of farmers gathering to watch. We pushed through to the front, where the pack waited.

It was a day for the history books that would change everything, for better or worse. I could sense the tension in the air, the farmers watching and chatting in hushed whispers as they waited for my instruction.

Jayleigh squealed next to me as she pressed her nose into the window, trying to get as close to the action as possible. Lora's hand gripped mine so tight that it could have been glued, a nervous smile on her lips. She squeezed my thumb, and I squeezed hers in return.

Hail watched over my shoulder but crouched slightly to whisper into my ear, "Bro, are you sure we'll have enough food for everyone?"

I laughed, "I've been to level -2 and seen our food supply.

Don't worry. Marshall was certainly a hoarder. There's plenty to go around."

Daniel stepped through the growing crowd on the bridge behind us. "Everything is in order," he confirmed and nodded in my direction.

I took a deep breath and held Lora's hand a little tighter. My spare hand was gripping my mother's necklace, feeling the grooves of the unusually shaped pendant.

"Then it's time," I said.

Time to fix my mother's mistakes.

Time to honour Father's and Marshall's legacies.

Time to go to war…

My eyes fell on Lora, still needing her confirmation. "Tell me that this is a good idea?"

She gave me a reassuring nod, "The best we have."

And then I looked back to the hundreds of hibernating Titaniums and Venos.

One.

Deep breath.

Two.

Release.

Three.

"Then let's wake them up," I turned to the farmers, dropping Lora's hand and tapping a few buttons on the screen of my tablet. "It's time to put an end to the apocalypse."

To be continued...

REAP
The Titanium Trilogy - Book 3

FOR THE GREATER GOOD

Coming 2023

Sign up for the

Kirsty Bright

Newsletter

Don't miss out on the next thrilling novel in the trilogy. Sign up to the author newsletter for first chapter reads, release dates and more!

For more details, visit

www.kirstybrightauthor.com

Love this book?
Leave a review!

With special thanks,

Kirsty.

#	TITLE	ALBUM
1	Take It All Valley Of Wolves	Take It All
2	Born for This CRMNL	II
3	Ain't No Sunshine Saint Chaos	Ain't No Sunshine
4	The Hunter Adam Jensen	The Hunter
5	Wolves Jake Daniels	Wolves
6	The Great Escape Boys Like Girls	Boys Like Girls
7	Freaks Like Us Sleeping Wolf	Freaks Like Us
8	PSYCHO AViVA	VOLUME I
9	Little Poor Me Layto	Little Poor Me
10	I'm Dangerous The EverLove	Walk Through Fire

Search

Revive (The Titanium Trilogy, Book 2) - Soundtrack

0:24 2:56

ABOUT THE AUTHOR

Kirsty is a British small-town girl with a big love for coffee and spicy food. She spent her childhood on the border of England and Wales, surrounded by vast countryside where she enjoyed horse riding and time outdoors with her family and friends.

She found herself drawn to the creative arts in her early teens, especially music, drama, and writing; and she still continues to sing locally from time to time. But reading or writing, with a candle lit and a mug of coffee in her hand, is where she feels most at home.

www.ingramcontent.com/pod-product-compliance
Lightning Source LLC
Chambersburg PA
CBHW010446310726
48979CB00018B/2834/J

* 9 7 8 1 7 3 9 9 9 7 8 3 0 *